Amélie Rives

Herod and Mariamne

Amélie Rives

Herod and Mariamne

ISBN/EAN: 9783337194161

Printed in Europe, USA, Canada, Australia, Japan

Cover: Foto ©Andreas Hilbeck / pixelio.de

More available books at **www.hansebooks.com**

A TRAGEDY.

BY

AMÉLIE RIVES,

AUTHOR OF "THE QUICK OR THE DEAD?" "VIRGINIA OF VIRGINIA,"
ETC., ETC.

PHILADELPHIA:

J. B. LIPPINCOTT COMPANY.

TO MY HUSBAND.

LIPPINCOTT'S
MONTHLY MAGAZINE.

SEPTEMBER, 1888.

HEROD AND MARIAMNE.

ACT I.

SCENE I.—*A hall in* HEROD'S *palace.*

Enter JOSEPH *and* SOHEMUS.

Joseph. It hath come, good Sohemus. 'T hath come.
Sohemus.   What, brother?
Jos. The king is summoned by Antonius
Unto Laodicea concerning——
   Soh.   Well?
Jos. Lower, I pray you—why, concerning, sir,
The death of Aristobulus.
   Soh.   Heaven save us!
What saith the queen?
   Jos.   Which queen, my Sohemus?
There are so many queens in Herod's palace,
We needs must name them when we speak of them.
By Moses' beard! the wild bees have more wisdom:
They have one queen, where Herod houses four.
There is his mother Cypros, and his sister
My wife Salome: they do hate most violently
His consort Mariamne, and her mother,
The old king's daughter, Alexandra.
   Soh.   Nay,
All this I know by demonstration, sir.
The information that I crave concerns
Queen Mariamne. Doth she think her brother
To have been murdered?
   Jos.   There, sir, lies the matter.
She doth not think so, while her mother doth.

They have been wrangling o'er it all the morning,
And wrangle yet. My wife and Cypros sulk
Within their own apartments; and the king
Is closeted with Antony's messenger.
    Soh. Where is Hyrcanus?
    Jos.   Sleeping, sir, I think.
The kind old king hath but that refuge now
When the queens quarrel.
    Soh.   A most fitting refuge!
For when queens quarrel kings are kings in vain.
Soft, friend! is that not Mariamne's voice?
    Jos. It is,—and Alexandra's. Let us go,
Ere we be dragged into their mad dispute.   [*Exeunt.*

Enter MARIAMNE *and* ALEXANDRA.

    Alex. Art thou my daughter?
    Mar.   If thou dost tell truth.
    Alex. Insolence! Wilt thou mock me? God of Moses!
Almost I think that I unknowing lie
And that thou art a changeling! Sure no blood
Of mine makes blue those traitorous veins o' thine!
To call him brother, and yet love the king
Who murdered him!
    Mar.   Madam, I will not think it.
    Alex. Not think it? Will not think it!
    Mar.   No, madam.
Nor hear it said. Therefore be silent.
    Alex.   Silent!
This unto me, thy mother? Silent? Oh,
Would I were tongued like nature! thou shouldst hear
A hundred thousand voices utter, " Murder!"
Why, I do tell thee I have knowledge of it
From ten reliable sources. It was planned—
Ay, planned from first to last. And he, thy brother,
So young, so fair, that even thou didst show
Old and uncomely by his side!
    Mar.   Good mother,
None loved my brother more than I did love,
And love him: therefore go I quietly,
Thinking how did he live he would prefer
That we should mourn him, not with cries and curses,
But in the stillness of our hearts with prayer.
    Alex. Prayers for his murderer? Oh, 'tis well! 'tis well!
Thou art so eaten with unnatural love
For this thy kingly sinner, that thy heart
Hath no unoccupied cranny where might lodge
Love natural for him whom he hath murdered.
    Mar. I will not hear that word again.
    Alex.   Not hear it?
Canst command deafness, that thou wilt not hear it?

I say that Herod hath thy brother murdered,—
Murdered! Ay, murdered! murdered! Dost thou hear?
Or, being queen, canst thou command thy ears
That they drink not unwelcome sounds?
 Mar.   No, madam;
But I can twenty hands command to take thee
Where thy voice cannot reach my ears.
 Alex.   Ay, do it!
Do it, I say! 'Twere well that Herod's wife
Took Herod's way; 'twere well Hyrcanus' daughter
Should be o'er-daughtered in Hyrcanus' palace;
'Twere well the blood of Aristobulus
Should not cry out, lest Herod seeking sleep
Should be disturbed. O God of Israel,
God of the widowed and the childless, hear!
To Thee I turn, to Thee shall mount my grief;
Thine ears shall drink this murder, and Thine arm
Destroy the murderer.
 Mar.   Madam, have done.
 Alex. Have done! Have done, didst say? When hell is
    finished,
Packed full, and the gates locked against new-comers,
I will have done.—O Aristobulus,
This was thy sister, and is wife to him
Who had thee murdered.
 Mar.   Mother, be advised.
My duty as thy daughter hath a limit.
 Alex. Thy duty unto Herod hath no limit.
What! wilt thou take his hand, lie by his side,
Be mother of his children, and the blood
Of the high-priest thy brother red between ye?
I tell thee, woman, thou wilt know my pangs
When thou hast brought forth sons for him to slay!
 Mar. Mother, here comes the king! 'Twere best indeed
He did not hear thee.
 Alex.   Ay, now it were best;
But there will come a time, I tell you, girl,
He'll curse the day that he was born with ears!
 Mar. In truth, you'd best be silent.
 Alex.   I will go;
Fear not but that I'll go. God blast these eyes
If ever they are willing witnesses
Unto thy dalliance with Herod!   [*Exit.*
 Mar.   Nay,
God knows I loved my brother, and do mourn him
With a sore heart; but when my mother thus
Doth lay his death upon the king my husband,
She doth divide my pity with her hate,
And makes my grief half Herod's. Ay, by heaven!
Though he be rash, hot-natured, mad in wrath,

And prone to take occasion by the throat,
He is as little capable of murder
As this my heart of killing the great love
That I do bear him.   Ah, he comes, and anger
Hot at his heels!

Enter HEROD.

Herod. [*Not seeing* MARIAMNE.]   Herod commanded by a
    Roman turn-coat!
Antony summon Herod!   Antony,—
The by-word of all nations, the last toy
Of an Egyptian wanton!   Who that reads
In future ages will believe it?   Oh
That Antony had summoned me in person!
The Egyptian harlot had been loverless
In less time than she takes to make a kiss.—
Ah, Mariamne!
Mar.   Shall I stay, my lord?
Her. Hath Herod ever bid thee from him?
Mar.   No.
But I can well imagine that this summons
Hath left thee with a love of loneliness.
Her. Come close.   Give me thine eyes.   Dost think with
    Antony
Concerning this affair?
Mar.   With Antony?
Her. Ay,—that thy brother's blood is on my hands.
Thou dost not think it?
Mar.   As I live, my lord,
If I do think it, let me live no longer.
Her. Then I care not who thinks it.   Mariamne,
I am not Herod when I am with thee.
Mar. What then, my lord?
Her.   Why, Mariamne's lover.
I am no longer king, no longer soldier,
No longer conqueror, unless in truth
I rule thy heart.
Mar.   Thou knowest that my heart
Is but thy throne.
Her.   Let me be king of thee,
And God is welcome to the sway of heaven.
Mar. Do not blaspheme.
Her.   Away! thy veins run milk
And make thy heart a baby.   Not blaspheme!
Love cannot utter blasphemy, for Love
Is his own god and king of his own heaven.
Well, dost thou love me?
Mar.   Thou dost know I do.
Her. Thou dost not!   Thou dost make a pet of Duty,
And fatten him on what should be my food.

Love me?   Not thou!   Thou lovest the cold peace
That's child of frozen virtue.   I have fire
To melt the Sphinx, but not to warm the blood
Of one chaste woman.
   Mar.   Chaste I am, my lord,
Yet for that chasteness do but better love thee.
   Her.   I tell thee no!   Thou dost but use the word
To play with, as a child its father's sword.
Thou hast ne'er seen it scarlet with joy's death,
Or smoking with the heart's blood of a thought.
What! thou lie 'wake o' nights?   Thou scorch thy brain
With bootless wishing?   Thou eat pictured lips?
Thou feed regret with memory, and then rage
Because he is not satisfied?   Thou love?
Nay, girl, the sun will set the sea afire
Ere thy cool heart be set aflame with love.
Moreover, look you, sooner shall the waves
Of that same ocean cool the thirsty sun
Than thy pale humor make me moderate.
   Mar.   I would not have thee love me less.
   Her.   Thou wouldst not?
Why dost thou shrink, then?   Look how thou dost pale
And redden when I touch thee.   Come, thine eyes,
Thine arms, thy lips, still shrinking?   Israel's God!
Shall Herod coax his lawful wife for favors?
I say thou dost not love me, yea, moreover,
That thou dost lie when thou wouldst have me think
Thou dost not blame me for thy brother's death.
I know thou thinkest that I had him slain.
   Mar.   I do not think it, Herod.   Dost thou think
I would be here if I believed it?
   Her.   Where,
Where wouldst thou be, then?   Not here, say'st thou?
Where then?   Speak, woman! where?
   Mar.   Why, dead, maybe;
But not with thee.
   Her.   Thou liest!   Didst thou die,
I'd have thy body brought into my chamber
And make my bed thy sepulchre.
   Mar.   Ay, Herod,
My body, but not me.   Nay, my dear lord,
Why waste such moments as are left in strife
And harsh dissension?   Soon thou wilt be gone,
And Mariamne but a recollection.
Why dost thou doubt me?   Why should I not love thee,
Who art the chief of men and lovers?   Nay,
If, as thou sayest, I shrink, it is because
My love doth fear the violence of thy love,
Not I thyself,—not Mariamne Herod.
   Her.   Love is not blind, as the Greeks fable it,

For he doth look from these fair eyes o' thine,
Else am I Pleasure's bondman.
  Mar.   Nay, not so.
Thou'rt husband to the truest wife in Jewry.
  Her. And the least loving.
  Mar.   Wilt thou wrong me still?
I know not how to dress out love in words.
I can but tell thee o'er and o'er again
The naked fact, I love thee.
  Her.   Would to heaven
I knew what loving means to thee!
  Mar.   I'll tell thee:
It means to put myself beyond myself,
To think of him I love in that self's stead,
To be sleep's enemy because of him,
Because of him to be the friend of pain,
To have no thought, no wish, no dream, no memory,
That is not servant to him; to forget
All earlier loves in his,—all hates, all wrongs;
Being meek to him, though proud unto all others;
Gentle to him, though to all others harsh;
To him submissive, though unto high heaven
Something rebellious. Last, to keep my patience
And bear his doubts, who have his children borne.
  Her. Enough, enough. Thou most magnificent
Of queens and women, I will never doubt thee
After to-day.
  Mar.   Alas, my lord, to-morrow—
To-morrow'll be to-day.
  Her.   I will not doubt thee
So long as I do live.
  Mar.   Oh that thou wouldst not!
Doubt is the shaft wherewith Love wounds himself:
Doubt me no more, and be no more unhappy.
  Her. Alas! unhappiness doth wait below
To ride with me, seeing I must leave thee, love,
And that for such a summons! Jewry's throne!
Antony summon me? It is as though
The dog did whistle for his master.
  Mar.   Ay,
It is most insolent. But need'st thou go?
Is it imperative?
  Her.   More than thou knowest.
Let us not talk of it. Tell me thou'lt miss me.
How wilt thou spend the hours when I am gone?
  Mar. In wishing for the hour when thou'lt return.
  Her. God's heart! how I do love thee!—Ha! a step!
Cursèd be any that doth interrupt us,
Though it be mine own mother!
  Mar. [*Starting away from him.*] 'Tis thy mother.

Love me not in her presence, lest she hate me
The more for thy much loving.

Enter CYPROS.

Cyp. Good my son,
Thy horses wait for thee.
Her. Do thou likewise.
Seest thou not that I am occupied?
Cyp. A wife should urge her husband to his duty,—
Not keep him from it.
Her. Out! Such musty maxims
Affront the air. Leave me. I'll send for thee
When I desire thee.
Cyp. Madam, wilt thou hear this
And say no word?
Her. Think'st thou that I'll hear that
And say no word? Depart o' the instant!
Mar. Nay,
I'll wait below. Thy mother hath some message,—
Some special word for thee. I will be there,
Fear not, to give thee my last love and blessing.
Now let me leave thee, as I love thee.
Her. Go, then.
Mar. Why dost thou say't so harshly?
Her. If thou lovedst me
Thou wouldst not be so ready to be gone.
Mar. Doubt'st me again? Remember what thou saidst
A moment past, and to thy word be true.
Her. Well, go. I will believe thee. [*Exit* MAR.]
How now, mother?
What reason shall make good of this offence
To plead thy pardon?
Cyp. Love, my son.
Her. What love
Can pardon plead for interrupting mine?
Thy love, sayest thou? The love of all the mothers
Back counted unto Eve, and smelted down
In one huge mass, would not so much as make
My love a weapon.
Cyp. Then I'll say my pride,
Which guards thy dignity as 'twere mine own.
Her. My dignity?
Cyp. Thy honor and thy dignity.
Her. My dignity? My honor? Quick, give word!
What wouldst thou touch?
Cyp. But that which touches thee.
Her. My honor! By the throne of God, thy honor
Shall not survive this moment of thy speaking,
If thou hast played with me.
Cyp. Nay, good my son,

Think you a woman so infirm as I
Would take a lion-whelp for plaything?   Nay,
Did I upon my knees approach the throne
Of great Jehovah, I were not more serious.
   Her. What then? Give word. Who is it?   Hath some one
Proved treacherous in the household?
   Oyp.   Ay,—the one
Who should above all else be faithful.
   Her.   What!
Joseph?—my treasurer?—thy son-in-law?
What hath he done?   Speak, madam: I've no time
To tarry information.
   Oyp.   Nay, not Joseph.
   Her. Not Joseph?   Then 'tis Sohemus.   By heaven!
Trust hath denied herself if ·he be false!
   Oyp. Neither is Sohemus the guilty one.
   Her. Who is it, then?   Delay no longer, woman.
I'll have it, though it blast me!   Who is it?
. *Oyp.* Mayhap I had best tell thee the offence
Ere naming the offender?
   Her.   No, I say,
I'll hear the name.   Who is it?
   Oyp.   Mariamne.
   Her. Thou liest! Dost thou hear? Thou liest! Stop!
Keep from me.   Come not near me.   Thou'rt my mother,
But tempt me not with nearness,—tempt me not.
Dost know what 'tis to anger Herod?   Answer!
What! Mariamne?   Mariamne false?
How false?   False to my bed?   Were this proved false,
I'd have thee burned to warm her bedchamber!
False?   Mariamne?   How?   With whom?   How false?
Down on thy knees and swear it!
   Oyp.   I do swear it.
But she is false only in thought, not deed.
   Her. In thought?   In thought?   How canst thou know her
      thought?
This is a lie, and thou shalt die for it.
—Without, there!
   Oyp.   Herod, hear me.   Call no witness
Unto thy shame.
   Her.   My shame?   Away!   Away!
   Oyp. Salome'll prove it.
   Her.   Though great God Himself
Came down as witness, I would not believe it!
   Oyp. My son, if thou wouldst only let me speak——
   Her. Speak, then.   But I do warn thee that thy life
Hangs in the balance.   One thin thread of gold
From Mariamne's temple would outweigh it.
   Oyp. I have had certain knowledge that thy wife
Hath sent her picture——

Her.   Ah?
Cyp.   To Antony.
Her. Woman, dost thou crave death, that thus thou tempt'st it?
To Antony? To Antony? Her picture?
Hath sent her picture to Mark Antony,
The Egyptian harlot's lover? She, my wife,
The queen of Jewry? Mariamne? She,
The wife of Herod? Oh, if thou hast lied,
I'll have thy heart cut out and thrown straightway
Beneath the feet of Mariamne!
Cyp.   Nay,
Thou sham'st thyself, my son, more than thou dost thy mother,
To give thy wrath the rein. I have had word.
I know the thing I speak. Salome, too,
Doth know it.
Her.   That she hath her picture sent
Unto Mark Antony?
Cyp.   Ev'n so.
Her.   That she——   .
God! she shall come herself and answer this.
Cyp. Not so; but wait until thou art arrived
In Laodicea, and then, in off-hand manner,
Bring up the subject to Mark Antony,
Or Gallius, or some one of his picked friends,
But carelessly, as though thou found'st it matter
For mirth.
Her.   Ha! now I see why Antony
Hath summoned me.
Cyp.   For what, my son?
Her.   For what?
To take my life, that he may take my wife!
I see it all. It is a plot between them.
I see it! Ha! ha! ha!
Cyp.   Is this a time for laughter, Herod?
Beseech you, quietly. At what dost laugh?
Her. I laugh to think how I will foil them, madam!
Where's Joseph? Where is Sohemus?
Cyp.   My son,
Sure thou wilt not word this to Sohemus,—
To Joseph?
Her.   I will word it to Beelzebub
If it doth pleasure me! Out of my way!
Oh, I will play into their hands! I'll aid them!
I'll make them merry! Ha! ha! ha! Oh, I'll make them
    merry!   [*Exit, laughing.*

          Enter SALOME.

Sal. Why laughed my brother?
Cyp.   At what should he laugh?
A Herod laughs where a mere man would weep.

Sal. Hast told him of the picture?
Cyp.   Ay.
Sal.   What said he?
Cyp. He laughed, and asked me where thy husband was.
Sal. Asked thee where Joseph was?
Cyp.   Ay.
Sal.   God above!
This will ruin all.   Joseph would take her part
Against great heaven.
Cyp.   But he cannot deny 't.
Sal. He'll find some means to soothe him.
Cyp.   Well, so be it.
I've done all in my power to ruin her.
Sal. Insolent vixen!   I would give one-half
Of my young life, could I but spend the other
In watching her abasement.
Cyp.   Soft!   Come on.
Herod returns this way.   [*Exeunt.*

.

Enter HEROD *and* JOSEPH.

Jos. What!   Sent her picture to Mark Antony?
Thy mother told thee this?   Wilt thou believe it?
Her. Whether or not I do believe it, uncle,
I've a command for thee.
Jos.   In all, my liege,
I'll prove obedient.
Her.   Thou knowest, sir,
This summons is a dangerous one.
Jos.   My lord,
God's kinghood watches over Israel's kings.
Her. But Israel's God hath naught to do, good uncle,
With Roman Antony.   Look! this command
Is one most sacred.
Jos.   I will keep it, sire,
As mine own soul.
Her.   Then, Joseph, if that Antony
Doth take my life, do thou take Mariamne's;
For even in death I would not be without her.
Jos. Dear my lord——
Her.   Say no word.   Thou hast thy orders.
Jos. But kill her, sire?—thy queen, whom thou so lovest?
Her. 'Tis for that reason I would have her slain.
Jos. But sure, my lord, this is a savage love.
Her. As savage as the heart it quickens.   Look, sir!
Thou wilt be faithful?
Jos.   As unto my God.
Her. [*Taking off a ring.*]   Thus, then, I seal thee to me.
          Wear this ring,
And never look on it but what thou thinkest
Of that which thou art sworn to.

Jos. I'll remember.
Her. Commend me to my mother and thy wife,
Also to Alexandra and Hyrcanus.
My queen doth wait for me without. Farewell.
Remember thou art sealed to this.
Jos. My lord,
Death will forget ere I do.
Her. Then farewell. [*Exit.*
Jos. How he doth love her! Yet a love more cruel
Than hottest hate. I know not, on my soul,
If Herod's hate or Herod's love be crueller.
Ay, to be Herod's wife were punishment
Enough for a she-angel grown rebellious,
Where Lucifer was hurled into a hell.
Sealed to his orders? Sealed unto a murder!
Yet he hath ever used me kindly,—ay,
With trust and courtesy. It is this love,
Which makes a madman even of a king,
That hath so spurred him. Now would unto heaven.
Salome did not so abhor the queen!
For, though imperious, she is a woman
To win the liking even of a woman.
She send her picture to Mark Antony!
Why, sooner would she scar her wondrous beauty
Than so unveil it to the eyes of lust.
She send the fool of Cleopatra love-tokens!
Nay, let the sea turn traitor to the moon
And fill some reedy pond for love! Well, well,
Her innocence doth wait to welcome him
In Laodicea. [*Exit.*

Enter ALEXANDRA *and* HYRCANUS.

Alex. What, father! thou art with this Herod too?
Thou think'st him guiltless? Thou canst speak of him
With kindness, and thy only grandson dead
At his command? Oh, are there mothers in heaven
Who have so suffered upon earth? If so,—
If any such there be, to them I kneel,
To them cry out, to them denounce this Herod!
Hyr. My daughter, thou hast heavy grief to bear.
Alex. Help me to bear it, then! Take thou thy share,
And help me to my vengeance! Thou art king,
Thou art the king of Jewry,—not this Herod,
This low-born conqueror, this thief o' crowns,
This son of scorned Antipater! Oh, I marvel
That thou canst eat, and drink, and sleep, and wake,
And call thyself Hyrcanus, and yet bear it!
Whence came his greatness? Whence his power? Yea,
And whence his crown? The first two were thy gifts,
The third he stole to show his gratitude!

What, sire ! wilt thou endure 't, wilt sit so calm
While Fortune strips thee to make rich this traitor?
Rise, be a king once more ; nay, be a man !
Appeal unto the people ; they do love thee.
Resume thy throne, resume thy dignity,
Denounce this Herod !   Seize this Herod !   Slay this Herod !
  Hyr. More gently, good my daughter.   I am old.
  Alex. Ay, old in patience !   Make me but thine heir,
And I'll defy him.
  Hyr.   Nay, I crave but peace
As pillow for my age.   My time to rule
Is past, and Time is ruler over me.
Believe me, thou dost somewhat wrong the man.
He is ambitious, but hath not kept all
Of this my kingdom.
  Alex.   What ! not all?   Not all?
Oh, noble generosity !   Not all ?
Thy kingdom is thy spouse, and is there beggar
So lost that he would share with any man
His lawful wife ?   Hyrcanus, O my father,
By thy white hairs I charge thee honor them
And give them back their crown !
  Hyr.   Dear daughter, patience.
Had I the wish, the means were not with me.
  Alex. Take thou thy part, and God will give thee means.
Oh, would I were Hyrcanus, and a man !
Thou soon shouldst see this Herod made a slave !
  Hyr. Hast thou forgot he is thy daughter's husband ?
  Alex. Forgotten it !   Though memory were worn
So full of gaps 'twould not hold yesterday,
That should be recollected !   What ! forgotten
A Herod's blood doth mingle in the veins
That should be clogged with it as with some poison ?
That my grandchildren are half Herod ?—she,
My child, their willing mother ?   No, O God !
When I forget this thing, forget Thou me !

Enter Cypros *and* Salome.

  Cyp. Madam, thou dost talk loudly for a palace.
  Alex. Madam, thou dost talk pertly for a commoner.
  Cyp. How !   Commoner !   The mother of King Herod ?
  Alex. Common for that, if not a commoner.
  Cyp. Insolent shrew !   dost not thou fear to word me?
  Alex. Insolent citizen !   dost not thou fear
To word me ?
  Sal.   Madam, best you have a care.
  Hyr. Ay, good my daughter, pray you guard your tongue.
Who rouses Hate must look for hell to follow.
Come with me.

Alex. Nay, not I. Let these go forth,
If they would not be worded.
Cyp. We go forth
At thy command? Let God obey the devil.
Go thou forth, shrew.
Alex. Let God obey the devil,
For I will not.
Sal. Dost thou insinuate?
Cyp. Ay, dost thou dare?
Hyr. Good Cypros, good Salome,
Good Alexandra——
Alex. Ay, call evil good!
It is thy trade, since thou'st called Herod generous.
Cyp. The king shall hear of this on his return.
Ay, instantly!
Alex. He hath not yet departed.
Here is the lawful king of Israel [*points to* HYRCANUS],
And here his daughter.
Cyp. Herod shall know of this.
Alex. Ay, tell the shoe that the foot chafes with it.
Do, gentle commoner; do, citizen; Cypros, do.
Hyr. Oh, daughter, daughter, you do dig a pit
And rush into it.—Please you, madam, patience.
Cyp. Dost tell me patience? Thou hast heard her? Come,
Salome : if the king be not yet gone,
He shall have word of this.
Sal. Ay, as I live!
[*Exeunt* SALOME *and* CYPROS.
Hyr. Oh, woe is me, my daughter, that my life
May not glide onward stilly to its silence,
But thus by words be lashed into a storm
To toss this frail old bark that bears my soul.
Canst thou not feign a peace, though set for war?
Surely thou need'st not use such taunting terms
As those with which thou hast just heaped the mother
And sister of the king.
Alex. The king again?
And thou dost call him king? More sovereignty
There is in this my tender woman's body
Than e'er was topped by thy lost diadem.
Let us begone. The very air's infected
That they have breathed. [*Exeunt.*

SCENE II.—*Before the palace gates.*

MARIAMNE, *with her two sons,* ALEXANDER *and* ARISTOBULUS.

Mar. How long he tarries! Run, my boys, run quickly,
And see if ye can glimpse him. [*Exeunt boys.*]
This delay
Hath signs that make me fearful. What if Cypros

Hath poured some falsehood in his jealous ears
To poison love? He's here. I'll meet him. Well,

Enter HEROD.

At last thou'rt come, my lord.
  Alex. [*Running to his mother.*] Oh, mother, mother!
He flung me from him, that I tripped and fell!
  Mar. Herod, was this well done?—Hush, hush, my boy:
King's sons weep not for scratches.—Good my lord,
Wilt thou not answer?
  Her.   'Tis a comely boy.
Think you that Antony could father better?
  Mar. Mark Antony? How should I know, my lord?
  Her. How shouldst thou know? That's well, that's very well.
How shouldst thou know? Ay, ay, there is the riddle
The Sphinx hath failed to answer. 'Tis for that
He turns from Egypt for its solving.
  Mar.   Sire,
Thou art in merry mood for sad occasion.
Goest thou in truth to Antony?
  Her.   Ay, madam.
Wilt thou come with me?
  Mar.   No, not if I could.
  Her. Ha? Wherefore not?
  Mar.   Because I'm weary, Herod,
Of thy fierce humors.
  Her.   Weary of my humors?
Weary of me? Thou wilt confess it, then,
Unto my face?
  Mar.   I said not I was weary
Of thee, but of thy humors. As to that,
When they do touch me only, I can bear them;
But when they touch my children, I am roused
Above submission. See how thou'st bruised him, sir!
And he doth look to thee as unto God,
And loves thee above God,—ay, worships thee,—
And thus thou usest him!
  Her.   Come to me, boy.
Thy mother, doth she speak the truth?
  Alex.   Ay, sire,
My mother always speaks the truth.
  Her.   So! does she?
Thou lov'st me, then?
  Alex.   Yes, sire.
  Her.   With all thy heart?
  Alex. With all that's not my mother's.
  Her.   Dost not know
Herod will not take part of anything?
Well, tremble not. So! Let me see thine eyes:
What color are they?

Alex.   Mother saith, like thine.
Her. Ay, doth she? Look! how wouldst thou like a brother
With Roman eyes?
Alex.   What are they like, my lord?
Her. Like Antony's.
Alex.   Is that the Antony
My mother talks of?
Her.   Dost thou say so, boy?
Doth she talk of him? Soft, soft, soft! no tears!
This Antony thy mother talks of,—soft!
No tears, I tell thee,—come, what doth she say
Of Antony?
Alex.   That he's a bad, bad Roman,
Who hath sent here to take thee from us.
Her.   Hold!
Look at me. Thou hast honest eyes.
Mar. [*Coming forward.*]   Ay, Herod,
And he is honest. Wilt thou doubt thy son,
As well as her who mothered him?—Sweet boy,
Come close to me.—Why should he not be honest?
He is Hyrcanus' grandson, and the son
Of Mariamne.
Her.   Not of Herod?
Mar.   Now
Shame on thee, doubting king! I will bear all
But that which slurs my honor. Darest thou stand,
Look in my eyes, and hint me wanton? No,
Thou dost not dare to do it.—Come, my sons,
These are no words to fill your innocent ears:
Bid God-speed to the king your father.
Alex.   Sire,
God speed thee on thy journey.
Aris.   God be with thee.
Mar. Farewell, my lord. God be with thee indeed,
To mend thy doubting heart.   [*Exit with her sons.*
Her.   Stay, Mariamne!
No, I'll not call her back to melt resolve
With love's quick fire. I will be firm in this.
And yet was guilt ne'er forcheaded like that.
The child, too, said that she named Antony
But to abuse him. Yet that is no proof,—
He may have been instructed so to speak.
I will proceed unto the truth in person.
How if it were some trick? My mother hates her,—
Salome too. But then they dared not trick me;
Moreover, they do know that proof awaits me
Whether of their dishonesty or truth.
Be that as 't may, if she hath sent her picture
Unto Mark Antony, by Israel's God,
I'll send her to his wanton as a slave!

ACT II.

SCENE I.—*Laodicea. A room in* ANTONY'S *house.*

Enter ANTONY *and* HEROD.

Ant. Nay, say no more about it. I'm content
Unto the full with what thou'st told me. Tut!
I might have known 'twas woman's babble.
Her.   Ay,
These women that are kin to those we love!
Methinks that Satan was a married man,
And his wife's mother egged him to rebel,
Seeing that heaven would not hold them both.
Ant. Well said! Well said! Thou hast the trick o' humor.
Thou canst trim old facts with invention, sir,
Until they seem not worn. Thou'lt be well missed
In Laodicea. But look you; it is said
Arabia doth not give willing tribute.
How's that?
Her.   Thou'st tapped a cedar, Antony,
And look for it to give forth balsam.
Ant.   So?
Arabia's king is niggardly?
Her.   Good sooth,
As covetous of his gold as Earth herself,
And tighter holds it.
Ant.   So? I have heard as much
From Cleopatra. What's the tribute? Know you?
Her. It was two hundred talents, but of late
It has been less,—considerably less.
Ant. Less? That's not well,—not well. I like not that.
I have no time to war against Arabia.
Two hundred talents? That rich country's veins
Could spare ten hundred drops o' gold, nor beat
One pulse-stroke weaker. If there must be war——
Her. Well?
Ant.   If there must be war, I'll look to thee
To manage it.
Her.   So be it. [*Aside.*] He shrinks from murder
Of one alone, but to secure his death
Would order thousands unto theirs.
Ant. [*Muttering.*]   'Tis pity.
'Tis pity. I'd not have it so. [*Rousing.*] What say you?
Her. Nothing.
Ant.   If there be war, I look to thee,
Remember.
Her. I'll remember.
Ant.   Hold a little,
There are some papers,—those I told thee of.
Wait for me here.   [*Exit* ANTONY.

Her.   Thou Roman hypocrite!
Wait for thee?   Ay, I'll wait, I'll wait.   Fear not
But that I'll wait.   Thou cunning plot-maker!
Make war against Arabia?   Thou'dst make war
Against red hell, if Satan's wife were comely.
And yet this man doth take my hand and clasp me
His closest friend, speak of the things that irk him,
Quote Cæsar freely, whistle Cæsar's Rome
Into my Jewish ears, make light or serious
As the mood takes him ; and doth brood withal
O'er schemes to have me butchered.   Israel's God,
If such is friendship, be not Thou my friend !
Here comes the Roman lover o' Jews' wives.

Enter ANTONY.

Ant.   Here are the papers : please you look at them :
They can be sealed again.   Note this, and this,
And this particularly.   Is't not strange?
Here, too, is something strikes me inconsistent,
And here again.   Dost thou return to-day?
I do not willing spare thee.
    Her.   And I go
Less willingly for thy unwillingness.
When shall I look to welcome thee, my lord,
In Jewry?
    Ant.   Why, ere very long, I trust,
If all works as I'd have it.
    Her. [*Aside.*]   Ay, ay, ay
If all works as thou'dst have it.   Verily
I do believe thee.
    Ant.   What say'st?
    Her.   That these errors
Are strange indeed.   Who drew up these reports?
    Ant. Athenion.
    Her.   With his own hand?
    Ant.   I think so.
    Her. Best thou madest certain.   Then thou'lt come to Jewry,
If all doth work as thou wouldst have it, sir?
    Ant. Indeed, most joyously.
    Her.   Be sure o' that.
    Ant. What, Herod?
    Her.   That thou'lt come most joyously.
    Ant. Why, I am sure of it.
    Her.   Sure?
    Ant.   What's the matter?
Thou makest a mountain of this mole-hill.
    Her.   Ay,
But 'twere a task as difficult, Antony,
To make a mole-hill of a mountain.

Ant.   Well,
Thou'rt in strange mood to-day.   And thou wilt go?
Her. Ay, Antony.
Ant.   I do suspect thee, friend——
Her. Of what?
Ant.   Of being somewhat in my plight.
There is one only difference.
Her.   And that?
Ant. Thou callest thy Cleopatra Mariamne.
Her. Antony!
Ant.   What! So moved at the mere name?
Her. Not at the name, but at the way of naming:
Name not the wife of Herod and thy wanton
In the same breath.
Ant.   How, sir!
Her.   Yes, I repeat it,
And do but ask what I myself fulfil.
Thou hast ne'er heard me name Octavia
In such connection.
Ant.   By the gods! thy pride
Would make Jove's throne its footstool! Have a care!
Dost brave me?
Her.   Thou mayst call it as thou wilt,
The fact remains, I will not have my queen
Come near thy wanton, even in a sentence.
Ant. Gods, sir!
Her.   I know I'm in thy power. Yet, Roman,
I've done but what in my place thou hadst done.
Ant. Well—well—well—well. She's fair enough, in truth,
To make a lover even of a Herod.
Her. How dost thou know she's fair? By hearsay?
Ant.   Ay,
By hearsay and by demonstration both.
I have her picture.
Her. [*Calmly and with tightened lips.*] Ah! thou hast her
              picture?
Ant. And well done, too. One Procrius, a Greek,
Hath limned it. I have oft bethought me, sir,
That thou shouldst have it.
Her. [*More calmly and more rigid.*] Hast thou so, indeed?
Ant. Ay, from the hour I knew it had been sent
By Alexandra, I did purpose to——
Her. By Alexandra! God! by Alexandra?
Didst thou say Alexandra?
Ant.   Ay. What then?
Her. Did Alexandra send it to thee? Speak!
Hyrcanus' daughter, Alexandra?
Ant.   Ay.
What, man! art going mad?—Without, there! ho!
Wine! Water! Anything to drink! Wine, there!

Her. [*Aside.*] (And I have doubted her, have thought her
false,
Bid her a cold farewell.) I cry you grace.
Give me to drink some water. No, not wine !
Water, I tell you ! 'Tis the air, I think,
The closeness of the day. Notice me not.
The picture, thou dost say, was sent to thee
By Alexandra ?
    Ant.   Ay, by Alexandra.
    Her. Dost thou know, Antony, I lied just now ?
    Ant. Lied ?
    Her.   Lied ! I gave thee, friend, to understand
That my wife's mother stood not in my love.
    Ant. And so thou didst.
    Her.   Well, hear me, Antony :
Before the one great God of Israel,
I dote upon her !
    Ant.   Well, of all thy moods
This is the strangest.
    Her.   Yet the welcomest ;
Look you,—the picture,—can I see it now ?
    Ant. I will go bring it to thee.
    Her.   I'm thy debtor. [*Exit* ANTONY.
Oh, Mariamne, Mariamne, Mariamne !
Thou shalt set foot upon my neck for this,
Loll on my throne, and take my diadem
To girdle thee.
And I did bid her cold farewell, and thus
Am one kiss short for all eternity !
And the boy, too,—I hurt him. A brave boy,
So proud he would not weep, although I gripped him
To hurt one tougher by a good ten years.
A valiant boy. And she so fierce for him ;
Ay, ay, she hurt me well for hurting him.
Oh, I'll invent some higher name than prince
To give her sons !
Good Joseph !—he believed in her. Now, truth,
I am half envious of Joseph's goodness.
But he shall not outdo me after this :
Herod the king shall as a warning take
Herod the husband. Yet without a cause
I was not jealous. No, by Jewry's throne,
I was not jealous without cause ! My mother——
Ay, but she did not lie in everything.
No, Alexandra, Alexandra, she——
Hyrcanus' daughter ! Ha ! there's mischief here,
Though of a different temper. She to send
The picture of my wife to Antony ?
To Antony ? Ah, let me think on this !
This hath, in truth, a twang of treachery,

False, scheming Jezebel !   Yet I'll forgive her,
That 'twas herself, not Mariamne,—yea,
Not Mariamne !   But she must to prison,—
To prison, for a time at least.

Enter ANTONY.

Ant. Here is the picture : it is something rough
In certain parts : a taking roughness, though.
Her. Ay, ay, 'tis like, 'tis very like : her eyes
Unto an eyelash, yet not to an eyelash :
There's margin here for the imagination
To make perfection out of, almost.   Why,
I like it for its lack o' sleekness, man.
'Tis only God who can afford to finish !
'Tis like her, but as sunlight's like the sun.
The color's here, but not the radiance.
I thank thee, Antony.   This thought o' thine
Shall father many deeds.   As to Arabia,
I will do all that thou couldst there desire :
Fear not the issue.   Now give me the papers ;
Thou hast not sealed them, though.   Here is a lamp ;
Despatch, I pray thee, for I must begone ;
Or shall I seal them ?
Ant.   Oh, I'll do it for thee.
Gaze on thy pictured queen in peace meantime.
As to the tribute from Arabia,
'Tis in thy hands.   All such auxiliaries
As thou didst purpose for my army's strengthening,
Take in this cause if needs be so.   These papers
Are now as tight as is my trust in thee,
And, like that trust, stamped with my seal.   Commend me
Unto thy queen, thy mother, and thy household ;
Farewell, if thou wilt go.
Her.   I must, my friend.
In everything depend on me.
Ant.   I will.
Her. Then, once more thanking thee as to this matter,
The likeness of my queen, farewell.
Ant.   Farewell.   [*Exit* HEROD.
'Twas well imagined.   Ay, 'twill serve a turn.
Fate hath by this woven his very heart-strings
Into the pattern of my destiny.
He will remember I returned that picture,
Where, otherwise, myself would be forgot.
Ah, well, so goes it.   Yet, as I'm a Roman,
'Twere almost worth my while to turn a Jew
Could I by so becoming fall in love
With mine own lawful spouse.   Yet, after all,
The Jews' God is a bachelor, therefore wise
In that respect above our Roman Jove :

There's nothing quicker rouses envious spleen
Than to behold a man who's deep in love
With his own wife !   [*Exit.*

SCENE II.—*A room in* HEROD'S *palace.*
Enter JOSEPH *and* SALOME.

Jos. Ay, madam, I repeat it,—I repeat it ;
I know thou art my wife, and I repeat it.
God wot, I know that thou'rt my lawful wife,
And yet I do repeat it.   Heaven witness
That I remember Cypros is thy mother,
Thyself my wife Salome, yet again
I do repeat it : ye are both unjust,
Unwise, unwomanly, in this your hatred
Of noble Mariamne.
Sal.   Sir, be warned :
Thou hadst best guard thy tongue.
Jos.   Do thou, then, wife,
Set me example.
Sal.   This to me ?—to me ?
Jos. This unto any one who hates the queen.
I say 'twas base in thee to run to Herod
With this tale of the picture.   Ay, moreover,
That I will ne'er believe she knew 'twas sent,
Till Raphael be commissioned so to say !
Sal. Sir, I do tell thee——
Jos.   Madam, I tell thee
I will not rest till this be set at rights.
She send her picture to Mark Antony !
She would as soon have Satan for a lover.
Ay, that I'll swear to.   She to send her picture !
Salome, in God's name—all praise be His !—
Wherefore, in God's name, as I said, do ye,
Your mother and yourself, so hate the queen ?
Sal. Wherefore ?   Didst say wherefore ?   Thou dost observe
            her,
Her insolence, her arrogance, her scorn,
Her sideward smiles, her upward eyebrows, ay,
Her hints and innuendoes, and then ask
Wherefore ?   Away !   Thou art so blind with doting
Upon this virtuous queen, thou canst not see
When she insults thy wife.
Jos.   I can well see
When that my wife insults me.   Come, be careful :
No more o' that.
Sal.   No more of what ?
Jos.   Of that
I shame to mention,—how much more to hear !
Woman, see that thou dost not drop again
Into such wicked hinting.   Nay, no word :

I will not hear it. God protect the queen
From thy tongue's venom! In the mean time, I,
Being His servant, will do what I can
To keep her happy. Nay, I tell thee, peace.
I will not hear so much as one foul word
Against Queen Mariamne!
Sal.   Will not?
Jos.   Ay,
Will not.
Sal. Thou wilt not hear me speak? Thou?—thou?
Thou wilt not hear me speak?—Salome?—me?—
Thy wife, and Herod's sister?
Jos.   Herod's self
Should not to me insult his queen.
Sal.   Out, slave!
Jos. Slave, maybe, but unchained. Therefore be still.
Here comes the queen herself.
Sal. [*Muttering.*] A crownéd baggage.

   Enter MARIAMNE *and her two sons.*

Mar. Let us sit here, sweet boys.—Madam, good-morrow.
Fair greeting to thee, friend.—Come, Alexander,
Bring me thy bow, I'll string it.
Sal.   Pray you, madam,
Whence came that bow?
Mar.   It was my husband's, madam,
When that he was a lad.
Sal.   He will ill take it
That thou hast fingered o'er his trappings thus.
Mar. Ah! dost thou think so?—Not so hard, my boy;
Set thy knee to it steadily. Now, now,
There goes the string! Now see if thou canst bend it.
Alex. Almost. 'Tis stiff. Whew! but it stung my wrist!
There. Is that better?
Jos.   Good, good, good, my lad!
Thy father will be boy again to watch thee.
Well done! Well done!
Alex.   What sayest thou, mother?
Mar.   Why,
Well done, indeed, my warrior.
Sal.   Have care;
I know thy father's humor, boy. Beware
Lest thy fine weapon turn into a rod
For thy chastisement.
Alex.   Madam, dost thou think
A son of Herod would be beaten?
Sal.   Ay,
If Herod snuffed occasion. Ay, young sir,
I do, most surely.
Mar.   Then thou art mistaken.

He is not only Herod's son, but mine.
Think you I'd see him beaten?
 Sal.   What wouldst do?
Close thine eyes, girl?
 Mar.   No, but have closed in death
The eyes of any who did try it.
 Sal.   Ay,
Were it the king himself. I can believe thee.
 Mar. Thou talkest idly, madam, and beyond
Thy mark o' freedom.—Come here, pretty one.
         [*To* ARISTOBULUS.]
Wouldst thou shoot, too?
 Aris.   Ay, mother, that I would.
But that's too big for me.
 Mar.   I'll have one cut, then,
Fit for thy dainty grasp. How's that, my heart?
 Aris. Oh, well, well, well! I will shoot too. Oh, ay!
Brother! oh, brother, look, I'm going to shoot,
Better than thee! I'm going to kill a tiger
And sleep upon his hide. And then another;
That shall be mother's. Then another yet
For Uncle Joseph. Uncle, wouldst thou like it?
Thou wilt not mind the hole my arrow makes,
Wilt thou? Look, uncle, big as this. Look, mother,
As big as this!
 Mar.   Sweet chatterer, come here.
Thou'rt treading on thy aunt Salome's robe.
 Sal. What's that? Let him tread on. His mother, truth,
Sets foot upon my neck: then why not he
Upon my garments? Go on, boy, go on.
 Alex. Why, what's the matter, aunt? What has he done?
 Sal. What is the matter? Out, thou babbling brat!
I'll answer thee. [*Cuffs him.*]
 Mar. [*Seizing her wrist and swinging her to her knees by a
   sudden movement.*]
      Ask thou his pardon, there.
Do as I bid thee. It were best for thee.
Look in my eyes, and thou wilt know 'twere best
For thee and thine that thou obeyed'st me! Quick,
His pardon.
 Sal. [*As if cowed.*] Well, I ask it, then.
 Mar.   More, more.
Say, " Alexander, son of Mariamne,
I crave thy pardon with all humbleness."
Say it!
 Sal. I say it.
 Mar.   Woman, speak those words!
Speak!
 Sal. Alexander, son of Mariamne,
I crave thy pardon.

Mar.   With all humbleness.
Sal. Well, with all humbleness.
Mar.   Now crave thou mine.
Jos. Nay, madam.
Mar.   Crave thou mine!
Sal. [*Sneeringly.*]   Ay, Joseph, plead!
Mar. Crave thou my pardon, woman!
Sal.   Well, I crave it. [*Rising to her feet.*]
But better for thee hadst thou cursed high heaven
Than dared Salome's vengeance!   [*Exit.*
Jos. Good madam, if it had been possible,
I would thou hadst left this undone.
Mar.   Good uncle,
In that she is thy wife, with all my heart
I wish so too. But it was written so.
Think on't no more. Thou hast my trust and love
In everything save in thy spouse, good uncle.
I cannot feign. Therein is my chief fault—
Or virtue, as you will.—Look, little one,
Go with thine uncle: he will see thy bow
Doth suit thee.
Aris.   Wilt thou truly, uncle dear?
Jos. Ay, that I will. Come on.—Sweet niece, I thank thee.
                    [*Exit* ARISTOBULUS *and* JOSEPH.
Alex. Mother, I loved thee when thou flungest her down!
How strong thou art! Oh, thou art very queen
Without thy diadem, as night is night
Without the stars. Sweet mother!
Mar.   Ah, my boy,
Thou dost not know——
Alex.   What, mother?
Mar. [*Absently.*]   What it is
To be a Herod's wife.
Alex.   How dost thou mean?
Mar. [*As if to herself.*]
Doubted at every turn,—insulted, braved
By those who most should cherish me,—my children
Subject to slights which I could better bear,
My mother scorned, her father set at naught,
And I not even queen over his moods.
Alex. What art thou saying, mother? Please remember
That which thou saidst thou'dst tell me.
Mar.   What, dear?
Alex.   Why,
How thou first saw'st my father! How he threw
The javelin! how rode the Arab horse!
Oh, thou dost know. Wilt thou not tell me now?
Mar. How I first saw thy father?
Alex.   Ay. Please do it.
Mar. It is so long ago.

Alex.   Oh, mother, please !
Don't say thou hast forgotten it, sweet mother !
Think !
   Mar. God in heaven ! it is the one last thing
That I would do. Nay, never heed me, child ;
I do remember what thou'dst have. So, then,
Sit there. How like, how like thine eyes are, sweet,
Unto thy father's ! Well, I'll on. Let's see :
How was it, now ? His very trick o' lip.
Well, well, I'll tell thee. 'Twas a summer day,
And I a maid of Spring. Canst thou think, boy,
Of me as being some sweet little maid
Such as thou'lt some day woo and marry ?
   Alex.   Nay,
I will not wed her unless she be in truth
Thy very copy as thou art this instant.
   Mar. Oh, darling ! thy old mother?
   Alex.   Old ! Thou old ?
But tell the story, for thou shalt not tease me.
   Mar. 'Twas Nisan, then, a day o' cloud and shine,
Yet all the clouds condensed would scarce have dyed
One o' thy swarthy locks. There was a festival,
And there were promised many feats of strength
And skill in various ways, especially
Casting the javelin. Thou knowest, sweet,
Samaria was my home, the lovely " vale
Of many waters,"—so they call it. Oh
To see the great pomegranate-trees in bloom
Once more—but once ! It was in very truth
As though the heart's blood of the year had stained them.
I'm coming to thy father ! I was then
Affianced to him only, ne'er had seen
Even his pictured face, and greatly feared
To think of how he might appear. At last,
When almost we were tired o' watching youths
Draw bows or brandish spears, he came. His horse,
A coal-black Arab, trapped in beaten gold,
As though dark Night had borrowed of bright Day,
Chafed at the reins and reared. At that the king,
Herod, thy father, dashed his mighty fist
Against the brute's strained crest, then, loosing rein,
Poised lithely, with his javelin aloft,
Keen on the changing air. Onward they swooped,
Straight on, with singing hair and hoofs a-thunder,
Like to a wind made visible.
   Alex.   On, mother !
Tell me the rest ! Please, mother ! mother ! mother !
Don't stop to think of it ! Tell me the rest !
   Mar. He cast the javelin. The severed air
Shrieked with its wound, and, lo ! the last shot arrow

That marked the target quivered, cleft in twain
By that sure-hurléd blade.
 Alex.   He cleft the arrow?—
The shaft itself? Oh, mother, dost thou think
I could so cast.a javelin some day?
Not now, but when I'm bigger? Dost thou think it?
 Mar. I know not if thou couldst excel withal
To such extent as did thy father, dear :
He is world-honored for such feats. But, truth,
I think thou couldst in part approach his skill.
Thou hast his very swing o' carriage.
 Alex.   Well,
What next? What did he then?
 Mar.   Leaped from his horse
And caught me in his arms.

      Enter HEROD.

 Her.   As he doth now!
What! trembling? Oh, my queen! my wife! my life!
Tremble no more! Give me thy lips! Look up!
Nay, sweet, look down. [*Kneeling.*] Here is my rightful place;
Here let me kneel forever!
 Mar.   Nay, my lord,
Thy place is something higher, for 'tis here.
         [*Touching her heart.*]
 Her. Then lift me to it, for I dare not rise
Of my sole self unto such happiness.
 Mar. [*Lifting him.*] Come, then.
 Her.   Oh, God! to love like this is pain.
Give me thy shoulder for a moment, sweet.
All of me that's not Herod is in mine eyes.
 Mar. And all that's Herod or not Herod, love,
Is in my heart.
 Her. [*Taking her face into his hands.*] In nothing changed :
  the same
Deep, maddening eyes; lips curled for love ; rich locks
That tempt the fingers. Ay, the same, the same,
Even to that flutter in thy throat when touched,
As though thy heart were some wild, wingéd thing
That struggled to be free. Wild heart, I'll kiss thee
For being wild. [*Kisses her throat.*]
 Mar.   Ah, Herod! ah, thy corselet!—
It cuts my arm.
 Her.   Let my lips plead its pardon.
[*Kissing her shoulder.*] God's heart, girl, thou art twenty times
  more sweet
Than all thy dear Samaria's sun-kissed fruits.
Thy lips! Once more thy lips!—thy lips !—thy lips !
 Mar. Nay, Herod! Herod! thou forgett'st the boy.
This is not seemly.

Her.   Ho ! Not seemly, say'st thou ?
Herod and seemly harnessed, were as well
As were a tiger lashed unto a dove.
 Mar. Yet doves, the Greeks do tell us, draw Love's chariot.
 Her. The chariot of Love's queen.   The king of love
Guides heel-winged tigers with a sword of flame.
Talk not to me of doves : it is as though
One little, milk-white cloud did near the blaze
Of some red sunset.   Heaven is in my heart
Because of thee,—but heaven on fire.   Look, boy ;
Come to my knee.   Thou art a well-knit lad :·
Wouldst learn to cast the javelin ?
 Alex.   Oh, father !
 Her. That's well,—that's well.   Ay, call me father, boy :
I like it better than more stately terms
From thy young lips.—He hath thy brows, my queen.
 Mar. Nay, thine—unto a hair.
 Her.   Why, heart, look here :
For th' dark original of this proud arch
I first did love thee.   Mine ?   Thou knowest well
Those were ne'er copied from my shaggy front.—
Look thou, to-morrow ere the sun be high
I'll teach thee how to cast a javelin.
 Alex.   Sire !
 Her. Nay, father, or no javelin.
 Alex.   Dear father !
 Her. Thou rogue ! that knack o' sweetness, without ques-
          tion,
Was from thy mother gotten.   Well, come kiss me.
Now off.
 Alex.   Ay, father.   Mother dear, farewell !   [*Exit.*
 Her. Now to my lips !
 Mar.   My lord.
 Her.   Nay, do not speak.
 Mar. I cannot breathe.
 Her.   Ah, peace !
 Mar.   Nay, let me breathe.
 Her. Presently, by and by.   Why, struggle not.
I would not hurt thee.
 Mar.   But thou dost,—thou dost.
Thou art so strong thou dost not know.
 Her.   Well, there.
Come lean against me.   Look ! what thinkest thou
That I have here ?   [*Touching his breast.*]
 Mar.   I cannot think.
 Her.   But try,
To please me.   Come.
 Mar.   A lock of hair ?
 Her.   Ay, that,
Since first I loved thee ; but there's something else.

Mar. Indeed I cannot think what 'tis.
Her. [*Taking out picture.*]　　　　Why, here,—
What dost thou think o' this?
Mar.　　　　　　　　Why, 'tis myself!
When didst thou have it done?　And where?　By whom?
Am I as fair as that?
Her.　　　　Is moonlight fair
As starlight?
Mar.　　　Nay, my eyes are not so large.
Her. Larger.
Mar. ·　　　Oh, Herod, no!　And see what lips!
Her. I'd rather feel them.　Nay, shrink not, shrink not:
Thou dost not know how 't chafes me when thou shrinkest.
Mar. I will not, then.　Who painted it?
Her.　　　　　　　　A Greek
Named Procrius.　Here, take it in thy hands.
'Tis well done, is it not?　[*Aside.*]　She is as true
To me as I was false to her.　I'd swear
By every goddess in the Roman heaven
That she ne'er eyed that picture in her life.
Ay, 'twas all Alexandra.　God of Israel!
Would to Thy mercy that, like Adam's wife,
All others could be mothered by a rib!
Mar. [*Coming towards him.*]　　　　It is most wondrous.
In truth, my love, it gladdens me at heart
That thou'st so good a copy of myself,
To help remembrance when thou'rt absent.
Her.　　　　　　　　Nay,
Memory needs no aid from Mariamne.
But how thinkest thou I got this picture?
Mar.　　　　　　　　Truth,
It is beyond me.
Her.　　　Whose dost think it was
Ere it was mine?
Mar.　　　I cannot dream.
Her.　　　　　　　　Why, then——
Mark Antony's.
Mar.　　　Mark Antony's!　Thou jestest.
Her. I do not jest.　Thy mother sent this picture
Unto Mark Antony.
Mar.　　　No! no!　Why should she?
Her. I know not; but for no good,—that I know.
Mar. What wilt thou do?
Her.　　　　Thou knowest as well as I
That for offence so grave imprisonment
Were a light punishment.
Mar.　　　　Ah, for my sake
Forgive her.　Thou dost know how rash she is,—
How hot o' temper.　'Twas a crime, indeed,
To bare my face unto the Roman's eyes;

But I, who bare my very soul to thee,
Do crave her pardon.   Look, my lord, I kneel.
    Her. No, by my soul ! thou never shalt bend knee
To any save thy God.   She was forgiven
At thy first asking.
    Mar.   Now thou'rt king indeed,—
Now Herod at his best.
    Her.   Come, prove it, then,
Upon my lips.—Who comes?

Enter JOSEPH *and* ARISTOBULUS.

    Aris. [*Brandishing a little bow and arrow.*]   Oh, mother,
        look ! look ! look ! [*Seeing the king.*]   Oh, uncle !
    Her.   Soft !
Come here, boy.   Why, thou art most bravely weaponed.
Canst bend that monstrous bow?—Good uncle, greeting.
    Jos. I knew not thou wert back, my lord, indeed.
When didst thou come?
    Her.   Why, some few moments gone.
Uncle, I would have word with thee.—My love,
Farewell until this interview be o'er.
Wait for me in our chamber.
    Mar.   .   Ay, my lord.
Come, little archer.   [*Exit with* ARISTOBULUS.
    Her. Good uncle, thou wert right in all thou saidst :
The mother of my queen, and not herself,
Did send her picture to Mark Antony.
    Jos. Praise be to God for this ! And, good my lord,
Let it be long ere thou again dost doubt her.
    Her. Is never long enough ?
    Jos.   Ay, if thou'rt serious.
But close thine ears against the slanders, sire,
My wife and thine own mother are most sure
Again to bring thee.
    Her.   Death's not deafer, sir,
Than I will be.
    Jos. Nor let looks stir thee.
    Her.   None,
As I am king.
    Jos.   As thou art man !
    Her.   Ay, then,
As I am man.   Not one, not one.   Rest, uncle ;
I will be staunch.   But look you, sir : what object
Dost think Hyrcanus' daughter had in this?
    Jos. Nay, I know not.   Some woman's muddle, surely.
Thou'lt not stir up dissension when 'tis napping,
For such small cause ?
    Her.   Small cause, say you ? Small cause !
Just heaven ! it hath never seemed so great
As by this "small" o' thine.   Small cause, that she,

My queen, hath been unveiled unto the eyes
That are a wanton's daily mirrors ! Oh,
Small cause had God to punish Lucifer,
If that my cause against this shrew be small !
   Jos. What wilt thou, then ?
   Her.   I would have 'prisoned her,
But that my queen did plead against it, sir.—
Unto less heart-near matters : Antony
Has given Cœlosyria to his jade.
   Jos. That's better for Judea than for Antony.
Sawest Cleopatra while in Laodicea ?
   Her. Ay. How she hates me !
   Jos.   Thou wert safer, nephew,
In Cleopatra's hate than in her love.
   Her. Ay, but she works against me.

Enter CYPROS.

                          Greeting, mother.
How dost thou ?
   Cyp.   Well in body, but in mind
Something less easy. Sir, I crave your leave.
[*Aside.*] Bid him go forth. I have some news for thee.
   Her. Is it so musty now it will not keep ?
   Cyp. It doth concern Hyrcanus' daughter, Herod.
If thou'st no care to hear it, I will go.
   Her. Nay, stay. Of Alexandra ? I will hear it.—
Uncle, thy leave.
   Jos.   Nephew, thy promise.
   Her.   Ay,
I will remember.
   Jos.   Heaven aid thee, then !   [*Exit.*
   Her. Mother, thou art not in my love just now.
How camest thou to state so falsely, madam,
This matter of the picture ?
   Cyp.   Good my son,
How dost thou mean ?
   Her. Thou knewest all the while
Hyrcanus' daughter sent it,—not my wife.
   Cyp. Nay, Herod, as I live. But how dost know
'Twas only Alexandra ?
   Her.   That's no matter.
Suffice it that I know. What's this thou saidst
Thou hadst to tell me ?
   Cyp.   While that thou wast gone,
Reports did reach us thou wert slain by Antony ;
Whereon this woman strove to coax thy uncle
That he would set forth straightway from Judea
And seek protection with the Roman legion.
   Her. She did ?
   Cyp.   Ay, by my soul !

Her.   Thou hast once lied :
How shall I know if once thou speakest truth ?
Cyp. Here comes Salome : ask her.
Her.   Hath Salome
The writ of truth about her ? [*Enter* SALOME.]
                              Look you, sister,
What of this flying to the Roman ensigns ?
Sal. True.
Her.   Wilt thou swear it ?
Sal.   Ay.
Her.   God knows ye women
Would swear hell heaven, to win the devil over.
How shall I know ?
Cyp.   Ask Joseph.
Sal.   Nay, not Joseph.
Her. Why not ?
Sal.   Because he would swear wet were dry,
To win one smile from thy chaste queen.
Her.   What meanest thou ?
Sal. But what I said.
Her.   Why saidst thou " my chaste queen" ?
Sal. Is she not chaste ?
Her.   Softly ! No insolence !
Why should I not ask Joseph ?
Sal.   Ask him, then :
'Tis naught to me.
Her.   But 'tis not naught to me !
Woman, give word.   Why dost thou simper ?   Speak !
What dost thou smirk at ?
Sal.   Why, at mine own thoughts.
Her. Are they so merry ?—Mother, dost thou know
Why thus she Josephs me ?
Cyp.   'Tis not unnatural
A wife should feel some jealousy when——
Her.   Ay,
When what ?   This ' what's' the thing.   Sister, have care,—
Have care : I am more Mariamne's husband
Than I'm thy brother.
Sal.   Think'st thou that is news ?
Her. Then answer.
Sal.   I have answered.
Her.   Trifle not.
What dost thou hint at ?
Sal.   Hinting's not my way.
Thank God, I have the courage to be honest.
Her. Then demonstrate it.   What didst mean just now,
By saying that Joseph would swear wet were dry,
To win a smile from Mariamne ?
Sal.   Why,
That he would do it.   There's no mystery there.

Her. Pernicious vixen! I'd not husband thee
Though on our wedding-day I were to pose
God of the hundredth heaven! What dost thou mean,
Thou smirking obstinacy? Speak, I say!
If that thou dost not word it o' th' instant,
I'll give thy vaunted courage work to do.
Sal. If thou wouldst hear thy shame told as a tale,
Pardon me if I would not so hear mine.
Her. My shame and thine? My shame? Have care! have
care!
Herod is Herod, though ten times a brother.
My shame? My shame? My shame? Ay, let thy blood
Forswear thy poisonous lips, as that of thee
In my hot veins forswears thy poisonous self.
Mother, begone! we'll have this out alone.
No word! Depart! [*Exit* CYPROS.]
                                      Now, woman.
Sal.   Why dost glare?
'Tis not my fault.
Her.   Fault? Fault? Who spoke of fault?
Just now 'twas shame. Well, shame's a fault, that's true.
And faults are shameful when found out. Come, hasten,
Madam, this matter.
Sal. [*Pulling out a bracelet.*] Hast thou e'er seen this?
Her. Ah, 'tis the bracelet I gave Mariamne
At our betrothal. Jade, how didst thou get it?
She wears it ever on her left arm.
Sal.   Nay,
Did wear,—not wears it.
Her.   Girl, where didst thou find it?
Sal. In Joseph's closet.
Her.   May that lie thrice damn thee!
What! thou wouldst have me think——oh, devilish harpy!—
Have I e'er called thee sister? Look, Salome,
If thou hast jested, I'll forgive thee.
Sal.   Nay,
If I had jested, I would not forgive
Myself.
Her. Oh, devil!—devil!
Sal.   Why, just powers!
Let me begone ere that I am quite murdered
For doing what's my duty.
Her.   Move no step
Until I wring that poisonous mind o' thine
Of its last drop. Thou say'st thou found'st this bracelet
Within thy husband's closet?
Sal.   Ay.
Her.   Then thou
Didst steal and put it there!
Sal.   Brother!

Her.   I say,
If thou didst find the bracelet of my wife
In Joseph's closet, thou didst steal it thence
And put it there for reasons of thine own !
Sal. Herod !
Her.   Ay, that's the name of Jewry's king.
Doth any dare to brave him who doth bear it?
Look you, if this be false,—nay, it is false,—
Why, mark you, then, if when I show this bracelet
Unto my queen, with word of thy foul slander,—
If, when I tell her this, she pleads not for thee,
To have thee pardoned, dear as is this toy
For all the memories that it doth enring,
I'll have it beaten to an arrow-head,
And send it through thy false and shrivelled heart
With mine own hand !   [*Exit.*
Sal.   Accurséd be ye both !

ACT III.

SCENE I.—*A room in* HEROD'S *palace.*

Enter MARIAMNE *and* ALEXANDRA.

Mar.. Mother, I do but ask thee be advised.
Alex. Thou dost but ask me be advised? Indeed !
So thou dost only ask me be advised ?
Well, am I not a docile, patient mother ?—
A gentle, good, obedient, humble queen ?
Thou ask'st me be advised ! Now, let a babe
Advise its mother how to suckle it,—
The stars grow independent, and turn back
Upon their courses to instruct high God
How they should move,—earth rail at heaven's method,—
The entire and changeless system change about,
Until at last the nations rule their kings,
Not kings their nations ! · Thou advise me !
Mar.   Madam,
Thou must acknowledge that it was not seemly
To send my picture to the Roman general.
What purpose hadst thou ?
Alex.   What is that to thee,
Since 'twas unseemly ? Thou wouldst not seek, surely,
To learn unseemly matters ?
Mar.   Good my mother,
Wilt thou not see that all my care in this
Hath been to place thee beyond scorn or danger ?
Thou ran'st a risk almost as terrible
As when thou soughtest to convey thyself

And Aristobulus to Cleopatra
Concealed in perforated coffins.
 Alex.   Risk !
What risk ? Of what ?
 Mar.   Of being imprisoned.
 Alex.   I ?—
I be imprisoned ?—I ?—Hyrcanus' daughter ?—
The sometime queen of this usurping king ?
 Mar. Mother, have care.
 Alex.   He to imprison me ?
He—Herod—to imprison Alexandra ?
Out ! I will not believe it.
 Mar.   Best thou didst.
 Alex. What ! thou wouldst suffer it ?
 Mar.   To be a queen
Doth mean to suffer many things, good mother ;
And who should know this better than thyself ?
 Alex. Ay, who indeed, O God !
 Mar.   Then for my sake
Be warned in time. For there may come an hour
When even Mariamne 'll plead in vain.
 Alex. What wouldst thou ?
 Mar.   Be but careful. Make no plans
To follow secret ways. Thou knowest well
Thou'rt watched at every turn.
 Alex.   Ay, well I know it.
But what's more exquisite than by thy skill
To make the watcher watch in vain,—outwit him,—
Baffle him utterly ?
 Mar.   But recollect
How thou hast ever failed unto this moment.
 Alex. We must thrice fail to be successful once.
I have once more to fail.
 Mar.   Believe me, mother,
That " once" might never live to breed success.
Here comes the king. I'll ask thee now to go :
'Twere best he did not now see us together.
 Alex. I'll think of what thou'st said, but will not promise.
No promises.   [*Exit.*
 Mar. She is my body's mother,
And yet she seems as daughter to my soul.
Oh, would to God that she would be advised !
There's something ominous to me of late
In very silence, and my urgent heart
Cries, " Herod ! Herod ! Herod !" till the night
Is vibrant with his name. Would unto God
I knew to what extent he loveth me,
Or could but sift his passion through his love
And note how much the one outweighs the other !
Joseph doth hold unto the theory

That he doth cherish me above ambition ;
And yet I doubt :—men so oft love the pleasure
Above the pleasure-giver.   Love lives on trifles,
And we can lose him wholly with an eye,
A broken tooth, an arm, our tresses' gold.
How if some day this face which now he worships
Were by some grievous accident scarred o'er,
Made hideous ?   How if mine eyes were blurred
By some fierce, sudden blight ?—my figure mangled ?
How if—oh, God !—I were a leper ?   Then—
Would he then love me ?   Nay, a leprous soul
Were easier borne of men than that one lock

Enter HEROD.

Should lose its beauty !   Yet, withal, how Joseph
Doth dwell upon his constancy !   Good Joseph !
His wife's the only evil thing about him.
Good, faithful Joseph !
 Her.   Madam, I am come.
Is Joseph here ?
 Mar.   No.   Dost thou wish for him ?
I'll have him called.
 Her.   Nay, but I heard his name ;
I'm sure I heard his name.
 Mar.   Why, so thou didst :
I spoke of him.
 Her.   Spoke of him ?   What of him ?
Do thy thoughts oft run Joseph-wards ?
 Mar. Indeed they do, my lord.
 Her.   Ha !
 Mar.   I am certain, sir,
He is the faithfullest of those about thee.
 Her. The faithfullest ?
 Mar.   Ay.   Why dost thou so stare ?
 Her. Know'st thou this bracelet ?
 Mar.   Oh ! where didst thou find it ?
Thank God 'tis found !   How strange that thou shouldst find it !
 Her. Strange ?
 Mar. Ay.   What then ?
 Her.   Wherefore is it so strange
That I should find thy bracelet ?
 Mar.   'Twas my thought,—
My woman's way o' conjuring coincidence
Out of a leaf-fall.   I did say 'twas strange
Because it is the bracelet thou didst give me
At our betrothal.   Aristobulus
Did slip it from mine arm this very morn
While playing, and I have not seen it since,
Though every servant hath been erranded
Throughout the palace to make search for it.

Her. Where is the boy?
Mar.   With Joseph.
Her.   Is there none
Save Joseph to amuse him?
Mar.   Nay, thine uncle
Doth love our boys.
Her.   And our boys' mother,—yes.
Mar. I think he doth. He is the only one
Of all thy household who is civil to me.
Her. Insinuations?
Mar.   Dost insinuate
That I insinuate?
Her.   Why not? thou art—
A woman.
Mar.   And a queen.
Her.   By heaven, thou lookest it!
See that thou act it, too. Have the boy called.
Mar. Who?—Aristobulus?
Her.   Ay.
Mar.   Wherefore, sir?
Her. Have the boy called, I say.
Mar.   I pray you, Herod,
If that he hath offended,—if (more like)
Thy sister and thy mother have borne tales
Concerning him——
Her.   Away!
Mar.   If thou'st been urged
To harshly deal with him, do not, I pray thee.
Her. Peace!
Mar.   He's so young, so frail, so timorous,
So fearful of thee.
Her.   It were well his mother
Took lesson by that last. Call him, I say.
Mar. And I, that I will not, unless thyself
Dost tell me why thou wishest him.
Her.   Thou wilt not?
—Without, there! [*Enter Servant.*]
                         Tell the young prince Aristobulus
To wait on me immediately. Hasten!
Mar. If 'tis thy purpose to ungently use him,
Myself shall stand between ye!

Enter ARISTOBULUS.

                                        Come, my heart;
None shall entreat thee.
Aris.   Is he angry with me?
Mar. I know not; but he shall not hurt thee.
Her.   Boy,
When didst thou have this bracelet?
Mar.   Ah!

Aris.   This morning.—
Oh, mother, who did find it? I'm so glad!
Did the king find it, mother?
  Mar.   I know not.
  Her. Where didst thou have it last?
  Aris.   I don't remember.
  Her. Thou dost not?
  Aris.   No. I think——
  Her.   Well, out with it!
What dost thou think?
  Aris.   I think my uncle Joseph
Took us into his chamber, and I think—
I think—I think——
  Her.   Gods! what dost stammer at?
I will not eat thee.
  Mar.   Thou dost eye him so.
  Her. What, then! shall I not look at mine own son?
What is it that thou thinkest, boy?
  Aris.   'Twas there
I dropped it.
  Her.   Come to me.
  Aris.   Oh, mother!
  Her.   Come.
  Mar. Nay, go, my boy.—If thou dost hurt him, Herod,
From that same moment I'm no more thy wife!
  Her. So be it, then.—Come to me, boy. Now up,—
Up for a kiss. Here, take this chain with thee:
'Twill make as bright a plaything as the bracelet.
Now, dost thou love me?
  Aris.   I—I—think so. Oh!
I mean, I do. Don't hurt me. Put me down.
  Her. Go, then.
  Aris.   May I go, mother?
  Mar.   Ay.
         Exit ARISTOBULUS.

  Her.   My queen,
Come, let me new-betroth thee.
  Mar.   First, my lord,
Tell me the meaning of this most strange scene
Through which we have just gone.
  Her.   For what wouldst know?
  Mar. For that I am thy wife and Jewry's queen.
Thinkest thou, my lord, that thou canst doubt me—ay,
In any way—and that I'll meekly bear it?
I tell thee thou hadst better doubt thyself
Ten thousand times than Mariamne once!
  Her. I do not doubt thee.
  Mar.   Thou hast doubted me;
And once to doubt is ever to be doubtful.
Thinkest thou I did not mark the hidden meaning

With which thou didst enweigh the boy's least word,—
How thou didst question and cross-question him,
Frighten, soothe, frown, and smile all in an instant?
Why didst thou summon him—my child, my last-born—
To answer what his mother had replied to?
Ay, wherefore didst thou that? And as thou entered'st,
Why didst thou eye me when I spoke of Joseph?
There's more in all of this than Joseph only.
Can it be Joseph's wife?
Her.   How if it were?
Mar. Then farewell happiness, farewell peace, hope,
Life, joy, content,—ay, Herod, fare thee well!
Her. How dost thou mean?
Mar.   If Herod once hath listened
Unto Salome, Death may wed with Life
Ere Mariamne be again a queen!
Her. Why, what dost mean?
Mar.   That thy trust was my throne,
Thy love my sceptre, and thy faith my crown.
Shall I be queen and yet despoiled of these?—
A beggar of small favors in the kingdom
Where I was wont to reign? Not I!—O God!
I'd rather be Thy humblest slave, than queen
Unto a king whom a Salome rules!
Her. Nay, Mariamne.
Mar.   Am I Mariamne,
And yet my child made witness 'gainst me? Mariamne,
And yet Salome heard before me? Mariamne,
And yet by Herod doubted?
Her.   By my kingdom,
I do not doubt thee.
Mar.   Then why brought'st my child
To prove me? Yea, if that the flesh were false
From whence he sprung, why should he be more true?
How didst thou know 'twere not a lesson taught,
That guiltiness might look like innocence?
Who is there in the breadth of Israel
To prove that Mariamne is not false?
Her. Herself! He who could meet thine eyes and doubt thee
Would prove himself the very core of falseness!
Mar. He who Salome trusts doubts Mariamne.
Thou canst not both believe in Jove and Jah:
Honor to one doth mean to one dishonor,—
For one a throne, for one a sepulchre.
Her. Madam, I swear to thee.
Mar.   Swear unto God:
His throne is sure.
Her.   No surer than thine own.
Mar. Then heaven's kingdom rocks.
Her.   Nay, be assured.

Mar. Of what? Of my abasement? Would to God
I were as sure of ultimate content!
Her. Nay, Mariamne, hear me. Let me speak.
I never was suspicious without cause.
Mar. And such a cause!
Her.   Why, there was reason in't.
Mar. One grain of reason leavens a huge mass
Of inconsistency. Of what, my lord,
Am I suspected?
Her.   I was told to-day
This bracelet had been found in Joseph's closet.
Mar. What if it had? What then? In Joseph's closet?
What if it had been found in Joseph's closet?
Her. Why, sure thou seest where conclusion points?
Mar. He points into a blackness where mine eyes
Are sensible of naught but blackness.
Her.   .   Why,
Thou knowest how mine uncle worships thee,
Is ever ready to defend or serve thee,
Doth in the least thing find thee love-worthy.
Mar. And so he doth. What then? What hath my bracelet
To do with this?
Her.   Why, 'tis self-evident.
Thou hast ne'er parted from it till to-day,—
Not once since I first clasped it on thee. Well,
Then, when I hear—dost mark me?—when I hear
It has been found in Joseph's closet,—ay,
When I hear where 'twas found, was it but natural
That I should think—should find it strange—should wonder——
Oh, thou must understand what I would say.
It is all past : let us not think on it,—
Let us not think.
Mar.   I will be queen to Death
When I have ceased to think upon it. What!
Thou didst suspect me with thine uncle? Me?
Thy queen, thy wife, the mother of thy sons?
Thou hast suspected me, and with thine uncle?
—Now, God in heaven, commemorate this day
By pardoning Satan, for Thou mayest withal
Unjustly have condemned him!
Her.   Hear me, madam.
Mar. Hear thee, to have mine ears more blasted? Nay,
Let deafness rescue me from further words
That thou mayst utter!
Her.   Madam.
Mar.   Out! Away!
I will not hear thee! False with Joseph? False?—
False with his treasurer? Nay, God, with any?
Why, I must laugh at this! The world must laugh!

Oh, God! Oh, God! I am indeed unqueened!
My heart and sceptre both at once are broken!
Her. Weep not.
Mar.   I do not weep! Tears, such as women
Do shed for lesser causes, I would scorn
To offer this my sorrow. The red drops
Shed from my riven heart, no man may witness,
Though he were ten times tyrant, ten times king,
Ten times a Herod!
Her.   Mariamne.
Mar.   Ay,
Murder my name, now thou hast slain my honor!
Cry, "Mariamne," till the west doth ring
An echo to the east, north unto south,
The earth to heaven, until the very stars
Cease in their song, to shriek, "Adulteress!"
Her. Why, thou art mad!
Mar.   Oh, would to God I were!—
That this my reason had not joy survived,
To view my misery as a thing apart!
—O God! Shame is chief torturer in hell:
Kill me outright, and be more merciful
Than hadst Thou spared more lives than I have griefs!
Her. Wilt thou not listen?
Mar.   Shall I tutor God?
Since He is deaf to me, I unto thee
Will be deaf also!
Her.   Mariamne, stay.
Mar. She was the queen of Jewry, and was slain
By one of Herod's words. I am the queen
Of my sole self; therefore I will begone.   [*Exit.*
Her. How she defies me! Yet I swear I love her
The more for her defiance. She were one
To sit beside Jah on His throne and nod
At quits with Juno. She hath scourged me bravely,
Yet from each wound my heart's blood leaped with love,
To kiss the hand that smote. And she was proud,
Held herself loftily, and veiled her eyes
Beneath her haughty lids, as who should say,   ·
"Thine halves can view sufficiently this Herod."
Israel's God! her mind is virgin yet:
I've never wedded save her body. She
To word me thus,—she,—Mariamne,—she,—
The conquered daughter of a conquered king?
And yet I love her for 't. Yea, were I God,
And able to fill space with Mariamne,
Compact the stars into her diadem,
Darken heaven to give her light, and of eternity
Make one embrace, I were an-hungered still!
                                        [*Enter Servant.*

Serv. A messenger, my lord, from Antony.
Her. From Antony? Command him hither. [*Exit Servant.*
                                            So!
Shall public warfare chafe the ill-shod heel
Of private strife? Can I not rest a moment?—
                                    [*Enter Messenger.*
Papers from Antony? What can they treat of? [*Opens them.*]
What's this? What's this, I say? Knew'st thou of this?
Lysanius of Syria put to death!
Leagued with the Parthians! His rule given o'er—
Given to the Queen of Egypt,—Cleopatra!
Know you the contents of these papers, sir?
    Mess. In part, my lord.
    Her.   All this since I have left!
And is Lysanius dead?
    Mess.   Even so, my liege.
    Her. Lysanius dead, and Cleopatra queen
Of his domain? God! let me on—on—on!
What! More donations? The Nahalacan kingdom,—
The sea-coast—what! Palestine's sea-coast—all—
From Eleutherus even unto Egypt,
With only Tyre and Sidon, sir, excepted?
This greedy wanton would storm heaven itself
Were Babel's tower standing! What! More yet?
Jericho, too?—Without, there, ho!   [*Enter Attendant.*
                                    Thou, sir,
Bid Sohemus and Saramallas hither——
Stay, let them wait within my audience-chamber.
                                    [*Exit Attendant.*
While I fold these, sir, know'st thou if the queen
Went into Syria with Antony?
    Mess. She did, my lord.
    Her.   Ah! Say you? There's the germ
Whence sprung this crooked tree o' knowledge. Come.
Let's to my audience-chamber.   [*Exeunt.*

SCENE II.—*Enter* ALEXANDRA *and* HYRCANUS.

Alex. But why not write to Malchus? Is not Malchus
Thy friend? Hath he not proved himself thy friend?
Now, as Arabia's governor and lord,
Is he not placed to take the part of friend
In verity towards us? Thou must know it!—
Ask that he send some horsemen to escort us
In safety from Jerusalem's boundaries.
What's in a letter? Thou couldst find some ten,
Ay, twelve, to bear 't in secret. There's Dositheus!
I'm sure Dositheus loves thee.
    Hyr.   So he doth;
Ay, so he doth,—he doth,—I'm sure he doth.

But as for writing unto Malchus,—why,
It is too much to ask of friendship.
 Alex.   What?
What is too much? That he do send us horsemen
To aid us in our flight? Call'st thou that much?
Why, 'twere an office he would claim with gladness.
As for the multitude, thou knowest well
They are with thee,—not Herod.
 Hyr.   Daughter, daughter,
Why wilt thou not let peace sleep peacefully?
Quiet doth seem to me a boon, good daughter,
That kings might place before their diadems.
I am too old to plan new orders.
 Alex.   So?
Then let me do 't. The future race of kings
That yet may spring to power from Mariamne
Will never find that fault, believe me, father,
Among the virtues of their sovereignty.
Come, here is pen; come, here is parchment. Write,—
Write,—write.
 Hyr.   To Malchus? That he send us horsemen?
 Alex. Ay, escort to the lake Asphaltites.
Write, sire, as thou wast king and wilt be! Write.
 Hyr. Soft, daughter, soft! How would it be if Herod
Should by some means discover I had written?
Would it not anger him? Hast pondered that?
 Alex. Oh, wilt thou pause to think of Herod's anger,
When thine should make thee pitiless? Plunge thy pen
Into my veins, that my resolvéd blood
May of itself form the important words
And save thy dubious hand the trouble!
 Hyr.   Nay,
Nay, nay; be not so violent, good daughter.
Canst thou not give me time to ponder this?
If Herod finds thou hadst a part in it,
How then? How then?
 Alex.   Let then take care of then.
This now is in our charge. Oh, father, write.
Think on thy murdered grandson,—think on him,
The boy thou loved'st, so fair, so pure, so holy,
So all that Herod is not! Think on him,
And on his fate, on what our fates may be,
And write to Malchus. See, here is the parchment
Close to thy hand, and wax made ready. See—
I'll write it for thee,—That he'll send straightway
A troop of horsemen to escort us hence.
That's all. Look! thou hast but to sign thy name
And seal it with thy seal: unto Dositheus
I will myself commit it privately.
As for Dositheus, thou knowest, father,

He could not prove unfaithful. He knows well
What 'tis to lose kinspeople by this means,—
This Herod-plague. Ay, ay, Dositheus
Will be as true to thee as thine own arm.
Fear not. Wilt thou not sign?
 Hyr.   How if I sign—
My death-warrant?
 Alex.   Think not such woman thoughts:
They do unsex thee. Naught can come of it
But good to thee and thine.
 Hyr.   Sometimes death's good
When life is evil.
 Alex.   Oh, delay no longer!
Sign, as thou lovest me,—as I love thee,—
As God doth love us both! Sign,—sign, Hyrcanus.
 Hyr. Thou'rt sure thou hast not asked but that?
 Alex.   But what?
 Hyr. That he send horsemen to escort us?
 Alex.   Ay,
As I'm thy daughter, that is all. Now sign.
Good father, sweet, sweet father, sign the letter.
Wilt thou not sign to please me, father? Look!
I have not had a pleasure since the day
On which we lost our Aristobulus.
It will so please me.
 Hyr.   Well——
 Alex.   Oh, do it! do it!
Some one may come. There is no time.
 Hyr.   Thou'rt sure
Thou'st only asked for escort?
 Alex.   Sure,—sure,—sure.
Now sign it, father,—dearest father.
 Hyr.   Well,
If thou art sure thou'st asked no more than that——
 Alex. I swear it by my dead boy's murdered body!
 Hyr. Soft! not so shrilly,—not so shrilly, daughter.
There [*signs letter*], will that pleasure thee?
 Alex.   Ay, God alone
Doth know how much! Oh, dear my father, trust me,
When we are safe beyond these listening walls,
I'll tell thee how I thank thee! Some one comes.

    Enter MARIAMNE, *slowly.*

Sweet father, say no word to her as yet:
She must not know of this till by and by.
Why, gods! how pale she is!—Daughter, good-morrow.
What ails thee?
 Mar.   Nothing. Mine own spirit. Ah!
How farest thou, dear Hyrcanus?
 Hyr.   Why, my sweet one,

As old men fare who have no occupation
Save thinking on what occupied them once.
Mar. 'Tis a sad way to live.
Hyr.   Think you?
Mar.   Ay, sire;
But to live any way is sad.
Alex.   How now?
What sour experience gave that maxim birth?
What hath gone wrong?
Mar.   My destiny.
Alex.   Why, girl,
I never saw thee in such plight before.
Mar. Nor I myself.
Hyr.   Dost thou feel ill, my star?—
But then how rustily old wits do work!
Stars are exempt from maladies and ailments,
As thou shouldst be, my blossom.
Mar.   Thou'rt so good,
So gentle ever, I do love thee. Here,
Give me thy hand. Doth not my forehead burn?
Hyr. Ay, ay, it doth.—What's well for fever, daughter?
The child hath fever.
Mar.   There's no cure for this.
Alex. Now, by my faith, thou hast a fever, girl!
This comes o' too much roof-walking by night.
Thou knowest I warned thee not to stay so late.
But then I have a drink of balsam-flowers
That savors more of magic and strange arts
Than doth beseem a Jewish beverage.
I'll give thee some to drink.
Mar.   'Twill do no good.
Alex. How dost thou say? I tell thee that it will.
Come, be not obstinate.
Hyr.   Ay, go, my lamb,
Go, take thy mother's brew. Go, pretty one:
She makes rare brews. There's one she hath of late,—
'Twill stop an aching back,—'tis wonderful.
Mar. Hast one will stop an aching heart—for aye?

Enter JOSEPH.

Jos. [*To* HYR.] My lord, the king would speak with thee.
Hyr.   Well, Joseph——
Be docile, pretty one: thy mother's brews
Are brewed with strange discretion. Best you hearkened.
Wilt hearken, daughter?—Yes, I come, good Joseph.—
Fair health attend thee, fair one. Take the brew.   [*Exit.*
Jos. Sweet niece, how pale thou art!—How is't, in truth?
Is she ill, madam?
Alex.   Why, I know not, sir.
Mayhap she'll not acknowledge it. She looks so.

Mar. Nay, I am well enough, good uncle.—Mother,
Reach me my needlework.
    Alex.   What! wilt thou work?
Best that thou took'st the air awhile.
    Jos.   Ay, madam.
Wilt thou not walk?
    Mar.   Good uncle, let me rest.
    Alex. How? peevish?
    Mar.   Possibly. Despair, good mother,
Dons strange disguises.—Seemed I peevish, uncle?
I'm sorry for it.
    Jos.   Tut! tut! tut! 'tis nothing.
I mean, thou wert not peevish.
    Mar.   Nay, I was.
    Alex. Ay, ay, thou wert indeed. What hath gone wrong?
Haply thy Herod hath his favors stinted,—
Doth not so hotly love thee?
    Jos.   Madam, madam,
The king's love doth not wane with lesser fires,
But, like the sun, burns steadily, always,
Though sometimes by a cloud 'tis darkened.
    Alex.   Pshaw!
It twinkles like a star; is no more fixed
Than torch-reflections in a restless sea;
Waneth and waxeth ever with the moon;
Needeth, like any lamp, to be refilled
With flattery's oil; flares with the wind o' passion,
Like any earth-born flame.
    Jos.   Wilt thou, sweet niece,
Hear this of thy fond lord, and yet be silent?
    Mar. Whom is he fond of?
    Jos.   Madam, canst thou ask it?
    Mar. Sir, canst thou answer it?
    Jos.   Ay, that can I.
With all my heart I'll speak in his heart's cause.
If ever man loved woman, Jewry's king
Doth love the queen of Jewry.
    Alex.   Pah! go to!
Go to, I say! He'd love her ten times better
Were she the queen of somewhere else.
    Jos.   Nay, lady,
Man were a god could he love more than Herod.
    Alex. Ay, ay, ay,—more than Herod loves himself.
I can believe thee.
    Jos. [*Turning to* MARIAMNE.] Madam, sure thou knowest
How dear thy husband holds thee.
    Mar.   No, good uncle.
    Jos. No! Ah, thou meanest thou wouldst make me think
'Tis past thy comprehension.
    Alex.   Pshaw, I say!

He loves her by the moment, by the mood,—
To fill the gap 'twixt war and war.
  Jos.   Why, surely
Thou dost not think so, madam?   As I live,
There are ten thousand proofs he loves his queen,—
Ay, more, that Herod doth love Mariamne
Till Antony and Cleopatra's loves
Seem like as sparks blown off from his great fire.
  Alex. Sparks that may scorch his robe of self-esteem
Some windy day.   What are ten thousand proofs?
Give me but one, and all the doubtful rest
Shall sleep beneath my blessing.   Where's a proof?
Come, proof, sir.
  Jos.   Proof?   And is there need of proof?
Not that I have it not, but marvel, madam,
That thou wouldst have it.—Lady, pray thee listen.
Dost thou too wish a proof?
  Mar.   If such there be,
I will not close mine ears against it.
  Jos.   How!
If such there be!   If such there be!   Just heaven!
If there be proof that Herod loves thee?   Why,
I have one single one that would outsize
Ten thousand thousand!
  Alex.   Oh, there's room for it.
Come, yield it,—yield, good Joseph.
  Jos.   Thou, my queen,
Wilt have me speak?
  Mar.   Ay, if thou carest to.
  Jos. Why, then,—but speak not of it to the king:
I know not if he'd like its mentioning,
Though 'twere to prove his love,—ere he set forth
To Laodicea, he did instruct me, madam,—
Commission me——
  Alex.   Well, on: this wondrous proof,—
I thirst to hear it.—Say you, daughter?
  Mar.   Ay,
Tell on, good uncle.
  Jos.   He commissioned me,
So dearly did he love thee, that should death
Be meted him by Antony——in fact,
Should he be put to death——
  Mar.   To death?   What then?
  Jos. So doth he worship thee, so doteth on thee,
That he commissioned me, in such event,
In case, as I have said, that Antony——
Who's there?   Is't no one?   Nay, I saw a figure.
Some one moved near the door, and, o' my word,
This must be kept with us.

Mar. Well, on ! on ! on !
What did he tell thee?
Jos. That if Antony
Did order him to death,—did slay him, madam,—
If Antony——
Mar. If Antony did what?
Good uncle, thou'st a Cleopatra tongue,
That thus thou dinnest ever Antony
In Mariamne's ears. They'd hear of Herod.
Jos. Well, then, in short, he did commission me,
If such were his sad fate, to send thee after.
Mar. How, sir? Not slay me?
Jos. Ay, that was his order.
So dearly did he love thee that in death—
Even in death—he would not be without thee.
Mar. Oh, mother, mother, take me to thy breast!
I'm but thy child again,—no wife! no wife!
No wife!
Jos. Why, lady!—
Alex. Dost thou mean to say
That crownéd devil bade thee murder her?—
My daughter?
Jos. Nay, not murder.
Alex. He hath murdered,
Why not again? Blood-lust doth grow with tasting,
And murders breed as summer locusts do.
He hath her brother murdered, why not her?—
Why not the sister? Shall there be a limit
Unto a Herod's thirst: when he cries out
For blood to slake it, doth that being live
Who'd dare deny him? Yea! For I am she,—
I, Alexandra, rightful queen of Jewry!
What! call you this a proof?—a proof of love?
That she be murdered? Oh, how he doth love her!
So that's thy proof? Oh, how he worships her!
It is thy proof, you say? Witness, O God,
How he must dote upon her! Mariamne,
Up! up! Wilt thou bear this? Ah! she hath swooned.
Some water, pray you. Toss me that cushion quickly.
Here, place it here. Water, I pray you, sir. [*Exit* JOSEPH.
O God of Gods, whose brow is bound with justice,
Whose loins with vengeance,—Thou whose changeless shadow
Breaks on the edge of Space, whose sheltering wings
Enroof the windy temple of the stars,
To whom the stars themselves are but as gold-dust
From noiseless wheels of thy Triumphal Car,—
Thou who of Thine Omnipotence madest man
Visible in Thine image, and invisible
Of Thine own essence,—let not his spilt blood
Cry out to Thee in vain. Judge Thou, O Jah,

The murderer of Aristobulus,
Of him who as my son was dear indeed,
But as thy high-priest precious beyond words!
Judge Thou in all the would-be murderer
Of this mine other child, the lawful daughter
Of Alexánder Thine anointed king!
Judge him by his desires, not by his deeds,
And Thou wilt have to make another hell
To scorch another Satan!

SCENE III.—*Another room in the palace.*

Enter SALOME, *laughing.*

Sal. Oh, fool, fool, fool! Oh, excellent, sweet fool!
Sweet husband fool! Sweet, simple, foolish Joseph!
How thou hast played into mine hands with this!
To tell her that,—ha! ha!—to tell her that,
Of all things in the world, to prove his love!
When thou art dead, mine own dear fool of fools,
I will turn Roman and erect a temple
Unto thy godlike memory! Oh, this—
This is beyond my utmost expectation,—
Mine enemy to toss into my lap
The ball of fate,—my loyal husband—oh!
I never loved him until now! ha! ha!
What wisdom's in the fooling of some fools!
Here comes my brother.—This will please you, brother,—
Sweet brother, this will please you when you hear it.
Wilt have the bracelet made to an arrow-head
To reach my heart, good brother? Nay, not yet,—
Not yet, by that of Herod that's mine own!
Farewell, sweet brother, till thou hear'st this news.
Oh, Joseph, thou hast made me bride again.
I am again in love with thee for this!—
Oh, darling fool! Ha! ha! ha! ha!   [*Exit, laughing.*

Enter HEROD, *folding some papers, followed by Attendant.*

Her. Run after Saramallas with these papers,
And bid the queen attend me.   [*Exit Attendant.*
                    How accursed
These quarrels that divide us! I am thirsty
Already for her lips. Her angry eyes
Yet paint the air with horror.—Death! that look—
That look she gave me! Yet I did deserve it;
Ay, ay, 'twas well deserved. How her lips curled,
Like threads that writhe in fire, and her thin nostrils
Sucked like a veil blown o'er an open mouth.
I swear, were she but angry with another,
I should more love her angry than composed!
Ah, she is here. My blood leaps hard to meet her.

Now, as I live, she shall be friends with me,
Or I will make an enemy of God!

Enter MARIAMNE.

My queen!
Mar. Not thine
In anything.
Her. What, madam?
Mar. Neither queen,
Nor wife, nor friend, nor slave, of thine.
Her. What, madam?
Mar. My name is Mariamne. I am sister
To Aristobulus,—that Aristobulus
Who died conveniently.
Her. Why, what is this?
Mar. The truth in person.
Her. Mariamne, thou—
Even thou mayst go too far.
Mar. How? To my grave?
Her. Hast thou gone mad?
Mar. If to face fate be madness.
Her. Is this some trick,—some fantasy?
Mar. Why, no.
It is my freedom's birthday.
Her. How? Thy freedom?
Mar. Have I not said? I am mine own and God's:
None other owns so much as the sixth share
In my least drop of blood.
Her. Dost thou defy me?
Mar. No, Herod; I despise thee.
Her. What?
Mar. Despise
And scorn thee.
Her. Thou art mad,—I'm sure of it;
Ay, thou art mad,—mad,—mad!
Mar. If it be madness
To scorn thee, I am mad.
Her. To scorn me? Thou?
To scorn me? Thou, whom I have loved!—God! loved!
Mar. Loved? Loved? Blaspheme not Love's most holy
name,
Lest he do blast thee. What, thou love? What! thou?—
Herod, and say thou'st loved? Oh, love most mighty,
Most infinite, most tender, to contemplate
The murder of the thing it loved!
Her. The murder?
Wert thou not mad——
Mar. The murder,—ay, the murder.
What! thou canst stand and bare thine eyes to mine,
And speak of love? Oh, wise to make my butcher

Him whom thou didst suspect me with,—ay, Herod,
The man whom thou didst think my paramour!
Her. What dost thou mean?
Mar.   That thou didst love me well
Most well and nobly, when thou ordered'st Joseph,
If thou wert slain by Marc Antonius,
To slay me also, whom thou dost so love!
Her. Who told thee this? Who told thee this, I say?
Mar. Joseph himself.
Her.   Adulteress!
Mar.   Sir——
Her.   Ay,
Adulteress! Now know I thou art false.
What! dost thou think a man would give such words
Unto a woman lest there were between them
A tie more strong than death?—would thus brave death,
Nay, woo death as a bride? Cursed be ye both!
Thou, woman, thou, whom I have called my wife,
May there be drought throughout thy treacherous veins
As in a land accursed! Ay, mayst thou shrivel
To a lank, eye-blasting horror day by day,
Until a million million lagging years
Have sucked thy blood, as babes once sucked thy breast
When thou wast Herod's wife!
Mar.   Thy coward curse
I do shake off as 'twere a stainéd garment.
God is with me. Thou, Herod, stand'st alone.
Thou hast scared even pity from thy side
With those foul words. There is my crown,—there all
Of Mariamne that remains to thee!
                    [*Flings her crown at his feet, and Exit.*
Her. Oh, God! I choke! Wine, there! Nay, blood,—
        blood,—blood!   [*Exit.*

ACT IV.

SCENE I.—*A room in* HEROD'S *palace.*

Enter HEROD, *laughing.*

Her. Am I called Herod, and shall Fate laugh at me?
No, I will laugh at Fate!——
Ha! ha! ha! ha! Oh, I have been well fooled,—
Herod the Fool, not Herod King of Jewry.
Who was the man in Egypt had a treasurer
Called Joseph? But that Joseph was not false.
Potiphar's Joseph unto Herod's Joseph
Was as the smile of God unto His frown.
God's frown? Ay, God can frown; but so can Herod.
And Herod's wife to Potiphar's? Ay, there—

There is the matter : my wife unto Potiphar's
Is as one drop of mud unto another !
Oh, curse her ! curse her ! What ! false unto me ?—
My queen, and with my treasurer ? Both false ?
Not even the cutting comfort of his truth
To hug ? Adulteress ! adulteress !
Now let such angels as cry " Holy !" thrice
Before the throne of God, so shriek that word
" Adulteress" that she may hear it ring
From heaven to hell, when she doth stand in pride
Before the throne of Satan ! May she live
To die ten times a pulse-beat ! May starved fiends,
With faces like her children's, gnaw her heart
And spit it in her eyes to dry her tears !
May she be Baal's drudge, and bear him devils
To rend her paramour ! God ! God ! God ! God !
That I were but Thyself, to revise hell
And multiply capacity for pain
By all the worlds in space !

Enter SOHEMUS.

Soh.   I am here, my liege.
Her. Go bid my mother and Salome hither.
Ay, let her come. [*Exit* SOHEMUS.] 'Tis well that she should
    come.
She shall this dainty pleasure share with me.
For every pang of anguish I endure,
She shall be torn with two,—ay, with a hundred.
Oh, devil, devil, to have told me of it !
And yet I'd know. But 'twas a devil's errand.
                 [*Enter* SALOME *and* CYPROS.
So, madam, thou hast come,—and thou ? Ye're welcome.
The day is fair.
Sal.   What mean'st thou ?
Her.   What mean'st thou ?
Sal. When ?
Her.   When thou brought'st me that bracelet ?
Sal.   Why,
My meaning was as easily observed
As was the bracelet.
Her. [*Seizing her by the throat.*] Darest thou, jade ? So ! so !
Cyp. Herod, hold off thy hands ! Thou'lt choke her !
Her.   Ay,
By God's help or the devil's, so I will.
Cyp. Thou'rt mad !—Help, ho ! The king is mad !
Her.   'Tis madness
To say a king is mad. Well, there she is :
Mayst thou rejoice in her !
Cyp.   Thou hast half killed her.

Her. Would it were wholly! Serpents die not thus.
Cyp. Thou art a fiend!
Her.   Else were I not her brother.
Look thou,—thou, madam, who art lying there,—
Die not ere thy reward be given thee.
I took thee for a liar, but in all
Thou hast been true,—I do acknowledge it,—
In all,—in all. I've somewhat roughly used thee,
But thou shalt have amends,—ay, ay, amends.
What thinkest thou 'twill be? Thou canst not dream,
Canst thou, poor dove? thou art so sadly ruffled
Since thou didst choose to preen thy dainty feathers
Betwixt a tiger's paws,—poor dove, poor dove!
But there shall be reward.
Cyp.   Speak what thou meanest.
Canst thou not see she is half dead—poor girl!—
With thy rough usage?
Her.   She shall have a toy
To soothe her waking,—ay, a pretty ball
To toss withal, of red and white and black.
Like you the colors?
Sal.   Dost thou mean in truth
Thou hast aught for me?
Her.   Ay.
Sal.   What is it?
Her.   Why,
Thy husband's head!—Without, there, ho!   [*Enter Attendant.*
                                            Send Sohemus
Straightway unto me.—What! dost pale?   What! thou,
A Joseph's wife, and pale? Thou! thou!   Oh, thou
Shalt feel what 'tis to suffer.—   [*Enter* SOHEMUS.
                              Sohemus,
Take forth this woman's husband, the Idumean
Joseph, sometime my trusted treasurer,
And let him not return.
Sal.   How! Banish him?
Her. No.
Sal.   What then?
Her.   Slay him.
Sal.   Never! thou wouldst not.
Her. Soft! shall I break a promise? 'Twas my word.
Thou shalt be paid in full,—in full,—in full.
By God! I am half minded that thy lap
Should serve as block for his beheading!—Sir,
Away unto thy office!—Ay, there, crouch,—
Crouch, thou foul, damnèd thing. What! still so white,
For all thy well-daubed red? Ere it be night
Thou shalt have blood for paint!
Cyp.   My son!—my son!
Her. No son of thine, to call that monster sister.

—Let me not thrice remind thee, Sohemus:
To work without delay. To work!
Soh. But, sire——
Her. Tempt me not thrice, I say. Begone!
[Sohemus *attempts to go, but* Salome *clings to him
and prevents him from leaving.*]
Sal. By God,
He shall not till I know what thou dost purpose.
Her. Why, then remain, good Sohemus; remain.
'Twill give me joy such as kings seldom know
To tell her what I purpose. It is this.
With the first western streak of evening red,
It is my purpose—wilt thou write it down?
Here are my tablets, if thou hast none. No?
So be it. As I said, with the first stain
Of blood from Night's wound on the brow of Day
The blood of thy sweet spouse shall stain likewise
The sword of him I shall appoint herewith
To strike his fair head from his comely neck.
'Tis now some minutes short of sunsetting.
Let Sohemus place a chair beside this window
Ere he goes forth. Methinks it is but just
That after all thy crafty painstaking
Thou shouldst enjoy results unto the full.
The execution will take place there,—seest thou?—
Beneath that date-tree.—Sohemus, a chair.
Sal. Thou wouldst not do it!
Her. No, I'll have it done.
From childhood I've abhorred the sight of blood,
Save when it's battle-shed: it turns me faint.
Wilt thou not have the chair?
Sal. Thou couldst not kill him.
Her. What didst thou think that I would do, sweet sister,
When thou hadst proved him false? Have him to sup?
A higher honor waits him, trust me, madam:
He shall be Herod's chief ambassador
To Satan, and his power unlimited.
There are some things in hell that I'd have changed,—
Ay, some in heaven. Thou'rt pale. Nay, have the chair.
Sal. If thou wouldst kill him, let her die with him.
Her. Make her ambassadress who was a queen?
It were not seemly.
Sal. 'Tis the law of Jewry
That both should die.
Her. Herod is Herod's law.
Sal. Brother, I lied! In all I lied! In everything
I was a liar!
Her. Ay, and thou dost lie,
In all thou liest, and in everything
Thou art a liar, still!—

Sal.   Good brother, hear me——
Her. A Herod hear a liar?
Sal.   'Twas her fault,—
Not his, but hers.
Her.   Devil! I'd shed his blood
To wipe those words out, if for nothing else!
What! thou art not yet satisfied? God's wrath!
I'll make thee drain a goblet of his blood
Unto my health! Away! The west is red;
The headsman's sword is thirsty.
Sal.   Herod——
Her.   Nay,
Remind me not that I am Herod, woman,
If thou wouldst gain thy plea.
Sal.   Brother——
Her.   That's worse.
Sal. As Jewry's king I kneel to thee.
Her.   As wife
To an adulterous hound I spurn thee.
Sal. [*To* Cypros.]   Madam,
Help me to plead.
Cyp.   Wilt thou not hear me, sir?
Her. No! for thou art her mother.—Sohemus,
Forth on my errand.
Sal. [*Clinging to* Sohemus.]   Nay, he shall not.
Cyp.   Sir,
Think what thou doest.
Soh.   Ay, in God's name, sire——
Her. In mine own name I do command thee forth.—
Unhand him, madam. Thou weak, snivelling wretch,
Unloose him, or I will compel thee,—thus.—
             [*Dragging* Salome *away from* Sohemus.]
Sohemus, forth upon my errand. Lo!
The west is yet more red! Ha! ha! ha! ha!

SCENE II.—*Enter* Mariamne.

Mar. Oh, God! that I were dead!—that I were dead!—
That I were dead!—or that I had not lived
To be the sepulchre of mine own heart!
What! Mariamne called adulteress
By Herod? Herod call me that? Just heaven!
All things are possible after this thing!
Oh, that foul name! Would he had sent his sword
To find the utmost secret of my heart,
Or ever my quick ears had sucked that poison!
Where shall I turn for comfort?—Is to live
Always to wish for death? Now, were it so,
And my veins nourishing an unborn child,
I'd spill their plenty unto lapping dogs
Ere breath should be its portion! Let me think,—

Ay, let me think. He shed my brother's blood,
And my blood feeds the hearts of his two sons.
What horror were beyond this horrible?
Ay, there is one. He hath been loved by me!
I've held his murderous hands, played with the curls
That warmed his murder-pregnant brain,—ay, kissed—
Oft kissed the lips that spoke the murdering words,
Lain down my head above the awful secret
His heart so well did keep! Oh, God! oh, God!
Must I know this and live? Sweet heaven, but rid me
Of this disgracéd body, and my soul
Upon the wind of knowledge may be blown
Eternally an alien and accursed,
Yet I will think Thee merciful.

   Enter ALEXANDER *with pomegranate-flowers.*

 Alex.   Look, mother,
Sweet, mother, look! Here are pomegranate-flowers,
To make thee think thou'rt in Samaria.
Are those more beautiful? Look, mother!
 Mar.   Nay,
Nay, do not touch me! do not speak to me!
Oh, look not so, my heart,—my life,—my son,—
Mine, and not his! Come, touch me! touch me! touch me!
Speak to me! kiss me! clasp me! let me hear
Ten thousand words of love!
 Alex.   Why dost thou hold me?
Thou'lt crush the flowers. And pray thee tell me, mother,
Why wast not pleased at first? Have I been naughty?
I thought thou'dst like the flowers so much.
 Mar.   I do,—
I do. The pretty flowers,—ay, they are lovely,
And colored like to blood,—like unto blood.
 Alex. Why dost thou say it so? The ugly word!
I hate that word,—that "blood." Wilt thou not wear them?
 Mar. Ay, ay,—upon my heart,—there is the place.
Look not at me out of his eyes. Dost hear?
Thou hast his eyes, I say! Do not look at me!
 Alex. Mother!
 Mar.   No, not that word! Dost hear me, boy?
Why, they're his very eyelids! Get thee gone!
Away with thee! Oh, God! Come back! come back!
I did not mean it. Look at me, nor weep!
I did not mean it. Look, I'll drink thy tears
With kisses. Would that they were poisonous!
Is this the dagger that I gave thee? Come,—
Give it to me again, and here——   [*Uncovering her neck.*
 Alex.   Nay, mother,
What dost thou mean? Take care! It is so sharp;
I sharpened it to-day.

Mar.   To-day is well;
To-day should every sword throughout Judea
Be newly whetted, and their edges proved
Upon one heart!
    Alex.   At what dost look so hard?
    Mar. Upon that glare of steel. Stand not like that,—
'Tis so he stands a hundred times a day.
Move,—walk,—change that position,—anything,
So thou dost not look like him. Yes,—thy flowers,—
Thy flowers. When hast thou seen thy father? Nay,
I mean thou must not name him unto me
So long as thou dost live. Dost understand?
    Alex. I must not name my father to thee?
    Mar.   Ay,
Thou must not.
    Alex.   Why? Dost thou not like his name?
I will not say his name.
    Mar.   Thou'lt not speak of him
In any wise. Dost hear?
    Alex.   Ay, mother, but——
    Mar. Where didst thou get these flowers? They are so fresh.
Didst thou think of it all of thine own self?
There is one pity : they have not a perfume.
Perfume's the soul of flowers. I think such flowers
As have no perfume will not bloom in heaven,
But perish, with the beasts. Thou hast not seen him,—
Thy father,—then, to-day? Nay, speak not! Look,
Here is the way the fruit begins to grow.
Did he speak to thee? Nay, no word,—no word.
There, go! go! go! Bring me some flowers, my heart,
That have sweet perfumes. Run! run! run!
                      [*Exit* ALEXANDER.

SCENE III.—*Enter* HEROD *and* DOSITHEUS.

    Her. A letter from Hyrcanus unto Malchus?
Malchus? What should Hyrcanus with this Malchus?
    Dos. My liege, I'd have thee read. My tongue rebels :
'Twill not be proxy for disloyal words.
    Her. Disloyal?
    Dos.   When thou'st read the letter, sire,
I think thou wilt agree with me.
    Her.   Disloyal?
He gave it to thee?
    Dos.   He and Alexandra.
    Her. Ah! Alexandra! Well, I'll read it. So!
An escort to Arabia! That's well,—
Excellent. Ay, I'm very glad to know
He's in such gallant health. An escort, sir,
Unto Arabia! He's somewhat aged—

Think you?—to look on travelling as a pleasure.
I'm glad his health's so good.
  Dos.   Was I right, sire,
To bring the letter to thee?
  Her.   Right,—most right.
'Tis at all times a cheering thing, Dositheus,
To know thy wife's grandfather is in health.
It cheers me, sir,—it cheers me, verily.
I thought he coughed of late.
  Dos.   And so he doth.
  Her. No matter: he'd ride double with his cough
Into Arabia.   It cannot, sir,
Be very heavy.   Come, re-seal this letter.
  Dos. Seal it?
  Her.   Ay, seal it.   And when it is sealed,
Bear it, as thou wast told to do, to Malchus.
  Dos. My liege?
  Her.   Sir, I have said.
  Dos.   That I this letter
Bear to Arabia's governor?
  Her.   Ay.
  Dos.   Sire,
Thou canst not understand its full import.
  Her. Possibly.
  Dos.   But, my lord, take it to Malchus?
How if he answers it?
  Her.   Dositheus,
It is not how if he will answer it,
But, if he answers, how it will be answered.
  Dos. I think I comprehend thy meaning, sire.
  Her. Think not, but act.   Take thou the fleetest horse
From out my stables, and to Malchus,—ho!
To Malchus ere 'tis night!   Dositheus,
Be prompt, and thou shalt win a higher place
Than even now thou hast in mine esteem.
Away to Malchus.
  Dos.   I will ride, my lord,
As lover to his maid.   Trust me in all.   [*Exit.*
  Her. [*Looking after him.*]   In all but all.   This works to
              thine advantage:
Therefore I trust thee.   Were Hyrcanus king,
Thou shouldst not be the letter-carrier
Of Herod, good Dositheus,—no, no,
I promise thee!   God! how my head burns!   Oh!
It is as though my skull were but a crucible
For flames to dance in.   Ha! ha! ha!   That's famous!
A crownèd crucible!   I've not the knack
Of fitting big ideas to little words:
I'm Herod,—more a poem than a poet.
Poets are mad, they say,—leastwise in Persia;

Well, I'm in Jewry, and I'm not a poet,
Ergo, not mad ; yet I've sometimes bethought me,
If the worst madness were not sanity,
To be most mad 's to think thyself most sane.
But if thou'rt sane and think'st thou mayest be mad ?
How then ?   Were it not better many times
To be unknowing mad ?—honestly raving?
'Tis not a pleasant task at hush of night
To daub upon the canvas of the future
Such scenes as thou mayst choose to conjure up
When thou shalt have declared a war 'gainst Reason.
'Tis better to dream sleeping than awake.
Traitors go mad sometimes, so I have heard,
For thinking on their sins ; beggars, they say,
Are sometimes starved to madness ; felons, too,
Rave in the galleys.   I do ofttimes wonder
If madness ever seized a king ?   Ay, ay,
Nebuchadnezzar grazed ; but Balaam's ass
Forsook his asshood and adopted speech :
It is a serious question which was madder,—
The man who took the ass's method, or
The ass who took the method of the man.
I'll have my chief interpreter take notes
Upon that theme,—if Balaam's ass was mad.
On his decision hangs a serious question :
Nebuchadnezzar's sanity.—What's that ?   [*A scream without.*]
What's that, I say ?

    Enter ALEXANDER, *running, pale as death.*

 Alex.   Oh, father, father, father !
 Her. What is it ?   Speak, I say !   Where is thy tongue?
Speak, o' the instant !   Is thy mother——   Ha !
What o' thy mother ?
 Alex.   Mother doth not know.
Oh, come with me,—quick,—quick !
 Her.   What is it, sir ?
God ! I will know.
 Alex.   Oh, sir,—I know it's false,—
But they have bound my uncle Joseph.   Oh !
The cords have cut him so !   They say, moreo'er,
'Tis thy command, and that he must be killed,—
His head chopped off.   Oh, father, come !—don't wait !
I know thou'lt come.   He kissed me ; and he wept ;
He said thou hadst his blessing ; and the blood
Was all upon his wrists, and on his robe,
And they are cutting off his beard and hair.
Oh, come ! come ! come !
 Her.   Well, boy, why should I come?
 Alex. Oh, father, please be different ; mock me not,—
Mock me not now : afterwards thou mayst tease me

Until my heart is like to burst, but now—
Oh, quickly, father, quickly give me leave
To have chopped off the heads of those who seized him.
Oh, 'twas so pitiful!
He'd just begun to show me how a storm—
A sand-storm in the desert—smothered men
And camels. Come! come! come!
The cord has cut so deep into his wrists!
Come, father!
    Her.   How if I told thee I had ordered this?
    Alex. Oh, do not mock! 'Twill be too late! Oh, come!
    Her. Thy uncle Joseph dies at my command.
    Alex. Oh, no! no! no!
    Her.   I say he doth.
    Alex.   And I,
That thou art mad to say it.
    Her.   Mad!
    Alex.   Ay, mad!
Oh, father, come! I kneel.
    Her.   It is too late.
    Alex. No! no! not if thou'lt hurry.
    Her.   I do tell thee
It is too late. [*Turns to window.*] Ha! there he is.—Good uncle,
Good-even to thee. Bear King Lucifer
Word of my everlasting fealty. So!
Up in my arms, boy. Look!
    Alex. [*Shrieks.*]   Oh, uncle! uncle!
Speak to him, father! Oh! the sword! the sword!
Make him put up his sword.—We're coming, uncle!
Uncle, we're coming.—Oh, why doth he kneel?
Why doth he bend his neck? Oh, God! oh, God!
The blood! the blood! the blood!
              [*Turns suddenly with a wild gesture.*]
                    Thou'rt not my father!—
Thou art a devil. Devils wear not crowns.
There, devil!
      [*Snatches off his father's crown and flings it out
           of the window, then swoons.*]
    Her. [*Dashing him down.*] Not thy father? I believe thee.

ACT V.

SCENE I.—*A room in* HEROD'S *palace.*

Enter SALOME *and* Cup-Bearer.

    Sal. The king returns to-day.
    Cup-Bearer.   Ay, madam.
    Sal.   Well,
Art sure thou knowest thy part?

Cup-Bearer.   Hear me, and see.
Sal. Be quick, then.   Soft! I'll draw this curtain first.
Now, quickly.
Cup-Bearer. First, then, madam, I'm to wait
Till thou send'st for me; then, on some occasion
When the king hath had words more violent
Than usual with the queen, I enter in,
Hastily, yet with a composéd mien,
That I may seem assured in every way
As to the service I'm about to render.
Next I do tell the king Queen Mariamne
Hath coaxed me to assist her in the mixture
Of a love-potion, all of whose ingredients
I do not know; that this was kept a secret
From all but us who brewed it; that I thought
My safest course, both for myself and him,
Was to confess it all.   Is not that right?
    Sal. Ay, ay.   But shouldst thou falter——
    Cup-Bearer.   I'll not falter,
Trust me, good madam, I have not forgotten
The day she had me scourged for making free
To pinch the ears of Aristobulus
For sprinkling me with water.   I'll not shrink.
Her servants' whips have sealed me to thy service.
    Sal. Well, go thy ways till I have need of thee.
Go with a usual face: purse not thy brows,
Nor look as though thy heart hung on thy ribs
A bag o' secrets.   Go: some one is coming.
Think of the gold that shall be thine.   That's well.
Now go.—Ha! it is she herself. Go quickly! [*Exit Cup-Bearer.*

                   Enter MARIAMNE.

Good-morrow, murderess.
    Mar.   Wouldst thou, poor wretch,
Raise anger from the dead?   Thy woes, Salome,
Make me forbearing.
    Sal.   So they make not me,
Proud-nostrilled harlot!
    Mar.   Darest thou?
    Sal.   Dare I?   God,
Help me to laugh!   Ha! ha! ha! ha!   Dare I?
    Mar. Nay, I forgot, — thou'rt mad.   Poor, fond, weak
          wretch,
In seeking my destruction thou hast compassed
Thy husband's death.
    Sal.   Wilt thou remind me of it?
Take that! [*Stabs at her.*]
    Mar. [*Quietly, holding her by both wrists.*]   Yes, I will take
          it, verily,
But not as thou didst mean that I should take it.

I am as far thy better in my body
As in my soul. There! get thee gone!—away!—
Ere I am tempted unto what I would not.
I'll keep thy dagger as a dear memento
Of this most gentle scene; and should my heart
Grow soft in thinking of thy grief, my soul
Shall profit by the lesson of this steel.
Go, woman.

    Sal.   Ay, I go,—to come again.   [*Exit.*

    Mar. Murderess? Yea, I feel a murderess.
Ah, Joseph, had I known,—had I but known,—
Torture could not have wrung those words from me,
For I'd have wedded dumbness on the rack.
O God, O God, is this Thy king?—this Herod?—
This Mariamne's husband?—this rage-buffeted
And passion-driven slayer of the innocent?—
This king whose humors rule him?—this fond fool
Who wears distemper's motley, and whose crown
Is but a badge of sin? Rather hath not
Some devil dispossessed his soul, to reign
Over his body's kingdom?
Oh, this is not the man whose bride I was,
The king whose queen, the conqueror whose wife!
Ah me! we women, how have we vexed Love,
That he doth scourge us speak we but his name?
I will be gentle with her, for the sake
Of him who was her husband; but this dagger
Shall keep me ever cautious.

Enter HEROD.

    Her.   What say you?

    Mar. I spoke, sir, with a ghost.

    Her.   Ha?

    Mar.   With a ghost
Which was thy handicraft.

    Her.   Woman!

    Mar.   A ghost
That wore a scarlet collar,—one whose head
Was plastered on with blood.

    Her.   Away, thou fiend!

    Mar. Nay, send me not away: I should much please thee.
There is the making of a pretty ghost
In me, my lord, and scarlet is my color.

    Her. Devil!

    Mar.   Nay, wife to one.

    Her.   [*Drawing a dagger.*] Begone, I say!

    Mar. Ay, strike! Thou hast a genius, sire, believe me,
For ghost-making. Strike! there is nothing—ay,
Nothing in all the world would so enchant me
As being made a ghost to haunt thee! Nay,

Glare not as I already were a ghost.
I see thou art not in a loving mood:
Therefore I will begone.　Great king of ghosts,
Good-morrow.　　　　　　　　　　　　　　　　　　　*[Exit.*
　　Her.　I said that I'd have blood,—I said so,—ay,
But there is not enough in all the land
To slake my humor's thirst.　Oh that I were
Another Pharaoh, and another Moses
Would turn the Nile to blood a second time,
That I might swim through its encrimsoned waves!
Oh that I were a thing of quenchless thirst,
A vampire monstrous, flattened at the throat
Of one vast body which should be the flesh
Incorporate of every thing alive!

　　　　　　　　　　Enter DOSITHEUS.
　　　　　　　　　　　　　　　　　　Dositheus,
Is't thou?
　　Dos.　My liege, the letter.
　　Her.　　　　　　　　　　　How?　From Malchus?
　　Dos. From Malchus, sire.
　　Her.　　　　　　　　That's well; that's well. Ah ha!
Look here, Dositheus: what think you, man,
Of that,—and that,—and that?
He will not only send an escort, sir,
To his beloved Hyrcanus,—dost thou mark?—
But will make welcome all whom he may bring,
Even all the Jews that may be of his party,
And he shall lack for nothing.　God of Israel!
There's one thing that he shall not lack for,—death!
　　Dos. My liege——
　　Her.　　　　　So the good Malchus doth agree?
　　Dos.　　　　　　　　　　　　　　　My liege——
　　Her. I'll show this letter to the Sanhedrim,
And he shall straightway suffer to the utmost
The law that deals with traitors!
　　Dos.　　　　　　　　But, my liege——
　　Her. Away!　Send me Hyrcanus and his daughter.
Bid them at once attend me.　　　*[Exit* DOSITHEUS.
　　　　　　　　　　　　Would to heaven
His withered veins held more of that red fluid
Which can alone quench my insatiate thirst!
Such drops as death may wring from his dry body
Will but make wet the door-way of a throat
That gapes for rivers.

　　　　Enter HYRCANUS *and* ALEXANDRA.
　　　　　　　　　　　　Thou art come, my lord.
I'm glad to see that thou'rt not more infirm.
I pray thee, sit.—Sit, madam.

Alex. No, I'll stand.
I can breathe better standing. What is it?
Her. Why, sure thou wouldst not hear before thy father,—
Thou who art courteous to thy waiting-woman
And cry thy needle pardon if thou breakest it?—
Thou'lt sit, sir?
Hyr. Yes, I thank thy courtesy,
I'm better friends with bed each day I live.
Her. Yet thou'rt industrious for an old man, sir.
Hyr. Industrious?
Her. Ay; thou doest many things
Which young men could not better.
Hyr. I, my son?
Alex. What dost thou mean?
Her. Softly, good mother-in-law:
I speak unto thy father.—Good Hyrcanus,
Thou hast a talent that I dreamed not of.
Hyr. Thou flatterest me, sir. I won a crown
From the Athenian senate once; but, truth,
'Twas long ago.
Her. The thing of which I speak
Might, sir, have won thee back the crown of Jewry,
Had it succeeded.
Alex. What?
Her. I speak, my friend,
Of this thy unsuspected talent——
Alex. Well?
Her. Of letter-writing. [*Shows him the letter.*]
I assure thee, sir,
I could not trace—upon my honor, sir—
Characters clearer or more shapely.
Hyr. Daughter,
It is some jest, is't not? Pray you, inform me:
I never had the trick o' jest-catching.
Alex. Father, come with me. Ay, it is a jest,—
It is a jest. Come, father; come, Hyrcanus.
Her. Stay, both of ye! Stir not a step!—A jest?
A jest to make hell merry!
What! wouldst feign ignorance, thou damnéd traitress?—
Thou, sir, dost thou in truth dare to pretend
Thou dost not recognize this letter?—this,—
The one thou sent'st unto Arabia's governor,—
To Malchus? Ha! I touch thee! Good my lord,
This Malchus is an honest friend o' thine.
Look! he will send thee escort. Look! thy party,
Even such Jews as thou mayest take with thee,
Will be provided for. Look here,—and here!
Thou shalt not want for aught. Oh, would to heaven
That I had such a friend!—that this same Malchus

Were Herod's friend [ALEXANDRA *sinks half fainting into a*
    chair].—What, madam, wilt thou sit,
Now that thy father stands? It is not seemly.
Up on thy feet: thou canst breathe better so. [*Laughing.*]
Methinks thou shouldst thank God with all thy breath
That thou dost breathe at all!
    Alex.   It was my fault:
Lay all the blame on me,—on me.
    Her.   Attend.
This is thy father's signature, is't not?
    Alex. I teased him to it. Oh, if any suffers,
It should be I!
    Hyr.   Nay, nay, thou must not suffer:
It was my fault to let thee bring me to it.
I am old, Herod, but not yet so old
As to have outlived courage. Weep not, daughter;
I'll bear the fullest consequence;—weep not:
Would I could weep!
    Her.   Thou shalt, and tears of blood.—
Without, there, ho! [*Enter Attendants.*]
                Lead forth this man straightway
Unto the palace prison, and send Sohemus
Unto me in my closet.
    Alex.   Thinkest thou, Herod,
While Alexandra still is Alexandra,
Her father shall be fingered by a slave?—
Thou knave, thou durst not touch him.—Father, come;
Come with me,—so.—Thou, sirrah, lead the way.—
Good father, lean on me.
    Hyr.   I'm very old;
Death hath been close to me for many years.
I am not frightened. Hath he naught to say?—
Naught of his reasons?
    Alex.   He hath none to speak of.
Come, come, come, come.
    Hyr. Well, I am old, and death is like a friend
Who comes disguiséd as an enemy.
Think'st thou he'll let me speak to Mariamne
And to her pretty boys?
    Alex.   Ay, ay. Come on.
    Hyr. Her boys are like her, but one hath his eyes.
Well, well, I've lived to be so old that death—
Even death will not seem new to me. Lead on.—
Farewell, Antipater.   [*Exeunt.*
    Her. That's over. Would it were to do again!
Her face—ha! ha!—her face was sure the servant
Of a most furious soul. I can believe it,—
That 'twas her plot; yet he must die for it.
And who can say Antipater is cruel
When he doth give another that one thing

Which he desires,—a swift and sudden death?
What's cruelty? A tree whose roots split hell,
Whose crest disturbs the stars. Methinks my star
Hath long since been a cinder, and its fire
Is all here in my brain. Do men go mad
For dreading madness? [*Enter* MARIAMNE.]
     Ha! What wouldst thou?
 Mar.   Madman!
Is this thing true?
 Her.   Why dost thou call me madman?
I am not mad.
 Mar.   Is this thing true, I say?
Hast thou given orders that he be imprisoned?—
Hyrcanus?
 Her.   Wherefore didst thou call me madman?
Thou never call'dst me so till now.
 Mar.   Till now
Thou ne'er wast mad. Give answer to my question.
Hast sent Hyrcanus unto prison?
 Her.   Ay.
 Mar. Thou hast?—O God, where is Thy justice?
 Her.   Look you,
Why said you I was mad? I am not so.
Was I e'er calmer?
 Mar.   Thou hast sent Hyrcanus
To prison, under charge of treachery?—
Hyrcanus,—he who was a king in all
To make thee seem his sceptre's shadow!
 Her.   Now—
Why, now, now, now—look now how calm I am!
Seem I a madman?
 Mar.   —He who is still king
By every right which cries thee wrong!—a man
To make thy memory a woman,—one
Beside whom thou dost show as black-ribbed clouds
Against an evening sun! Thou send Hyrcanus
To prison? Thou? Thou,—Herod? Now let Satan
Send God to hell that he may rule in heaven!
What! he in prison at thy order?—he
Who even with sin dealt ever holily,—
He whose white hair the very winds did reverence,—
He unto whom thy every dignity
Thou owest,—thy wealth, thy crown, thy throne, thy sceptre,
That very power which now doth wrong him! Oh,
Let me believe thee mad, ere that thy reason
Cried " Amen" to this deed!
 Her.   He is a traitor.
 Mar. And what art thou? thou who usurped his throne,
Who filched his crown, who stole away his sceptre,
Who hath his grandchild called adulteress?

Ay, what art thou,—thou, sir, whose name is Herod,
Whose heart is hell condensed?
Her.   Thou sayest, a madman.
Mar. No! no! thou art not mad! Look not like that.
' When thou didst order him to prison, then,—
Then wast thou mad. Not now; not now.
Her.   I am not?
Mar. No, no, I tell thee. What dost stare at? Come,
Thou didst not mean it: I am sure o' that.
Look! I'll forget my wrongs,—all, all, all, all,—
So thou dost not wrong him.
Her.   Why, it were madness
To set him free. I would not give the people
So good a cause to say that I am mad.
Mar. They could not have a better cause than this
That now they have in his imprisonment.
What! will the foulest beggar in the streets
Think that in sanity thou wouldst imprison
A gentle, fond, feeble, retired old man
For treachery? Nay, but believe me, Herod,
Thou'st ta'en the surest way to prove thy madness.
Her. Say it no more.
Mar.   Say what? That thou art mad?
Then give me no more cause to say it. See!
I've forgot all but what should be remembered,—
That I am Mariamne and thy wife,
Thy queen, the mother of thy sons. Take me,
And set Hyrcanus free!
Her.   What! wilt thou kiss me?
Mar. Yes.
Her.   What! be as my wife again?
Mar.   Yes,—yes!
All that I was, and more, I will be, Herod,
So thou dost set him free.
Her.   Wilt love me too?
Mar. I will be all to thee that thou couldst wish.
Her. Save loving?
Mar.   If thou dost find fault with me,
Send me to prison in Hyrcanus' stead.
Her. Then thou'lt not swear to love me?
Mar.   Oh, my lord,
What deed could better merit love than this one
I'd have thee do? As thou'lt some day be old,
Think on his age, and do him reverence.
Her.   Nay,
I am not old, and think of thee each moment.
Is that the way to calmness?
Mar.   What's his crime?
Or who hath slandered him? His innocence
I'll prove sire, with my life.

Her. [*Handing her Malchus's letter.*] Not with thy love?
Read that. The governor's reply is here,
On this side,—here.
    Mar. [*Reading.*] Would go to Asphaltites
And to Arabia. Would have an escort,
He and my mother. Signed Hyrcanus.—Well,
What's there of treachery? I see no harm here.
    Her. No harm? Thou seest no harm in it? No harm!
No harm! No harm! But soft! soft! soft! Read on.
Read Malchus' answer.
    Mar.   Escort granted them;
All done in's power to aid them; shelter promised
Unto his party.—Well?
    Her.   No,—ill, by God!
Give me the papers: thou wilt tear them, girl.
We'll see if that the Sanhedrim thinks with thee.
No harm! [*Laughing.*] 'Tis harm to think there is no harm.
    Mar. Thou canst not purpose to submit those letters
Unto the Sanhedrim?
    Her.   It is my purpose,—
This very moment.
    Mar.   Herod, hear me!—Look!
Look on me! Look, my lord!—I kneel; I kneel.
Am I less fair than when thou loved'st me?
    Her. Wilt swear to love me now?
    Mar.   All that a wife
Should be I will be.
    Her.   All save loving. Ay,
Thou dost not love me, and he shall not live
To take the love that should be mine!
    Mar.   Nay, hear me!
    Her. No more! no more! [*Enter Cup-Bearer.*]
             Ha, slave! what dost thou there?
    Cup-Bearer. My lord, I come on most important matters.
    Her. Important matters? Whom do they concern?
Hyrcanus?
    Cup-Bearer. No; the queen.
    Her.   The queen? What queen?—
Queen Mariamne? Well?
    Cup-Bearer.   Yesterday noon,
Your majesty, the queen did come to me
And ask that I would help her brew a potion—
A love-drink—for your majesty. Being won
By much fine gold, I did consent, but afterwards
Bethought me that, not knowing all the contents
Of that which she had given me, 'twere best
Both for my lord and my lord's faithful servant
That I should tell my lord concerning it.
    Her. A love-drink! Ha! for me?—Madam, what's this?
    Mar. As bold a lie as ever was well lied.—

Sirrah, hast thou forgot my eunuchs' whips,
That thus thou bravest me?
 Cup-Bearer.   Your majesty,
I've not forgotten them.
 Her.   A love-drink! So!
For me? Hast thou this drink?
 Cup-Bearer.   Not now, my lord.
Princess Salome hath it in her charge.
 Mar. [*Aside.*] Salome!
 Her.   Bid her here at once.
 Mar.   What, Herod!
Thou'lt hear thy slave and sister before me?
Canst thou not see he lies? Dost thou not know
He is in her employ and hired to lie?—
Thou craven hound! stir not until I bid thee.
Look in mine eyes and say those words again!—
Thou seest: he cannot do it. Mark him, sir:
He cannot look at me.
 Her.   Canst thou not so?
 Cup-Bearer. My lord, mistake me not; it is not fear
Which keeps me from returning the queen's look,
But that my duty unto thee, my liege,
Forbids that I should gaze upon thy consort.
 Her. Well said! Well said!—Madam, thou art rebuked.
 Mar. Rebuked! and by that worm? Thy queen rebuked!
And by thy cup-bearer?—Now long farewell,
Hyrcanus! Peace be thine,—as must be death.
I have done all for thee that woman could
And yet be woman.
 Her.   Nay, what dost thou mean?
Where art thou going?
 Mar.   Where I'll find honor, sir,—
Unto Hyrcanus.
 Her.   I forbid it!
 Mar.   I
Am not to be forbidden. Stand aside.
If thou art Herod, I am Mariamne,
And queen unto the end, though crownless.   [*Exit.*
 Her.   So
Then she is mad,—not I. I am not mad.
Who said so? No one. But they must not think so,—
Not think so, either. I will see a madman
And make comparison.—Ho, there! you, sir,
Do men run mad in Jewry?
 Cup-Bearer.   Ay, my lord.
 Her. Hast thou seen any?
 Cup-Bearer.   What? Madmen, my lord?
 Her. Ay, madmen.
 Cup-Bearer.   Scores, my lord.
 Her.   How looked they, slave?—

Seemed they to be in any sort acquainted
With their affliction?
   Cup-Bearer.   Some did, sire.
   Her.   Some did?
They were not mad, then—no! they were not mad.
A man may not be mad and know it, slave,
Think'st thou?
   Cup-Bearer.   Why, yes, my lord, sometimes.
   Her.   Away!
Away! thou traitorous hound! thou knave! thou villain!
Out of my sight! Dost hint that I am mad?
                               [Exit Cup-Bearer.
When Herod's mad, let God be writ a fool,
And wisdom's sucklings swarm the throne of heaven.
What! shall a man go mad and talk of it?
No! no! no! no! Cunning is twin to madness.
Madmen will swear unto their sanity
With th' self-same ravings that proclaim them mad.
Why, I am calmer than I was a month—
A week—a day—nay, even a moment past.
I let her go unhanded,—let her word me,—
Took even her insults calmly, where a madman
Had torn her into shreds,—ay, into ribbons!
A potion? A love-potion? Let me see:
That's not so bad. Methinks there's something here
Not altogether venomous. I'll ponder.
What if she loves me after all?—would win me
By crafty means? I've heard that such things happen.
If that were so,—if this love-drink were harmless,—
If——ah! if Mariamne loveth me! Why,
Though hell should burst in flames beneath my feet,
I'd take her back again, and with my kisses
Make its worst blaze seem cool! Oh, I'm on fire,—
On fire! But let me recollect. The potion,—
He said he thought 'twas best to tell me. Why?
Why was it best? Sure there could be no harm,
Unless—unless——ah! there's the thing,—unless
He did suspect that it was poisoned. Ay,
There is a possibility. No matter!
I will not think on it. She poison me?—
She, Mariamne, poison Herod? Well,
I'm glad I am not mad, since were I so
I might have fall'n into this snare. And yet
It is enough to make a Solomon
Cry Wisdom wanton, and as lawful wife
Clip easy Foolishness. Now would to God
That I were mad, to know not of this horror!
Sweet Madness, come, come, come! Scoop out my brains
To feed thy henchmen, and in this racked skull
Take up thy wild abode! Let every cranny

In my once-loving heart be packed with ravellings
From Fate's accursèd loom, snatch off my crown
To make the harlot Circumstance a zone,
And use my sceptre as a rod wherewith
To scourge all wise men to thy service!   [*Exit.*

SCENE II.—*A dungeon.*—HYRCANUS *and* ALEXANDRA.

Hyr. Good daughter, I am weary : loose these chains
A little.
Alex.   Oh, God help me, sir, I cannot!
Father, thou knowest with what joy of heart
I'd be there in thy place.   Thou knowest that,
Dost thou not, father?   Look! lean so, against me.
Is it not easier?   Here's water, sir,
If thou art thirsty.
Hyr.   No, I'm only tired.
Thou think'st he'll let me see my little grandsons
Ere I am led to execution?   Speak!
Dost not, good daughter?
Alex.   Nay, talk not like that.
He would not dare to kill thee.
Hyr.   Ay, ay, ay,
He would.   But Mariamne 'll plead for me?
Thou saidest so, didst not?
Alex.   Ay, father.
Hyr.   Well,
'Tis all with her.   Why dost thou weep, my daughter?
Alex. Alas! how canst thou ask me why I weep?
Dost thou not suffer for me?   Was 't not I
Who lured thee to thy ruin?   Did not I
Draw up that paper and then torture thee
Until thou'dst signed it?   And am I not free,
While thou art fettered?   I,—thy daughter,—I,
Who should have been the comfort of thy age,
The councillor of all to thy advantage,
Thy stay in time of trouble!   Look, Hyrcanus:
I brought thee to thy death.   Oh! curse me! curse me!
I kneel to hear thy curses as another
To receive blessings.   Let me no more writhe
Beneath thy gentleness.   Come, curse me! curse me!
Hyr. Good daughter, do not weep.   If it be death,
Why, Death and I are friends, and glad to meet.
And say not 'tis thy fault if that I die;
For in that letter there was naught, believe me,
To merit this the law's extremest course.
Alex. No: was there?   Was there?   Answer quickly, father.
Thou knowest I only wished to place thee, sir,
Beyond his reach.
Hyr.   I know it.   Do not weep.

I know it, daughter. Hark! I hear a footfall.
Hush! listen; listen.

Enter MARIAMNE.

Alex. Mariamne! Oh,
Thou'rt welcome, thou art welcome! Yet thine eyes
Are not as I would have them.
Hyr. Pretty one,
How will it fare with me?
Mar. As it should fare
With him who wrongs thee. Sire, he is a monster,
And his heart petrified long ere this hour
Into the corner-stone of a new hell.
Alex. And thou canst speak so calmly, Mariamne?
Knowest his doom, and yet can tell him of 't
With not so much as even one false note
In all thy soft voice-music?
Mar. Am I calm?
I think I'm mine own ghost; for I feel nothing
As I was wont to feel. I know the headsman,
And sent his wife a brew only this Nisan,
When she lay sick to death. There'll be no mis-stroke.
Thou art not feared, sir?
Hyr. No, my pretty one,
I am not feared of anything but life,
Now that I have made friends with Death. But, heart,
I'd say farewell unto our pretty boys.
Mar. I'll call them. [*Exit.*
Alex. Devil! devil! Oh, this Herod!
Lucifer were a paragon to him,
And Satan lovable.—O God! O God!
Instruct me how to demonize myself,
That I may meet him on equality
And curse him as a sister! Father, father,
Art thou asleep?
Hyr. Almost. I am fast drowsing
Unto the final moment, when my pillow
Shall be the block, and all my dreaming death.
Peace! peace! weep not.

Enter MARIAMNE, ALEXANDER, *and* ARISTOBULUS.

Ah, pretty ones, come here.
Thou lookest pale, my soldier. What's the matter?
Mar. He hath not yet recovered, dear Hyrcanus,
From witnessing his uncle's death.
Hyr. So! so!
Well, he must not see mine.
Alex. Oh, no! no! no!
No! no! no! no!
Hyr. There, there, my prince, thou shalt not.

Why, how thou tremblest! Look, I am to die,
And yet I tremble not.
 Alex.   I'd rather die
Ten thousand thousand times than see thee killed.
But then he cannot kill thee,—he cannot.
He is a devil, but he could not kill thee.
Say that he could not, mother,—mother, say it!
Oh, I did love him so! I loved him so!
And now, whenever I do think of him,
There is a shining redness comes between us—
Faugh!—and a smell of blood,—a thick, wet red,—
A damp, fresh, sickening, faint, far-reaching smell!
Oh, uncle! uncle!
 Hyr.   So! poor boy! poor boy!
And I must die?
 Mar.   Would I could die for thee!—
Who's there?

     Enter Attendant and Herald.

 Herald. Hyrcanus, thou art summonéd
To come straightway before the Sanhedrim.
 Hyr. Then kiss me, pretty ones. Come close to me.
Nay, daughter, do not weep. Come, Mariamne.
Kneel for my blessing,—all of ye; kneel there,
Where I can touch ye. Nay, come closer yet.
The God of Israel forever keep ye,
As I would keep ye, were I Israel's God,—
Forever love, bless, guard, and cherish ye.
Don't weep; don't weep! I can no more, my heart.
Unloose this bracelet,—I have missed the clasp,—
Wear it, and think sometimes of him who wore it.
This for thee, boy,—and this for thee,—and this
For thee, my daughter; all that's left, for Death.
Don't tremble, Alexander! this poor body
Hath not sufficient blood to fill a goblet
To Herod's health. Farewell,—farewell,—farewell!
         [ALEXANDRA *swoons.*
What, daughter! wilt thou go before me? Why,
It is not like thee so to lack in deference.—
Look to her, sweet, and if in truth she's dead,
See that she be entombed with me. Farewell,—
Farewell,—farewell! Why, I am young again,
To think how soon I will be quit of age.
Lead on. Hyrcanus is once more a king,
And goes to meet King Death as equal! [*Exeunt* HYRCANUS
  and Attendant.
 Mar.   Father?——
Nay, let me not disturb him. Come, my boys,
Let's to thy father,—let's unto thy father
With this sweet news. Let's to him with our thanks.

Let's take him kisses,—ha! ha! ha!—such kisses!
Let's fall upon our knees to honor him.
Was ever such a father?   Come, let's hurry!
Let's kiss, kiss, kiss, kiss, kiss him!   Run! run! run!
          [*Exit, running, leading her two boys by either hand.*

SCENE III.—*A room in the palace.*

Enter HEROD *and* SALOME.

Her. Thou canst not swear that it was poisoned?
Sal.   No;
But can there be a doubt?   .
    Her.   Ha!
    Sal.   I repeat it,
Can there be any doubt?   She knows too well
That thou art but her fancy's slave, her toy,
To brew thee merely love-potions.
    Her.   Her slave?
I'll make thee slave to her!   So? I a slave!
Thou hast a daring bent o' mind?   Look thou!
Unless thou prove this love-brew poisonous,
Thou shalt in prison rot.   As I am Herod,
I do believe thou'st lied from first to last
Concerning this affair and all that's touched it.
Thou art a most accomplished liar.   Prove it,
Or I will make her ten times queen again,
And brand the hideous story of thy falseness
With red-hot irons on thy naked flesh,
Then have thee whipped through every street and by-way
Of all the towns in Jewry, that all men
May read of it!   Away, and bring me proof,
Or look for death in agony unequalled!   [*Exit* SALOME.
What if I've been deceived in everything
From then till now?

Enter MARIAMNE *and boys.*

              What! Mariamne?
    Mar.   Ay.
Who looks like Mariamne, save herself?
And these, sir, are her sons.   She comes to thank thee—
She and her sons—for thy last kindness to them.
    Her. Wilt thou not sit?   Here is a chair.
    Mar.   Nay, Herod,
I'd have mine eyes at level with thine own;
And loving thanks are better proffered standing.
    Her. Why so?
    Mar.   'Tis hard to give thanks graciously.
    Her. Not when 'tis Mariamne thanking Herod.
    Mar. More then than ever.
    Her.   Say'st thou?

Mar.   Ay, my lord,—
More then than ever.
    Her.   Why, right well thou knowest
I'm always thankful to be thanked by thee.
Come, kiss me. For what wouldst thou thank me?
    Mar.   For
Hyrcanus' death! Nay, kiss me! I am sister
To Aristobulus. Nay, wilt not kiss me?
Thy treasurer Joseph loved me. Nay, now kiss me.
I am the grandchild of Hyrcanus!
    Her. What! what! wilt thou dare?
    Mar.   Then thou'lt not kiss me? Haply
I am not looking fair enough to-day?
I'll have a robe dyed in Hyrcanus' blood,
And 'broidered richly with the hair of Joseph
And Aristobulus, to wear withal
When I would please thee. Come, a kiss,—a kiss.
    Her. Devil!
    Mar.   Or, if that will not pleasure thee,
I'll make a feast for thee, and in thine honor
These thy two sons I'll have served up, with blood
For wine.
    Her.   Devil, I say!
    Mar.   Or, if that dish
Were something coarse for such a mighty king,
Their hearts alone I'd offer thee.
    Her.   God's heart!
Dost think I'll let thee live to mock me?
    Mar.   No:
Killing's thy forte. I pray thee send me, sir,
To Aristobulus, and Joseph, and Hyrcanus.
Haply thou hast some tender message, sir,
That I could bear them? 'Tis the only errand
On which for thee I would go willingly.
Come, send me,—send me.
    Her.   Can a man bear this
And not go mad?
    Mar.   Mad? Oh, no, thou'rt not mad.
I'm mad, the time is mad, earth, sea, heaven, hell,
The past, the future,—but not Herod! No!
He'll stand a monument to sanity
When for some excellent reason he hath slain
Everything save his reason!
    Her.   God in heaven!
    Mar. Nay, God is not in heaven! If He were there,
Herod would not be here! He travels, sir;
There's a rebellion on some distant star,
And He hath gone to quell it.
                              Ay, in heaven
Thou know'st but these three souls, Hyrcanus, Joseph,

And Aristobulus. Cry out to them !
Cry out to them ! cry out to them !
   Her.   Thou darest?
Woman !
   Mar.   Ay,—to my woe. The wife of Herod
Should have by justice been a dragoness,
Giving birth to monsters that had murdered him,
Not unto men for him to murder.
   Her.   Curse thee !
   Mar. Curse me, didst say?—curse me? Now, as I live,
May everything that hath on every world
Since the creation, died, be resurrected
To curse thee with a separate curse ! Oh, demon,
Thou'st found the core of sin and eaten it.
What ! thou wouldst curse me? Am I not accursed
Sufficiently in having been thy wife?
Didst thou not curse me with a curse complete
When thou didst make me mother of thy sons?
Be thou accurséd, Herod, ay, accurséd,
Beyond thy utmost knowledge of a curse.
Forget that I once loved thee. Recollect
My hatred only. Thirst, thou shalt have blood,
And blood alone, to quench thy torment. Hunger,
Thou shalt not eat, but be thyself devoured.
Cry out to heaven, and thy prayers rebounding
Shall hurl thee into hell; while death to thee
Shall be one dream of life most horrible !
   Her. Oh, God !
   Mar.   Ay, tremble ; for He hears not thee,
While Mariamne's curse is registered !   [*Exit.*
   Her. What ! Mariamne ! Mariamne ! Mariamne !
Return ! Thou canst not hate me ! No ! no ! no !
That's to be mad,—to say that Mariamne
Hates Herod. And I am not mad. I dreamed.
Then I am dead ! She said that I would dream
Of life in death. Who said so? Mariamne?
No,—one who looked like her. Yet there is none—
Not one who looks like her, saving herself.
She said that, too. Her eyes ! her eyes ! her eyes !
They were two fires ; they burned into my heart's core.
Nay, but my heart's a fire. My heart? What heart?
I gave my heart to Mariamne,—yea,
And she fed anger on it. Well, I'm glad,
I'm glad, in spite of all, that I'm not mad ;
Else might I think all this had really happened ;
And now I know I'm dreaming.

           Enter SALOME.

                 Good Salome,
Wake me, I pray you. [*Aside.*] But that's foolish : ay,

She's part and parcel of my dream.—Good sister,
How come you in my dream?
   Sal.   What! art thou mad?
   Her. No,—dreaming.
   Sal.   Why, that's madness on occasion.
Up! Rouse ye! rouse ye! Here's the potion.—Look!
   Her. Is 't poisonous?
   Sal.   Ay.
   Her.   Then give it me.
   Sal.   For what?
   Her. To drink.
   Sal.   Go to! Why, thou art mad in verity.
   Her. Would that I were!
   Sal.   I say thou art.
   Her.   Then once
Thou bringest me welcome tidings.
   Sal.   Brother.
   Her.   Well?
   Sal. What is the matter?
   Her.   Why, I'm mad, I hope.
Thou saidst that I was mad, but then, good sooth,
Thou art a famous liar lied about.
But look thou, there's a something in me, jade,
That whispers madmen may go madder.
   Sal.   Sir,
Rouse ye. Look here: this is the love-potion
That Mariamne brewed to kill thee.
   Her.   Ah!
   Sal. If it be not a poison, I implore
That thou wilt torture me for pastime.
   Her.   How!—
To kill me?
   Sal.   Ay: who else? Wake up! wake up!
   Her. Why, now, that's right. That is as I would have it.
I would not longer sleep.
   Sal.   Then rouse ye! Here,
Take 't in thy hand. There in thy palm thou holdest
What might have been thy death.
   Her.   Poison, thou sayest?
   Sal. Ay, ay.
   Her.   And brewed by Mariamne?
   Sal.   Ay.
   Her. By Mariamne for King Herod?
   Sal.   Ay.
All this thou knowest. Why wilt question me?
It is for thee to prove if I speak truth.
   Her. And I will prove thee, monster! Ay, by heaven!
The dream is past, and Herod is awake,
To sleep no more!—Without, there!

Enter Attendant.

Send me straightway
A slave from out the workers in the vineyard.
Thou shalt be proved. Fear not : thou shalt be proved,—
In all,—in all. But then I am not mad,
If this is not a dream.—So ! thou art come?

Enter Attendant and Slave.

Salome, here's thy proof,—a pretty proof.
—What is thy age ?
   Boy.   A score of years, my lord.
   Her. Dost thou hate life ?
   Boy.   No, sire. Why should I hate it ?
I'm very happy.
   Her.   Were 't not better, boy,
That thou shouldst part with it ere thou dost hate it?
Give me thy answer.
   Boy.   I know not, my lord.
   Her. I know, and will decide for thee. Drink this.
   Boy. [*Drinks.*] Unto thy health, sire.
   Her.   Ha !
   Boy.   Oh, God ! what's this ?—
—Water, I pray you.   [*Dies.*
   Her.   Thou art proved, Salome :—
Salome, thou art proved ! I will believe thee
Though thou shouldst say thou never wast a liar !
Almost a merry death this would have been.
It scarce had loosed my crown or stirred my sceptre.
Look how he's stretched,—as easily, I wager,
As were he sleeping in the vineyard sunlight.
I am not sorry that he's dead. No! no !
He might have lived to be a Herod. Ay,
He might have lived to have a wife.
   Sal.   Come, rouse thee !
Wilt thou hang thus above a dead slave's body ?
Away !
   Her. For what ?
   Sal.   For vengeance ! Dost thou ask me,
And that thou mightst have been, there at thy foot ?
Away ! to bring the would-be murderess
To justice.
   Her. No! let justice go to her !
I will not see her more, though we should live
A million years within our voices' sound !
   Sal. Live! dost thou speak of life as possible
Unto that demon ?—one who never loved thee ?—
Who made thy love a means unto her ends ?—
A traitress ?—an adulteress ?—Ay, thou'st said it !
Almost a murderess, quite one in heart ?—
She who seduced thy sister's husband ?—she——

Her. Enough ! enough ! thou hast named crimes sufficient
To make thyself seem holy in comparison !
Sal. Sir !
Her.   Oh, be satisfied ; be satisfied :
She shall not live.
Sal.   Now thou art Herod !
Her.   No,
Now I'm a madman !   [*Exit, laughing.*
Sal.   And now I have conquered !
She is already 'prisoned, and I'll follow,
To see that she doth soon meet death !   [*Exit.*

SCENE IV.—*A dungeon.* MARIAMNE *chained. Two guards, talking.*

1*st Guard.* She hath not said a word since I have watched her, ·
Nor moved.   I have not seen her weep,—not once.
2*d Guard.* Believe you all that's said of her ?
1*st Guard.*   Not I.
2*d Guard.* In thine ear, friend : I do suspect foul play.
1*st Guard.* Most like.   Here comes the sister of the king.

Enter SALOME.

Sal. Slaves, where's the prisoner ?
1*st Guard.*   There, madam.
Sal.   Ah !
Good-morrow, madam.   I do trust your queenship
Is in all things provided for ?   Not so ?
What ! sulky ?   Fie ! fie ! fie ! knit not thy brows.
I fear thou hast a temper, gentle queen.
A queen should not indulge in mortal passions.
And, by the way, if any ill befall thee,
I know 'twill comfort thee to think thy sons,—
Thy pretty sons,—Prince Aristobulus,—
The one who trod upon my robe,—rememberest ?—
And Alexander,—he who less resembles
My husband Joseph,—that into my charge
They will be given.   Ha ! have I touched thee, harlot ?
What !   No word yet ?   Well, thy blood speaks for thee :
It ne'er leaped readier to Herod's kisses
Than it doth to the words of Herod's sister.
Be honest, now : why didst thou lure my husband
From loyalty to me and to the king ?
'Twas madness.   Ay, thou mightst have known I'd trace it.
Come, now ; speak.   Tell me.   Didst thou truly love him,
Or was 't mere wantonness ?   Nay, do not die,
Of rage, before thy time,—thy time's so near,
Ha ! ha ! so near,—so near.   Well, of thy sons
I'll promise thee one thing.
Mar.   What ?
Sal.
                                 Ah ! thou speakest !

Thou art not dumb, as I began to fear?
I'll promise thee one thing,—but one, though.
 Mar.   Well,
What is it?
 Sal. Patience! patience!
 Mar.   What is it?
 Sal. I will not cuff them more than twice a day.
Ha! ha! ha! ha! Have care,—have care, good girl!
Thou'lt die, if thou so giv'st thy fury vent.
 Mar. Joseph! Joseph! Joseph! rise from thy grave
And blast this devil with thy festering horror!
Leap to her arms all headless as thou art,
And venge my wrongs: I, Mariamne, summon thee,
Who was and am the Queen of Jewry!
 Sal.   Fiend!
 Mar. [*Breaking loose and seizing* SALOME.]
O God! Make me the tool to venge his murder!
Off, cords! Be brittle as all joy! Off! off!—
Ha! wilt speak more of cuffing?
 Sal.   Help, there! ho!
The queen is mad! Help! help! The queen is mad!
 Mar. One other cry, and thou shalt stand straightway
Face unto face with thy wronged husband's ghost.
Ay, presently I mean to send thee to him,
No matter what thou doest. Dost thou hear me?
First cry me pardon, though,—pardon, dost hear?—
And then to bloody Joseph!
 Sal.   Hold thy hands!
Thou'rt choking me.
 Mar.   Presently,—but not yet.
My pardon.
 Sal. Thou art mad! Well, pardon,—pardon.
Now let me go.
 Mar. [*Stabbing her.*] Ay, unto Joseph! So!
Know'st thou this dagger? I return it to thee!
 Sal. [*Swoons.*] Oh! I am killed!

Enter Guards.

 1st Guard. Oh, heaven! what's this?
 2d Guard.   We will be put to death.
Mark how she bleeds.
 1st Guard. Softly! she is but wounded.
 2d Guard. Did the queen do it?
 1st Guard.   Ay, she must have.
 2d Guard.   Look!
She's stiller, sir, than ever.
 1st Guard. Well,—I know not,—
Mayhap the princess killed herself.
 2d Guard.   Soft! soft!

She moves.   She is not dead.   Come on, sir ; come.
                    [*Exeunt, bearing* SALOME *out.*
Mar. [*Staring at the blood left from* SALOME'S *wound upon the
        floor.*]
Why, her blood's red, like any other woman's!
I had thought it would be black,—black as her soul,—
As Herod's.

                    Enter SARAMALLAS *and* SOHEMUS.

Sar.   Look, friend, how she stares!
Soh.   In truth,
There's something here—— What! blood?   Look, Saramallas!
Sar. 'Tis blood, assuredly.   Look to the queen:
She may have stabbed herself.
Soh.   Would God she had!
Sar. Ay, Sohemus, Amen with all my heart.
Was his command to kill her final?
Soh.   Final.
Sar. And must she die?   Is there no way?—not one?
Soh. Thou knowest well that I would die to save her.
Sar. And thou'rt to take a napkin to the king
Dipped in her blood?
Soh.   Oh, speak not of it, man!
I love my mistress, and would kill ten Herods
Rather than look to see one single hair
Of her bright head disturbed.
Sar.   Well, 't must be done.—
Your majesty, the Sanhedrim——
Mar.   I know,
I know, good Saramallas.—Sohemus,
Good-morrow.   It is well.   I care not now.
She's dead: my sons are safe.   Thou, Sohemus,
Protect them all that's in thy power from Cypros.
Yet I do not much fear her, now the power
That urged her is subdued.   Good Sohemus,
Cypros without Salome is a hell
Without a devil.   See they say their prayers,
And do not break the Sabbath with their games,
And letter-cutting on the lintels.   Nay,
Thou wast a boy, and know how boys will do it,—
Even the gentlest.—Well, I'm ready.   Come.
Soh. Oh, mistress well beloved and always loving,
Thou knowest that I'd rather suffer death
Ten thousand times than see thee even unhappy.
Mar. Yea, friend, even so.   But once to suffer death
Is nevermore to suffer anything.
Therefore rejoice with me, whose not-long life
Hath been so full of pain, I would not purchase
Another day of life were 't purchasable
For the mere asking.   I will bear thy love

To Joseph. Nay, no tears, good Sohemus.
Mine eyes are dry as are these breasts of mine,
Which once did nourish princes. Cease, I pray thee.
I'll walk alone, a queen unto the last.   [*Exit.*

SCENE V.—*Enter* HEROD.

What ! she prepare a poison for me ! Oh,
Foul ! foul ! She, Mariamne ?—she, my queen ?
Nay, she was Joseph's wanton, not my queen.
Was not that vile ? But thus to seek my life,—
That's viler. No, not that : to slay my honor,—
That was more vile. And yet she might have known it,—
That I would pardon her. But she must die,—
She must die now. Die ? Mariamne ? Nay,
He who doth spill a drop of her rare blood
Shall kill his best-belovéd for my pleasure
Upon a holiday ! What ! die ? Her lips,
That I so oft have kissed, to rot i' th' tomb
Like any beggar's ? What ! an end of all ?
All our soft hours, our million-pleasured years,— ·
Even our quarrelling ? And yet, and yet,—
She plotted for my death. Soft ! is that sure ?
Soft, soft,—Salome ! But I saw him die—
Die, with these very eyes. Oh, God ! I care not :
One kiss would make a thousand deaths seem easy,
And there's no poison like to fruitless yearning !
I care not what she purposed, I'll forgive her,—
I will forgive her, and be writ forever   ˮ
Herod the happy fool of Mariamne !
Ay, ay, a happy fool is wise in all things
Above the sourest knowledge-wrinkled seer
That scoffs at him ! Yes, yes, I will forgive her,
And teach her not to hate me. [*Enter* SOHEMUS.]
                              Ay, sir, thou,—
Thou art the very man I seek. Good Sohemus,
Attend. I did speak rashly to thee, friend,
Some moments past.
    Soh.   Rashly, my lord ?
    Her.   Ay, Sohemus.
There is a burning here doth sometimes urge me
To violence whose half I do not mean.
I gave thee orders which I would retract,—
I would retract.
    Soh.   For God's sake, Herod, speak !
    Her. Why, what's the matter ? Here, sir ! wouldst thou
            swoon ?
What is the matter ? I would have the queen
Set free again. Dost hear ?
    Soh.   The queen is free.

Ay, Herod, she hath soared beyond thy reach
Forever. Here's the kerchief thou commanded'st
That I should dip in her warm blood.
Her.   Thou liest!
What! dost thou dare to show me that vile rag
And say 'tis stained with Mariamne's blood?
Soh. Ay, Herod: I have but obeyed thy order.
Her. Dog, thou dost lie! Who put thee to this trick?
Where is Salome? She hath hired thee to it.
Speak, sir! Where is she?
Soh.   Wounded unto death.
The poor queen, frenzied by her coward taunts,
Did burst her bonds and stab her nigh to death.
Her. The poor queen? What poor queen? What dost thou
          hint?
Dost dare speak thus of Mariamne? Go!
Bid her unto me. Bid her here, I say.
Away!
Soh. Nay, Herod, be convinced. Thy queen
No longer lives: that blood is hers indeed,
And I the most unhappy man on earth!
Her. Dost thou dare say thou art, when Herod's here?
Thou most unhappy? Thou? O dog, dog, dog!
Would thou hadst twenty lives, that I might take them
Each in a different way! She's dead, thou say'st?
And that's her blood? Back to her with this message:
" My chief fault was obedience; and Herod,
Being a madman, killed me for obeying."
                    [*Runs* SOHEMUS *through with his sword.*
Soh. I'm glad to go to her. Thou hast done well.   [*Dies.*
Her. That Mariamne's blood? Oh, God! let redness
Possess the earth, the heavens forswear their blue,
The sea its green! ay, let the very stars
Put on her color, and burn bloodily
To do her honor! I will build a pyramid
Unto her memory, and its littlest stone
Shall twice outsize Cheops' entirety;
While for a mortar I will mix the dust
Of emperors dead with blood of living kings!
To work! to work! for earth's foundation-stone
Must be the first in the tremendous pile!   [*Exit madly.*

          Enter two or three attendants, running.

1st Att. Was 't not the king?
2d Att.   I'm sure I heard him.
3d Att.   Ay,
And so am I; but he's not here. Look there!
Is 't not Lord Sohemus?
1st Att.   Ay,—dead, I think.

2d Att. Alas! alas! He had the kindest heart
In all of Jewry.
1st Att. So he had; and heaven
Now hath his soul. Let's bear him hence. Come on.
[*Exeunt, bearing the body of* SOHEMUS.

SCENE VI.—*Another part of the palace.*

Enter HEROD *and* ALEXANDER.

Her. Boy, where's thy mother? Where's thy mother, boy?
Speak, boy: I will not hurt thee. Look, I'm gentle,—
I am not angry. Look, I'll throw my sword
After my crown. Thou seest I recollect it,—
Thy insolent waggery,—ha! ha!—and yet am gentle.
Thou seest? Come, then, my pretty prince. Look here:
This ring for thee. Now tell me, where's thy mother?
Alex. In heaven, where thou'lt never be, vile king.
Call me no more sweet names; for I do hate thee!—
Hate thee!—hate thee!
Her. What's that, thou devil? Ha!
She taught thee that.
Alex. She never taught me anything
But what was good; nor could I teach myself
A better way of honoring her memory
Than by abhorring thee!
Her. Devil!
Alex. I tell thee,
Thou'lt be thrice damned, if after killing her
Thou seek'st to kill her honor! Slay me! do!
I'm not afraid. Thou'st thrown away thy sword;
Then take thy hands. I ask no more, by heaven,
Than to be sent to her!—Oh, mother! mother!
Her. Where is she, then? Where is she? Tell me that,
And thou shalt go to her. Don't weep; don't weep.
Look, I am sorry if I called thee devil.
Look,—for thou'lt see what no man saw ere this,—
Herod a pardon-beggar. Look,—I'm sorry.
Alex. Go beg of God; for I have naught to give thee
Save only hate. [*Exit.*
Her. Now know I thou'rt his son!
No! no! no! no! I did not mean it! Oh,
Return, return, my son, my Alexander,
My son and hers! Or if that thou dost hate me,
Be a dear hypocrite, and feign to love me!
What's that, though? Soft! if one may feign to love,
May not one feign to hate? Might she not so?
She doth not hate me: no, she hath but feigned it,—
This hatred,—that I may her love more value
When she confesses it.—Without, there! ho!

Enter Attendants.

Sirs,—bid the queen at once attend me.   Quick !
Why do ye stand there as though death had gripped ye?
Summon the queen at once!
     Att.   What queen, my lord?
     Her. What queen, dog? Wilt thou give me back my words?
What queen?   Know that there is one only queen
In Herod's catalogue.   Call Mariamne,
The Queen of Jewry ; bid her come to me
Here o' the instant.   Oh, away with ye!
                                        [*Exeunt Attendants.*
Now shall all nights to this night be as leaves
From Wisdom's tree, unto its golden fruit,—
As sparks to stars,—as stars unto God's crown !
Let some new God be born to conquer heaven,
Dethrone Jehovah, and create new worlds
For that prince who shall some day live as proof
Of this night's wonder.   Mariamne, come !
I'll shake the stars from out their blackened sockets
To light our bridal bed ; the choir of heaven
Shall chant us to our sleep ; and for thy coverlet
Thou shalt the mantle of God's glory.   Shout,
Ye tempest-riding spirits ; earth, give voice ;
Resound, ye forests, like to harps ; let ocean
Her cymbal-clashing waves send unto heaven
And sweep down echo from the halls of Zeus !
Yea, let hell on the forehead of this night
Be bound as torch to light our ecstasy !

Re-enter Attendants.

So, sirs !   Where is the queen?
     Att.   Thou must know, sire——
     Her. Must know?   Is that an answer for thy king?
Call me Queen Mariamne from the doors.
Call her, I say.
     Att.   Oh, sire, the queen is dead.
She was beheaded full an hour ago.
     Her. Damned be thy lying tongue !   Away ! away !
Or I will go myself to summon her !   [*Exit Attendants.*]
Beheaded?   Mariamne?   There was blood,—
Ay, there was blood,—but there's no sign in that.
A lamb's blood might stand proxy for a queen's,
And no one know the difference.   Dead?   Dead?
Were God to say it, I'd cry God a liar !
Stay ! something comes to me,—something comes back.
I did commission Sohemus——The napkin——
Oh, God ! it was her blood, and she is dead !
O Mariamne, Mariamne, Mariamne !
What am I who have slain thee?   Lucifer

Is holy unto Herod, for in truth
He was sin's victim, I the king of vice!
Beheaded? God! was there no other way
But death must roll that proud head on the ground
As children roll a ball? What! do I live,
And Mariamne dead? What! am I Herod,
And Mariamne slain at my command?—
That Herod whom men call the Great? Just God!
Herod the Great? Ay! Herod the great in sin!
[*Falls forward on his face.*

Amélie Rives.

THE END.

A FEW MORE WORDS ABOUT MISS RIVES.

IN literature, as in life, the candor of innocence is sometimes mistaken for that of intentional impurity. But our deception with regard to it is apt to be very short-lived, and is usually resultant from our own blunt or languid vision. I confess that a second reading of Miss Rives's remarkable story "The Quick or the Dead?" has made it evident to me just where the cause of the whole misunderstanding has lain; for there seems to be no doubt that in this work she has offended the tastes of readers whom her "Farrier Lass o' Piping Pebworth" and other tales of a like beauty and freshness had forcibly charmed. Miss Rives has steeped a love-story in realism, acted on by some peculiar force of her time, without stopping to consider what dangers, with a writer of her strongly romantic trend, must surround any such literary exploit, unless a good deal of discriminative caution be made to accompany it. But caution of this kind does not usually consort with authors of youth and inexperience. Had Miss Rives been commencing her career as a novelist about a half-century ago, she would have painted the episodes between Barbara and her lover in hues that no one would have found too glaring. But being inevitably a child of the period, she has told a modern story in the modern manner. Now, as it chanced, she had an extremely difficult story for a young writer to tell. It was one which George Sand would have delighted to deal with in French; it involved the question as to just how far human love is a physical magnetism and just how far it is an attraction of that finer and subtler sort which even materialists, for want of a better descriptive term, must call "spiritual." This whole _donnée_ is one of surpassing dramatic interest, and worthy to be treated by the greatest writers of fiction. Still, the appeal is constantly being made to Barbara through those fleshly qualities possessed by the man who so marvellously resembles her adored dead husband. Early in the work it is said of the heroine, on her first meeting with this extraordinary counterfeit presentment, "She began to think that she was in a dream,—the figure, the step, the pose, were so identically her husband's; but the greatest shock of all was when he spoke." In the very next line we learn that when he did speak "the voice was Val's voice." This living likeness of Barbara's husband is his cousin, and claims promptly a cousin's intimate privileges. They two are incessantly alone together in a great old Virginian homestead. He is filled with youthful vigor and fire, and almost hourly finds himself growing more and more in love with his kinsman's widow. She is a woman whose temperament has an almost tropical ardor, and whom we can imagine performing scarcely a single act in life without giving it the florid hues of her own rather theatric personality. Miss Rives means her for a very emotional being, and so she is; but her mentality is limited in an unfortunate degree, considering the numerous tempting opportunities with which she is presented by her creator for behaving in a silly fashion, and which she constantly embraces.

Apart, however, from Barbara's intelligence or lack of it, she has been prostrated by a fierce bereavement only to discover in John Dering's love a possible consolation for the treasured companionship that she has lost. Later along in the tale she becomes convinced that his bodily resemblance to Valentine Pomfret will not serve; it is a broken reed on which to lean the weight of her own bruised existence. But in Barbara's gradual realization of this melancholy truth do we trace both the circumference and diameter of a most unique achievement. Here lies the entire little history; and an infusion of the realistic method into those elements whose character I have sought to define was likely, unless directed by the hand of an adept, to produce highly inflammatory consequences. Indeed, "The Quick or the Dead?" would be, just as it stands, a valuable weapon in the hands of all confirmed anti-realists. "Here," they might cry, "is what comes of giving the reader too many minute details. When the subject is ordinary life they become paltry; when it is sexual passion they become salacious." Surely realism, to preserve consistency with its own tenets, never should shrink from details, no matter what may be its chosen theme. Between it and the naturalism of Zola there is no difference whatever except one of degree. Our American realists either fastidiously draw a line at "objectionable" disclosures or else restrain the excursional tendencies of their pens because the market which purchases their literary wares will refuse them if too careless a frankness be cultivated. It is in my memory that more than once an American writer of repute has said to me, "I would *like* to write fearlessly and with no gingerly concealments about my fiction; I regret being compelled not to call a spade a spade; I feel the cry of 'immorality' waiting for me, and hence I must repress an instinct to treat life as I see it and judge it, for the reason that if I do so I will meet a frowning publisher and perchance a still more frowning public." It has been the present essayist's good fortune to meet not a few writers of fiction in this country whose names are more or less distinguished as experts in their charming craft, and he can scarcely recall a single instance among these makers of novels and plays where the earnest craving was not evident for greater latitude in the discussion of matters which are often far too avidly gloated over by the French, but which assert, notwithstanding, a distinct claim to be treated rationally by more temperate chroniclers.

In the case of Miss Rives, however, I am reluctant to state that she has written with any deliberated observance of this or that school. She had doubtless read a large number of modern novels and was influenced by that prevailing *force majeure* which few of them have escaped. When a story-teller of her clime and tongue intentionally tries to "shock" the community, he is apt to reveal a hardness, a pert abandonment, a kind of saucy laxity which kills interests in his readers as surely as if he had committed some overt act of vulgar revolt against the decencies. In "The Quick or the Dead?" this premeditated spirit of mischief everywhere seems curiously absent. At times there are both extravagance and crudity in the narration, but these traits, regrettable though they must be declared, are manifested with a *naïveté* that often provokes a smile at their freedom from all operated, self-conscious effect and their positive childishness in the way of record and delivery. When, for example, after her absurdly particularized tussle with the hero to retain a locket which she has snatched from him, it is related of Barbara that while kneeling near her late contestant on the rug in front of the fireplace she felt her own " breath returned upon her face from Dering's trousers," we smile at the really juvenile simplicity which could present such a bit of spontaneous bathos instead of the winsome artistic touch we might have expected.   For Miss Rives has already shown us that she can surprise and charm by the deft use of phrase and simile; she has shown it only a page or so further back in her story, where the rape of the locket is about to occur :

" It was on a bitterly cold, gray afternoon in November that these two comrades, as they now called themselves, were engaged in a game of ' graces' in the large central hall at Rosemary.   The earlier day had been tempestuous and clattering with wind-whirled sleet, but a tawny cloud, that in streaming wildness resembled, perhaps, the flying mane of one of the Prophet's fiery steeds when in mid-heaven, now streaked all the upper sky and sent a gold-red light glowing in at the hall-windows.   There were eight of these tall, shrouded shapes, like uncanny mummies, and where the faces should have been, that furnace-like radiance shone through folds of sheer muslin. . . . The figures of Barbara and Dering were revealed, as they swooped among the shadows here and there, which glittered as with mica.   Now the rathe arm and throat of Barbara came into relief against the dusky formlessness, now it was Dering's gay crest of curls and straining shoulders.   The orange-ribboned hoops circled above, like two haloes uncertain as to which of those handsome heads they were to saint."

This may not be very accurate or painstaking writing, but it is certainly very excellent " impressionism."   It leaves a picture which would probably not stay in our recollection as long as it is fated to do were the workmanship less fervid, tumultuous, and heartfelt.   And so, again and again throughout the book, we come upon passages betraying the same immaturity and yet an equal fascination.   There is humor, too, and of a pungent quality.   Nothing can be better in its way than the despair of the lovers over Mr. Buzzy's quaint and maddening garrulity as he is driven in their company to the station.   They want to whisper sweet nothings in one another's ears—to sit with clasped hands—to be left unmolested there in the back of the lumbering vehicle during those few moments of intercourse which remain for them.   But Mr. Buzzy, impervious as regards all hints, rambles on, to the semi-distraction of his hearers.   Afterward, in the station itself, when this implacable fellow-passenger continues his tortures, Dering suddenly jumps up with frenzy and cries, " I have something of importance to say to Mrs. Pomfret, and I have now only thirteen minutes in which to say it.   Could you be so very kind as to leave us together ?"   But, as the author remarks, if Dering had thought to freeze Buzzy by this frigid and biting address, he was vastly mistaken.   The grinning, illiterate, boorish, but indestructibly good-natured creature at once consents to leave the waiting-room of the station, but not before he has responded, " Cert'n'y,—cert'n'y. . . Why didn't you tip me the wink ?

I'd er twigged. Reckon I'll go and git a snack." And then at last he goes.

"Buzzy" is apparently a triumph in the way of type-sketching. I am not prepared to state this positively, however, being unfamiliar with the region of which he seems a product. But he is most probably drawn with great correctness, for the whole key-note of the book is realism of a most unswerving fidelity.

In mentioning "Buzzy" I am reminded that his vernacular is never in the least fatiguing; there is just enough of it to make us want a little more, and in our age of dialectic surfeit that is surely a laudatory admission. Indeed, I think Miss Rives deserves the warm thanks of numberless readers who have had page after page of dissolute colloquial syntax thrust upon them by other Southern writers, and by not a few Western writers also, during the past decade. I am loath to believe that such novels create any save a lukewarm local interest. Negro and "hoosier" dialects have filled our magazines until there no longer seems to be common-sense in believing that weariness has not followed them. There is a kind of novel produced nowadays in which it would appear as if everything were fine except the English of the characters. Nature so far transcends human nature in what one might almost call a patrician excellence of deportment that we read on the one hand of delicate mists curling ethereally along mountain-sides, of prismatic sunsets, of valleys empurpled by twilight, and on the other hand encounter the whole English grammar in about as unpleasant a state of corruption as possible. We are reminded of the hymn-book, with its description of enchanting scenes in which "only man is vile;" our compassion and sense of justice alike are stirred by seeing the meadows and hills and trees and birds all getting along so beautifully, while such disastrous things are forever happening to the verb "to be." Happily, Miss Rives rids us of all anxiety on this latter point. I am afraid few of us realize just how exceptional it is to come across a Virginia novel that does not teem with negro-jargon from the first chapter to the last.

Dialect Miss Rives has employed in some of her shorter stories, however, though it is there far from being of the tiresome order. "The Farrier Lass o' Piping Pebworth," an excessively romantic tale of Queen Elizabeth's time, strikes a few false notes amid a general scheme of harmonious consistency. These are in giving the narrator, Humfrey Lemon, unnaturally elaborated expressions and sentiments, considering his unlettered condition. To make such a person say, for example, "He had eyes like pools o' water under a night heaven, wherein two stars have drowned themselves, as 'twere, and brows as black and straight as a sweep o' cloud across an evening sky," may be thoroughly poetic, but is misplaced as an utterance supposed to issue from uneducated lips. For like reasons a sentence delivered by the same Humfrey Lemon will not assimilate with the prevailing tone of his homespun rustic monologue: "Also a red came into her shadowy cheeks, like as though a scarlet flower tossed into a clear brown stream should rise slowly upward beneath the limpid surface and shine a-through." For a tippling peasant to address an ale-house companion in these terms cannot but place such portions of Miss Rives's prose on a level with Ouida's worst errors in the line of overdrawing and hyperbole. They prepare the reader but ill for bits as good as, "She was that brown, a bun looked pale i' th' comparison when she did lift it to her mouth to eat it;" or for, "'An thou tell it, the more fool thou,' saith she; and a draws up her red lips into a circle as though a'd had a draw-string in 'em, and a stands and looks at him as a used to stand and look at her dam when she chid her for a romp." The attempted wooing of the "farrier lass" by Sir Dagonet Balfour, with Keren's haughty rejection of this high-born gallant because of a previous unconquered attachment, has in it almost the airy, happy-go-lucky prettiness of old folk-lore. Yet it suits the Elizabethan atmosphere which encompasses the incidents, and is altogether as different from the realistic modernity of "The Quick or the Dead?" as an ivy-grown, mullion-paned window is different from a plate-glass one of to-day. Miss Rives's turn for the telling of archaic tales is an impulse to be commended. It is easy to pick flaws in the exactitude of her archæology, but, after all, she is plainly equipped as regards this form of flexible and practicable scholarship beyond the suggested powers of her most industrious detractors.

It has been my privilege to examine some of the advance-sheets of "Herod and Mariamne," and I find it a tragedy of uneven yet often astonishing vigor. Like almost everything which its gifted creator has thus far accomplished, it exhibits, I should say, more of fecund promise than of sterling accomplishment. Its gloom is unrelieved by any play of humor,—a criticism which can by no means be passed on such other work of hers as I have thus far seen. The character of Herod is too unrelievedly ferocious and lurid. Mariamne is more successful; Miss Rives can always draw women more firmly and satisfactorily than she can draw men,—an evidence, I think, that she "looks into her heart and writes," and that longer life and ampler observation will fortify her distinct literary aptitudes. I should call "Herod and Mariamne" the dramatic effort of a beginner; but it contains lines which insist on being recollected, and it bespeaks, throughout the whole richly-passionate scope of its composition, that same inherent vitality of organism which has already set her so high among our younger competitors for secure distinction in the noble art of letters.

Edgar Fawcett.

THE FADED PANSY.

M Y garden-beds are sweet with bloom;
　　Each flower its pride uprears;
But this faded pansy's faint perfume
Has drenched my eyes with tears.

Curtis Hall.

WITH GAUGE & SWALLOW.*

VII.—A CONFLICT BETWEEN CHURCH AND STATE.

"KIN I git ter see Mr. Swaller?" This inquiry came from a tall, lean man, clad in wool jeans and carrying a wide, soft-brimmed hat in his hand which rested on the railing by my desk. His face had a curious pinched expression, and the tobacco he was masticating had left a yellowish stain about the corners of his mouth and in the dull-grayish beard that straggled over his face. He had a subdued, almost furtive look, though his blue eyes were not without a gleam of shrewdness. He had wandered in and come to a halt near my desk, apparently because no one opposed his progress, asked him any questions, or seemed likely to do so.

"What is the name, sir?" I asked, smartly.

"'Tain't no matter 'bout the name," he answered. "The Cunnel never seed me, ner hearn tell o' me nuther, I don't s'pose. Ef I could jes' see him a minit 'twould be all I'd keer fer."

"If you will tell me your business," I said, patronizingly, "I will ascertain if he is able to see you. He is a very busy man."

"So I s'pose," said the stranger, deliberately expectorating on the carpet. "An' that's jes' what I was afeerd on. I tole Biah there wa'n't no sort uv use er tryin' ter git one o' these high-flyin' New-Yawkers ter so much ez look at his case. I reckon he must make a heap uv money," he added, inquiringly, as he glanced sharply about the office.

"Gauge & Swallow are pretty high-priced," I answered, feeling to the full the reflected glory of my employers' position.

"Wouldn't look at a case under a thousan' dollars, I reckon."

"They are not apt to engage in unremunerative labor." I smiled as I wondered what he would think of some of the fees they had received.

"Jes' what I tole Biah," said the stranger. "An' he hain't got no thousan' dollars ter spare, ner I nuther,—more's the pity. Ef I hed, Biah should hev it, kase he certin hev been badly used,—badly used. I don't pertend ter justify everythin' he's done,—by no manner uv means,—" the man expectorated with judicial severity and effusiveness before proceeding,—"but when a man hev repented an' done all that lay in his power ter comply with the laws uv God an' man, then ter jump on him an' tromp him down in the mire, jes' kase he happens ter be pore, that ain't right ner jestice. Is it, now, mister?"

I admitted that such conduct did not seem to be exactly in consonance with the principles of universal equity.

"Edzactly,—'zactly. Wal, that's Biah's case. Hit don't seem right, nohow; but his lawyer tells him thar ain't no chance fer him ter

* Copyright, 1888, by E. K. Tourgee.

git clar 'cept by an appeal er sunthin' uv that sort ter the Supreme
Court et Washington. Yer see, they found Biah guilty, the jury did;
an' the jedge *he* stood by the jury; an' the Supreme Court down ter
Richmou', they stood by *him.* Now, Lawyer Perrin says—an' he's a
right sharp sort uv a man, too—that there ain't no way ter git out on't
'cept by appeal ter the Supremest Court uv all in Washin'ton. An' ez
thet 'ud likely take 'bout all he's got left, yer see, he advises Biah—an'
I does the same when I hearn how 'twas—not ter make enny mo' fuss
'bout the matter, but jes' go 'long an' surve out his time an' be done
with it. But Biah's sot,—awful sot, mister,—an' he 'lows he hain't
done no wrong in the sight uv God ner man,—in the way he's accused
uv, at least,—an' he ain't gwine ter submit ter sech imposition jes' fer
tryin' ter do what's right. So, he 'lowed ez I should come hyer an'
see ef I couldn't git Mr. Swaller ter ondertake his case fer him; an' ef
I could, he'd jes' carry hit on up ter Washin'ton, ef it tuk the las' cent
he hed."

"Biah is your brother, I think you said?"

"Co'se, co'se: what ud I be here fer ef he warn't? Biah Wilkins,
uv Pittsylvany, suh, an' ez respectable a man ez ever lived in the
county, too, ef he is pore an' in jail this minnit, ef they heven't tuk
him ter the State prison, though I do say it ez oughtn't, bein' his
brother."

"What's the cause of your brother's difficulty?"

"That's jes' what I kem on ter tell Mr. Swaller, ef so be ez I kin
git speech with him fer a leetle while. An' Biah he sez ef I kin once
git this yere letter inter his hands, he's jes' boun' ter see me, even ef he
don't do nothin' mo'. Biah 'lows 't a gre't lawyer like Mr. Swaller's
boun' ter know a heap mo'n a little un like Mr. Perrin, not ter speak
disrespeckfully uv Mr. Perrin, who certain hev stuck by Biah like a
man."

He dropped his hat on the floor, and, after some search, drew from
his pocket a letter, which he held towards me.

"Oh, if you have a letter of introduction, Mr. Swallow will see
you, of course," I replied, cheerfully. "Have a seat, sir, and I will
take it to him."

"Thank ye: I don't keer ef I do," responded the stranger, sinking
into the chair I pushed towards him and drawing his hat carelessly
beside him so that the brim rested on the rung. "Tain't no letter uv
interduction, though; hit's one uv his,—Mr. Swaller's, ye know,—one
he writ ter Biah. Ef ye'd jes' be kin' 'nuff ter han' it ter him an' say
ef he's not too busy I'd like a word with him."

His language was apologetic, but his tone was confident rather than
supplicating.

I took the letter, went to Mr. Swallow's room, and handed it to
him, stating the request the stranger made. The Junior does not like
to be interrupted when he is at work, and he was working very hard
that day preparing his celebrated argument in the "Peterhoff Admiralty
Case,"—in which our fee, by the way, was twenty thousand dollars, with
about ten thousand dollars more granted for allowances, disburse-
ments, etc.

He drew down his brows as he took the soiled envelope, and, merely glancing at the superscription, drew forth the letter and ran over its contents. A single glance transformed him. " Where is he? Bring him here!" he exclaimed, excitedly. " No, I will go with you. Time? I should like to know anything that would prevent my having time for Abiah Wilkins's affairs!"

He followed me out, and literally fell upon the neck of the uncouth Southerner, as if he found it impossible otherwise to express his gratification.

" Why, Mr. Wilkins! what an unexpected pleasure! I hardly thought, when I wrote this letter almost twenty years ago, that I should ever have the pleasure of welcoming you to New York and personally showing my gratitude for your kindness to—to——"

Mr. Swallow choked at the word, and, while he wrung the stranger's hand, dropped the letter, and, drawing forth his handkerchief, began to wipe away the tears that were flowing down his cheeks. I looked on in amazement, and could see that the clerks were glancing shyly towards us, as surprised as I at this display of emotion.

" Naw," said the stranger, disengaging himself from this embrace, " I'm 'bleeged to ye all the same, Mr. Swaller, an' glad ter make yer acquaintance, but I ain't Biah,—only his brother John. Ef I'd been in his case, I don't s'pose ye'd been half ez glad ter see me. Not but what he done jes' right, more 'spechully ez things turned out, but most on us don't allers know jes' what is the right thing ter do at the time quite ez well ez we do atterwards. Biah's a pore man, an' hain't got much larnin'; but he hez his own notions 'bout what's right, an' when he's once made up his mind, 'tain't noways easy ter turn him from 'em. That's why he's in trouble now."

" In trouble? If there is anything I can do——" The Junior's tone told the rest.

—" Ef it won't be askin' too much, Mr. Swaller," said the other, hesitantly.

" As if Abiah Wilkins could ever ask too much from me!"

" That's jes' what Biah said," responded the other, with a smile of satisfaction. " He 'lowed the man ez writ that letter meant every word he said. I tole him mos' likely you'd forgot——"

" One never forgets some things," interrupted Mr. Swallow, reproachfully.

" Wal, sho' enuff," said the countryman, as he picked up his hat and stood revolving it constrainedly on the forefinger of his left hand. " I wanted ye to know, though, I'm doin' this only fer Biah's sake. I hain't got no right ter claim anythin' on my own account. Ef I'd hev known what was goin' on up ter the hill-place, I don't 'low I'd hev 'proved on't, thet's the truth; but Biah done it, an' now he's in trouble. I've done all I kin fer him, an' only jes' kem on hyer kase he 'peared ter hev sot his head on't thet you would either holp him or tell him 'twa'n't no use ter try an' do nothin' mo'."

" Well, come and tell me all about it," said Mr. Swallow, putting his hand almost affectionately in the arm of the awkward stranger and leading him towards his private room. His lashes were still wet with tears, and as the door closed behind them every eye was turned upon Burrill as the chartered depository of the secrets of the firm ; but the old man only shook his head, to intimate that his surprise was as great as ours.

It was as a result of this incident that I became familiar with the circumstances of the case entitled

IN THE SUPREME COURT OF THE UNITED STATES.

ABIAH WILKINS and ELENA WILKINS ⎫
             vs.   ⎬ *Error to the Supreme Court of Virginia.*
THE COMMONWEALTH OF VIRGINIA. ⎭

Abiah Wilkins was one of those who responded to the first call of the Confederacy for men to support the claim of the new republic to a place in the family of nations. He was a young man, hardly twenty years old, and felt ashamed to stay at home while others were in the army fighting his battles. He was one of a class whom it is the habit of many profound thinkers to declare were wheedled or forced into the army of the South, because we are told that the success of the Confederacy would have been inimical to their interests. If self-interest were the only motive which governs the action of peoples, or the measure of self-interest were always the same, this conclusion might be a correct one. That there is some weak point in the reasoning by which it is supported, however, is evident from the fact that such men composed the bulk of the Confederate army, and that a people can neither be led nor driven except in the direction of their own desires. It is no doubt true that slavery was a hard master to the non-slaveholding white man of the South ; but it is also true that he did not feel himself oppressed, and did not realize that he was deprived of any right or privilege. He had just as good an opportunity as his fellows ; and they are not the only people who have mistaken equal opportunity for the *ultima Thule* of civic right.

Though Abiah Wilkins was of what is known as the "poor-white" class, he was not lacking in independence or knowledge of his own preferences. His father had been a thrifty and capable overseer, whose services were always in demand at a good salary. Contrary to the usual Northern idea of those in his station, he was one of the most independent and self-respecting of men. Of profound religious conviction and blameless life, he was just, though severe, with those under his charge, and allowed no intermeddling with his functions on the part of the owner or any one else. If at the end of the year the owner were dissatisfied, he could employ another in his place ; but during that time there was no appeal from his judgment, and must be no interference with his plans. Though only a salaried foreman, he felt himself responsible for results, and had a reputation which he would not suffer to be imperilled by limitation of his judgment. His boast was that he could "raise more barrels of corn and a greater value of tobacco on fewer acres, with less stock and less labor, and leave the land, stock, and 'niggers' in better condition at the end of the year, than any other man on the Dan." This was not a vain boast nor an unworthy one, but a self-respecting assertion of thorough agricultural knowledge and high administrative capacity.

He had one ambition,—to start his two boys in life as their own masters. He wished them to belong to the universally-envied "planter aristocracy." With this in view, he bought, in his later years, a little plantation on the Shockoe and became the owner of three slaves,—an old man and woman, and a fuzzy-headed girl with a face of that curious lividness which marks the negro in whose cuticle the *pigmentum nigrum* is somewhat lacking. She was of mixed blood, but her mother was dark enough to show that the child was one of those freaks of nature which were not easily marketable. The overseer had bought her, therefore, almost for a song at an administrator's sale. As she grew older the albino tendency seemed to disappear, leaving her one of those curiously-marked types whose relation to either race is uncertain, but whose kinship to both is unmistakable. He purchased also a snug little plantation, forty miles away, at the foot of the Turkey-Cock Hills, which his sagacity told him would one day be valuable tobacco-land. It was understood that John, the elder, was to have the home-place, and Abiah, the younger, was to take the hill-plantation. The chattels-real were to be equitably divided also,—the old man and woman to John, and the girl Elena to Abiah. With this aid they were expected to lift themselves into the coveted social position.

The old man had raised his sons carefully, though they had little education. A few months in a neighborhood "contribution" school had sufficed to teach them to read, to write with difficulty, and to keep the rude accounts necessary in their station. As agriculturists, however, they were thoroughly trained. They had followed the plough from boyhood under their father's eye, knew what cultivation every crop required, and were adepts in the management of stock and the working of slaves. John had married and was working as overseer when the war began. He could not enter the service until his contract expired; but Abiah volunteered without hesitation. At the end of the year John did likewise, and his wife came to the home-place to live. A few months afterwards, Abiah returned, severely wounded. Soon after, his mother died; and when he recovered—so far as he ever would—from the effects of his wound, possessed with the spirit of unrest, generated partly perhaps by service in the army and partly by lack of harmony with his sister-in-law, he persuaded the old father to set off to him his portion of the estate, and, taking a horse and wagon, with a small stock of farming-utensils and the girl Elena, he set out to take possession of the hill-plantation, and, literally single-handed, to carve his way to fortune. He had still his right, and, in a half-boastful way, declared that, in spite of the crippled left, he was a better man than any of the skulkers who would neither fight nor work. He made good his boast, too, and the little plantation on the head-waters of Pig River soon assumed a thrifty and comfortable aspect.

There were few neighbors, and the "settlement" was more than a mile from any travelled road. They heard little of the movements of the outer world. Newspapers were not abundant, and were by no means considered a necessity of life. Now and then Abiah went to the city, twenty miles away, to market his produce. Whatever he raised brought enormous quantities of paper money, but what he had to buy seemed very dear. After the first season a colored man and woman who had been "refugeed" from the eastern part of the State were hired. They cost him little beyond their support, as the owner regarded their safety—or rather their lack of opportunity to escape to the enemy's lines—as an equivalent for their labor. As the fortunes of the Confederacy grew desperate, the mountains were filled with men fleeing from conscription and their pursuers. It was dangerous to be suspected of favoring the former, and quite as perilous to be thought to give aid to the latter.

Abiah Wilkins acted very prudently. As a wounded Confederate who had a brother in the ranks, he was free from suspicion of favoring the bushwhackers. On the other hand, Elena kept the keys of the smoke-house; and such was his confidence in her that he did not pry too closely into the amount of food required for the support of his family. While she saved him from the hostility of the deserters, however, she neither squandered his stores nor permitted her charity to imperil his reputation for loyalty. No doubtful characters were ever seen about his premises by the officials, and no hunted conscript ever suspected Abiah Wilkins of giving information of his hiding-place. He really had little sympathy with the conscripts. He would not willingly have assisted one of them to evade the service, but, good Confederate though he was, he managed to convince himself that he was not responsible for what the girl might do. She was only his slave, after all, though a most devoted and capable one. He hardly knew how he could have got along without her.

There came a time, however, when he could not thus easily shake off responsibility. It was a cold night in mid-winter when he was awakened by the whispered words of Elena:

"Mars' Biah! Mars' Biah! Won't you des come to de kitchen a minnit?"

"What is it, Lena?"

There was no answer, and he heard her swift, shuffling steps on the boards that formed the walk to the kitchen, rattling on the frozen ground as she went, and wondered what could have induced her to come out on such a night barefooted.

He rose hastily, and followed her, half dressed. As he reached the door he heard a dull, hollow cough. Opening it, he saw lying on a shuck mattress on the rude puncheon floor before the great fireplace a young man, pale, emaciated, and convulsed with that cough which it needs no technically-trained ear to know is the sure precursor of death. The girl was kneeling on the floor beside him, wiping the red line of his lips while he panted for breath.

"What's this?" asked the master, in an anxious tone, coming forward into the circle of light about the fire. The sufferer turned his great dark eyes upon the new-comer, and essayed to speak.

"'Sh! Don't try to speak, honey. I'll tell him," said the girl.

But the man would not be silent. Motioning to the girl to raise his head, he told the astonished planter a strange story. He was a

Federal soldier who had escaped from the Confederate prison at Salisbury and made his way thus far towards the lines of the Union army. His health, already broken, had been utterly shattered by the exposure of the journey. For some time he had been cared for as well as might be by the deserters in the bush, who finally, seeing that he could not recover, and being themselves compelled to flee to avoid an intended raid upon their hiding-place, had brought him to the house, hoping that the kind-hearted girl who had more than once brought him needed dainties might somehow afford him shelter.

"Ob co'se, Mars' Biah, I tole 'em he couldn't stay yere 'less you was willin', kase hit mought git you inter trouble."

"I wouldn't do that, after the kindness I've received," said the invalid, hoarsely. "I'll go away if you think——"

But Abiah did not allow him to finish the sentence.

"I'm a good Confederit," he said, "but ther' don't no man go outen my house en that condition,—friend ner foe."

He was as good as his word. The next day the sick man was removed to the house and placed in Abiah's own bed. Here he remained more days than it seemed possible that he could live. He even began· to hope for recovery ; but when the warm spring-time brought the news of victory for the Federal arms, he sank contentedly away. The story was common enough in those days, though it seems a strange one now. A mere boy, he had run away from school and enlisted under an assumed name to avoid paternal reclamation. Taken prisoner and confined in the fetid, overcrowded pen, he had sunk rapidly into consumption, and but for an almost miraculous escape would have been one of the twelve thousand nameless dead who sleep beneath the long ridges on the sunny hill-side beyond where the famous prison stood. He wrote an account of his wanderings ; and after he was dead and the war was over, Abiah Wilkins sent it to Mr. Swallow, with a brief ill-spelled note detailing the end. After a time the lawyer came—one of a great host of seekers for lost loved ones—and took away the remains of his son. When he had returned home and mastered the sorrow time could not assuage, he wrote the letter John had brought as his introduction.

Why had Abiah Wilkins appealed to the man whose dying son he had befriended almost a score of years before, for aid ? He had lived quietly enough upon the little hill-plantation, prosperous in a moderate way, contented with his fortune, and at peace with his neighbors. Almost too contented, some said, with a sly look which everybody seemed to understand ; but, for all that, he was highly respected, and more than one young woman of the neighborhood resolutely set her cap for the well-to-do bachelor, only to have her labor for her pains. With the downfall of slavery he increased the number of his hirelings, finding that his early training under the old overseer especially fitted him for the management of the negro in a state of freedom. Elena remained with her young master, and the keys which were the symbol of authority still hung at her girdle. She had not grown handsome with the years that had elapsed, but she had managed Abiah Wilkins's domestic affairs so faithfully that he felt his success was in great measure due to her co-operation. Another house had been added to the kitchen, in which she dwelt,—she and her children, a half-dozen of whom had grown up around her. Some of the elder ones had been sent away to school; the younger were with her yet. It needed but a glance at her surroundings to know why the neighbors wagged their heads at the mention of Abiah Wilkins's name.

Yet he was what is termed in the vernacular "a mighty straight man." Though not a member of the church, he was upright in his dealings, moderate in his language, and sober in his habits. He attended divine service regularly, and was one of the most liberal supporters of stated preaching at High Rock Meeting-house, four miles away; while Elena sustained a similar relation to the colored church at Elkin's Ford, two miles away in an opposite direction. Both were highly respected in the neighborhood, and, though some deprecated what was considered an impropriety, no one felt called upon to withdraw their countenance from either. Even John's wife, who had enviously rejoiced in the loss emancipation would bring to the fortunate younger brother, was fain to admit that there were not many such housekeepers as "that gal Lena" anywhere in the country. "Brother Biah," she declared, "owed more of his luck to her good management than to his own good sense."

The new plantation had grown old in the mean time. The trees which had been topped when the house was built had thrown out their protecting branches over it; porches had been added here and there, and a latticed way connected the house and kitchen with a branch that led to the well, and on this the ivy and honeysuckle struggled constantly for supremacy. Abiah smoked his pipe contentedly upon the porch, but supervised with diligence the work of the plantation. Neatness and comfort reigned about the house.

About this time a big meeting was held at High Rock Church after the crops were laid by, and, to the surprise of all, among others who went forward to the straw-strewn space before the pulpit under the arbor, asking the prayers of God's people, was Abiah Wilkins. The sight inspired those in charge of the meeting to renewed exertions. Long and fervid were the prayers which were offered in his behalf. If he was not a boisterous penitent, he was a persevering one. Day after day and night after night he was found kneeling in the same place. It was the talk of the neighborhood. Elena went once to see with her own eyes what she had heard so much about from others. When she returned home her eyes were red with weeping. After that she served her master silently, tearfully. She felt that her hour had come, yet she made no complaint, uttered no reproaches. So Hagar must have felt when her master put her forth in the desert.

At length, after seven days and nights of struggle, grace triumphed, and Abiah Wilkins testified with flowing tears of that love which taketh away sin. As in everything else, he was quiet and undemonstrative in regard to his religious experiences; but none the less did every one put faith in his sincerity. As he did not offer to join the church, he was urged to do so, and, upon expressing his willingness, one of the most persuasive of the preachers in attendance was deputed to confer with him in regard to a right ordering of his domestic life, so that the Church of God might not be scandalized by any show of evil.

"Brother Wilkins," said the chosen emissary, as they sat smoking upon the porch after having partaken of a bountiful repast prepared by Elena,—"Brother Wilkins, your past life has not been in harmony with the law of God."

Abiah bowed his head with a troubled look.

"This," said the mentor, sternly, "will have to be amended, so that the Church of God may suffer no harm from your example."

"Of course," said Abiah, shooting a stream of smoke out into the moonlight.

"What are you going to do about it?"

The new convert smoked on in silence. A whippoorwill, sitting lengthwise on the ridge-pole of the house, sent out into the night its melancholy song. The fire-flies danced up and down among the orchard-grass under the oaks, and the katydid shrieked its clamorous challenge into the night. Still Abiah was silent. The tragedy in which every man plays a leading part first or last had culminated, and the hero had forgotten his lines.

"What are you going to do, my brother?"

The soft persuasive tones of the man of God fell upon his ear and went by him into the silent night. Elena, crouching behind the vine-clad lattice, heard them, and waited breathless for the response. Still Abiah smoked on in silence. At length he took the long reed stem from his mouth, knocked the ashes from the bowl, carefully putting his foot on the yet glowing embers, and said,—

"Passon, I hain't edzactly concluded what I will do. I 'lows to do the fa'r thing; but the trouble is to know jes' what's the right thing to be done. What do you say, passon?"

"You must put away this woman with whom you have so long lived in open shame," said the minister, sternly. He thought it a case in which mild words and mild measures would be of no avail.

"She's stuck by me sick an' well," mused Abiah.

"Of course you will recompense her for her services."

"Jest 'bout half I've got's been owin' to her management."

"It's very creditable to you to acknowledge her merit."

"Ef it hadn't been for her, I'd 'a' died in my sins long ago."

He lighted his pipe and began to smoke again. The minister watched his face narrowly as the match flamed up from the glowing bowl.

"Were you afraid to die then, Brother Wilkins?"

"Nary bit, passon: jest felt as I do now, that I ought to do the fa'r thing; that was all."

"Did you do it?"

"Wal, sorter: I made my will."

"I suppose you made a good provision for the girl?" asked the minister, curiously.

"I left her all ther' was," answered the convert.

"What?"

"All ther' was, passon. You see, this is the way I felt about it.

She's done ez much ez I ; her chil'run is my chil'run. Ef there's been any wrong, I'm the one that's ter blame fer it; and what ther' is wouldn't be none too much fer her to git along with alone."

" It's fortunate you did not die at that time," said the minister, in a tone of relief.

"I don' know 'bout that," pursued the other ; "hit's a mighty sight easier ter do jestice when one thinks he's a-dyin' than when he's got ter keep on livin'. Yer see, what was jestice then ain't nothin' more'n jestice now."

" But no one would expect you to do as much as that for her."

" P'r'aps not ; but what's religion good fer if it don't make a man jest ?"

" But your idea is morbid and extravagant. The woman no doubt deserves to be treated liberally ; but you are not called upon to impoverish yourself. If she were a white woman, now, you might marry her."

"There ain't many women whiter'n she is, in this world ner the next, passon," said Abiah, solemnly.

" That may be,—in a way," assented the minister. " But you cannot marry her, of course. The law is dead against that."

" I s'pose 'tis," said the other, moodily.

" You ought to be glad of it, too, if you contemplated such a degrading act."

" P'r'aps I hed."

" Of course you should. Now let me urge you, my brother, to act in this matter with firmness and without delay. ' Cast aside the sin that doth so easily beset you.' Make a good provision for this girl, and pack her off. Then on next communion-day you can join the church and begin a new life."

" Wal, passon, I'll 'tend to hit right away, I'll promise that ; and whatever I do, you may be sure hit'll be right,—or ez nigh right ez I kin git."

" Well, don't let your impulses carry you so far that you might regret it : remember that justice, like charity, begins at home."

" So it do : I ain't likely ter fergit that," said Abiah. " Passon," he continued, earnestly, " what would you say ef I should jes' make over ter Lena an' her chil'run pretty much all I've got round me here an' start over in life fer myself,—a new life, ez you sed ?"

" I should say you were a fool," said the minister, bluntly.

" An' the others,—the church,—I s'pose they'd think so too ?"

" Of course ; every sensible person would."

" So I s'pose,—so I s'pose," mused Abiah. " But, passon, what d'yer think Jesus Christ would say about it ef he was here an a-jedgin' on't right now? D'ye think he would say it was too much, er—too little ?"

There was a moment's silence, and then the minister responded, solemnly,—

" My brother, there are some things every man must decide for himself; and this is one. May God help you to decide aright !"

" Amen !" responded Abiah. Then he struck a light and showed the minister to his room.

The next day Abiah drove to the city, taking Elena with him. They were absent nearly a week. It was thought he would return alone; but he did not. The Sabbath following, Abiah rode as usual to the High Rock meeting. It was the day he was to be received into the church. He arrived before the service commenced. The grove was fresh and green after a shower of the night previous. He felt that he ought to be happy, though his face was full of doubt. As he walked down the aisle, with his hat hung upon his crippled hand, he saw the table prepared for the communion, and wondered if he would be allowed to taste the elements the snowy cloth concealed. He knew that every one was regarding him with curiosity. Some of the light-minded winked and made remarks as he appeared, which the better-behaved pretended not to hear.

The minister saw him as he entered, and met him half-way down the aisle. Taking him by the arm, he led him out past the pulpit into the grove back of the arbor. After walking a little way, they sat down upon a log. The minister took out his knife, cut off a sucker, and began to trim it. Abiah still held his hat upon his crippled hand.

"Well, Brother Wilkins, how is it? What have you done with the woman?"

Abiah drew forth from the breast-pocket of his coat a paper, which he partly opened, with the curious skill the one-handed acquire, by pressing it against his knee, and extended towards the minister. The latter glanced at it, flushed, turned pale, and trembled with excitement.

"You don't mean to say——" he began, angrily.

"Yes, passon," said Abiah, humbly. "Thar didn't seem to be no other way ter do the right thing."

"Do you know what people will say?"

"I s'pose they'll think me mighty low-down. I don't blame 'em. Hit were pretty hard ter do, passon; but one can't expect ter be a Christian fer nothin'."

"But how did you come to do it? You promised me——"

"I did, passon, I did," interrupted Abiah, "an' I 'lowed ter do then pretty much ez you advised; but I thought I oughtn't ter be onjust ter ennybody. So when the lawyer tole me we could be married in the Deestrick of Columby, all straight an' reguler, I thought I'd give her a chance ter say she were an honest women, an give the chil'run a right ter wear their fayther's name. Then I 'lowed ter give her half uv all I hed, let her go off somewheres with the chil'run, an' I'd stay here an' never see nothin' more of 'em. That were my design, passon, an' I thought that were the best I could do; but when we stood up afore the minister an' I promised afore God ter 'take this woman' an' 'cleave only ter her,' I seed 'twouldn't do: I couldn't do jestice by halves. So here I be. Ef you think——"

"I think——" The minister interrupted himself as he looked into the patient face before him. "God judge you, my brother; I dare not. You have done a terrible thing. If it were known to the congregation, I fear you might suffer violence. I think you had better go home and —*go away.* God bless you!"

He wrung the convert's hand and walked back to the arbor. The

words of the opening hymn were echoing through the grove when
Abiah mounted his horse and rode homeward.

There was great excitement in the community when these things
became known. Fortunately, the court was in session at the county
seat, and, a true bill having been found, Biah and Elena were arrested.
This probably saved them from violence. As in very many States at
the North as well as at the South, the marriage of a white person
with one of one-eighth or more of colored blood was contrary to the
law, and this marriage, though solemnized without the State, being
between parties domiciled therein and visiting a foreign jurisdiction
simply for the purpose of marriage, was held upon the trial to be in
fraud of the statute, and therefore void. This view was also sustained
by the Supreme Court.

This was the state of affairs when appeal was made to Mr. Swallow.
" What Biah wants ter know," said the faithful brother who had
stuck to him " through evil as well as good report," " is whether the
law uv the United States is good over the whole kentry, er only three
miles one way and five miles 'tother from the Capitol. Er to put it in
a leetle diff'rent shape, he wants ter know ef Elena is his wife sure
an' fast in Washin'ton, why she ain't his wife in Ferginny? I ain't
stan'in' up fer Biah. Ef he was clar, I wouldn' own him ez a brother ;
he's gone an' disgraced hisself an' the whole fambly ; but this I will
say : he didn't 'low ter do enny harm, but only ter do in a lawful way
what he thought the Lord commanded. Now, what *I* want ter know
is, how is one gwine ter tell when he's right an' when he's wrong, ef he
can't foller law ner Scripter ?"

" These are very interesting questions, Mr. Wilkins," said the
Junior, suavely, " but I don't suppose Biah would care to stay in jail
long enough to have them decided. It happens that there is one thing
in his favor. The authority of a State court to disregard a marriage
duly solemnized under the laws of the United States, because inconsistent with the State law, has never been decided, and it is quite possible
that the authorities of the State would hardly care to press for an adju-
dication at this time. A lawyer's business is to serve his client rather
than settle legal questions. So we will apply for our writ of error, and
then, if the authorities are willing to let Biah go where nobody will
inquire about the pedigree of his wife, and he is willing to go, I don't
see but we have found the best way out of the trouble. If we have to
carry it up, of course we will ; but it's a mighty good rule never to
fight for what you can get without a fight."

We prepared the papers, and Mr. Swallow himself made the application for the writ. But the case has never come to trial. In the
court below, the indictment is marked " Nol. Pros.," and in the ap-
pellate court the entry stands, " Dismissed at Plaintiff's cost." So
the legal puzzle it presents remains unsolved. The great West has
swallowed up Abiah Wilkins and his shame ; " the peace of God and
the State" are no more threatened by his sin or his repentance ; and
those lawfully wedded in one State may still be adjudged malefactors in
another.

Albion W. Tourgee.

SOME FAMOUS HOAXES.

MANY etymologies for the word "hoax" have been suggested,—the most plausible making it a corruption from the first word of *hocus-pocus,* which in its turn is a corruption from the *hoc est corpus* of the mass. A hoax may be defined as a successful effort to deceive without any motive but fun. With a further limitation of its meaning as a deception of the many, a useful line of demarcation might be drawn between the hoax and the practical joke which is aimed only at individuals. This definition would exclude all the famous literary forgeries, from Chatterton to Lew Vanderpoole, where the object was pelf rather than amusement, such deliberate swindles as the South Sea Bubble, and even such famous instances as De Foe's story of the apparition of Mrs. Veal, which was written to sell "Drelincourt on Death."

When Sheridan completed the Greek sentence levelled against him —which the country members cheered, not because they understood it, but because it was quoted on their side—by saying that the passage should have been continued to the end, and glibly adding a screed of Irish, it is doubtful whether his jest rose to the dignity of a hoax. But the constant victimization of antiquaries by fabricated articles purporting to be interesting as relics of the past is clearly a hoax, except when it is done for profit. Every one will remember, in Scott's "Antiquary," the metal vessel inscribed with the letters A—D—L—L, which Monkbarns interpreted to mean *Agricola dicavit libens lubens,* but which Edie Ochiltree pronounced to be *Aikin Drum's lang ladle.* And every one will also remember the uneven and broken stone on which the Pickwick club laboriously deciphered this inscription :

+
BILST
UM
PSHI
S.M.
ARK

which turned out to be nothing more nor less than "Bil Stumps, his Mark." Here again the hoax is not perfect, because there is no evidence that either Aikin Drum or Bill Stokes had any deliberate intention to deceive. But the following inscription is a genuine hoax. It was sent to the secretary of an enthusiastic band of archæologists exploring the town of Banbury, as having been copied from the cornerstone of an old structure lately pulled down :

"SEOGEII SREVE EREII WCISUME VAIIL
LAII SEIIS SE OTREII NOS LLEIIDNAS
REONI FREII NOS GNIRES ROIIYER
GANOED IRYD ALE NIFAE ESOTS SOROY
RUB NAIIOT ES ROIIK CO CAED IR."

After the learned heads had been puzzled for a while, one of their number hit upon the expedient of reading the inscription backward, when it was found to be an ingenious transposition of the well-known nursery rhyme "Ride a cock-horse," etc.

The ever-amusing "Raikes's Diary" tells of a stone found near Nérac in 1838 which bore this legend: *Similiter causd-que ego ambo te fumant cum de suis.* After puzzling all the learned brains of the locality, it was about to be sent to Paris, when an old inhabitant remembered that the stone came from a building occupied by Russian troops during the invasion of 1814. The explanation that it was only a bit of military fun at once suggested itself, and finally it was discovered that by reading off the inscription with the proper French pronunciation of the syllables it became *Six militaires cosaques égaux en beauté fumant comme deux Suisses,* which translated means, "Six Cossack soldiers equal in beauty, smoking like two Swiss."

The archæologist Gough, at a curiosity-shop, came across a slab of stone with a curious inscription, bought it, and had it described before the Society of Antiquaries, and engraved for the *Gentlemen's Magazine.* The legend read, "Here Hardcnut drank a wine-horn dry, stared about him, and died." The evidence seemed to be in its favor. It had been found, so the shopkeeper asserted, in Kennington Lane, where the palace of Hardcnut is supposed to have been situated. At last it transpired that George Steevens, to satisfy an old grudge against Gough, had procured a fragment of an old chimney-slab, scratched the inscription in rude characters, and got the curiosity-dealer so to manage that Gough should see and buy the stone.

Traps of this sort are continually being laid for unsuspecting antiquarians by the waggishly-inclined, and many a supposed old coin has been found on investigation to be nothing more than a sou or a centime melted in the fire, battered with a hammer, punched with a cold-chisel in imitation of antique lettering, and then hidden in some place where it was sure to be discovered. "There is a cairn," says the Rev. J. G. Wood, "broken and battered, on the summit of the hills near the Vale of White Horse, and visible from the railway. A very well known author refers in a very well known book to that cairn as a Danish monument, whereas I built it myself; and, by the same token, there is in the middle of it a flat-iron without any handle. Jokes of this sort," he adds, "are very prevalent among scientific men. There is, for example, one of our best entomologists who prides himself on his skill in manufacturing insects. If they have wings, he discharges the color by chemical means, and paints them afresh. He substitutes various parts of various beings for those of the creature which he manufactures, cutting out from an old champagne-cork anything that may be found wanting. He once tried to palm off on me a most ingenious combination. The head was made of cork, the wings were real wings, only turned the wrong side upwards, and the body had been taken to pieces, painted, and varnished. Unfortunately for himself, this very clever forger of entomological rarities had visited one of those houses where the celebrated Cardinal Spider lives, and had added the legs of a spider from Hampton Court to the body, wings, and antennæ of insects from all parts of the world. The spider's legs betrayed him, but the author of the entomological forgery was not in the least disconcerted at the discovery of the fraud. There are no school-boys who enjoy a joke half as much as your celebrated scientific and literary men. Their reputation is too safe for cavil, and when they get together they are as playful as so many kittens. The museum of the late Charles Waterton was full of zoölogical jokes."

Many such hoaxes have been perpetrated for the purpose of silencing criticasters and exposing their pretensions. Thus, Michael Angelo, wearied of hearing modern sculpture contrasted with ancient to the disparagement of the former, hit upon the plan of burying a Cupid, having first knocked off an arm or so, and when it was dug up he had the satisfaction of hearing his former detractors praise it as a genuine antique. Muretus played a similar trick upon the critic Joseph Scaliger, a great admirer of the ancients, by palming off upon him some Latin verses as being copied from an old manuscript. Scaliger was delighted, ascribed them to an old comic poet, Trabeus, and quoted them in his commentary on Varro " De Re Rustica," as one of the most precious fragments of antiquity. Then Muretus wickedly informed the world of his deception, and pointed out the small dependence to be placed on the sagacity of one so prejudiced in favor of the ancients. A famous hoax of this sort was practised by Johann Meinhold upon the Tübingen school of critics. These gentlemen believed their judgment unerring in deciding upon the authenticity of any writing, and throughout the Gospels they professed to discriminate the precise degree of credibility of each chapter, each narrative, each word, with a certainty that disdained all doubt and a firmness no argument could move. In 1843 Dr. Meinhold published " The Amber Witch," professedly from a mutilated manuscript which had been found by an old sexton in a closet of the church at Usedom in Pomerania. It purported to be a contemporaneous chronicle, by the pastor of Coserow, of certain events that took place in his parish in the early part of the seventeenth century, and was accepted as such by the profoundest of the Tübingen *savants.* We know that Robert Stephen Hawkins deceived even Macaulay (an excellent judge of ballad poetry) by his " Song of the Western Men," with its refrain of

And must Trelawny die, and must Trelawny die?
Then forty thousand Cornishmen will know the reason why.

We know that Surtees deceived even Sir Walter Scott (a still better judge) with his ballads of " The Slaying of Antony Featherstonhaugh" and " Bartram's Dirge," which purported to be collected from oral tradition and were furnished with learned notes. Nay, Andrew Lang hints an uncomfortable suspicion that Sir Walter Scott, who was fond of forging extracts from " old plays" as citations for his chapter-headings, was himself the author of the ballad of " Kinmont Willie," which to this day is accepted as one of the finest of the old English ballads. The last ballad hoax of much note was a set of sham Macedonian epics and popular songs about Alexander the Great and other heroes, which a schoolmaster in Rhodope imposed on M. Verkovitch, and which for a brief period deceived the learned.

Prosper Mérimée was the most skilful of French literary forgers, using his talents for amusement rather than for deliberate deception. When a mere youth, he played a practical joke on Cuvier, by manufacturing for him an original letter of Robespierre, which delighted that hunter of autographs as well as truth. The deception was not found out until a rival collector held the autograph to the light and saw that the water-mark on the paper bore a date later than Robespierre's death. Mérimée's first published book was a collection of short dramas, pretended translations from a gifted Spanish lady, Clara Guzla, for whom he invented a biography. "Clara Guzla" was taken for a reality ; her genius was gravely discussed by critics, and a Spaniard, ashamed to confess ignorance of so gifted a countrywoman, declared that, although the French translation was good, it was inferior to the original. Afterwards Mérimée manufactured an Hungarian bard, songs and all, who made dupes of German as well as French critics, and set them to wondering why so brilliant a writer had never been heard of outside of Hungary.

A very different sort of hoax was recently practised upon English publishers and magazine-editors. A disappointed literary aspirant, weary of having his articles declined with thanks, and doubtful of his critics' infallibility, copied out "Samson Agonistes," which he rechristened "Like a Giant Refreshed," and the manuscript, as an original work of his own, went the rounds of publishers and editors. It was declined on various pleas, and the letters he received afforded him so much amusement that he published them in the St. James's Gazette. None of the critics discovered that the work was Milton's. One, who had evidently not even looked at it, deemed it a sensational novel ; another recognized a certain amount of merit, but thought it was disfigured by "Scotticisms ;" a third was sufficiently pleased to offer to publish it, provided the author contributed forty pounds towards expenses.

A hoax which did not deceive the learned, but sorely puzzled them, was that known as the Dutch Mail hoax. Some fifty years ago, an article appeared in the Leicester Herald, an English provincial paper, under the title of "The Dutch Mail," with the announcement that it had arrived too late for translation, and so had been set up and printed in the original. Much attention was attracted to the article, and many Dutch scholars rushed into print to say that it was not in any dialect with which they were acquainted. Finally it was discovered to be a hoax. Sir Richard Phillips, the editor of the paper, recently told this story of how the jest was conceived and carried out : "One evening, before one of our publications, my men and a boy overturned two or three columns of the paper in type. We had to get ready someway for the coaches, which, at four in the morning, required four or five hundred papers. After every exertion, we were short nearly a column, but there stood a tempting column of 'pi' on the galleys. It suddenly struck me that this might be thought Dutch. I made up the column, overcame the scruples of the foreman, and so away the country edition went with its philological puzzle to worry the honest agricultural readers' heads. There was plenty of time to set up a column of plain English for the local edition." Sir Richard met one man in Nottingham who for thirty years preserved a copy of the Leicester Herald, hoping that some day the letter would be explained.

Madame de Genlis tells a story in point. The Duc de Liancourt was an intimate friend of Abbé Delille. Both were at Spa, when one morning the Abbé was deeply chagrined by seeing some couplets on the birthday of the Duchess of Orleans, regular enough in manner, but foolish in matter, published with his name in a daily newspaper. The verses were in fact the duke's composition. We all remember the letter on American Philistinism which was credited to Matthew Arnold, the letter about public bores which was credited to Carlyle (and which Ruskin, by the way, endorsed as " not the least significant of the utterances of the Master"), and many similar forgeries, more or less clever imitations of style, which have gone the rounds of the press, provoked surprise, anger, applause, condemnation, and finally called forth vigorous denials from the supposed authors. A poem called "A Vision of Immortality," ascribed to William Cullen Bryant and copied as such into many papers, has been pasted into a host of scrap-books. The author had made a wager that he could write a poem which would deceive the general public into the impression that it was Bryant's. Poe has ever been a favorite subject for this sort of jesting, as the mannerisms of his style are easily caught; and every now and then a fresh imitation, claiming to be a genuine treasure trove, starts on its journey through the papers.

Perhaps this is only a fair *quid pro quo.* No man ever had a greater fondness for gulling the public. That gruesome tale, " The Facts in the Case of M. Valdemar," was worked up with an appalling verisimilitude of detail which imposed upon many people. Mesmerism at that time had just begun to be talked of. The Abbé Migne, in his " Dictionary of Popular Superstitions," seemed more than half inclined to believe in its truth. " We will not leave the subject of animal magnetism," he says, " without acquainting the reader with an extraordinary, we might say an incredible, incident which is just now creating a great sensation in the learned world," and then he translates Poe's story entire.

The " Balloon hoax" was Poe's most successful imposition upon the public. One day in April, 1844, the New York *Sun* astonished its readers with an article headed thus, in magnificent capitals:

"ASTOUNDING NEWS BY EXPRESS *VIA* NORFOLK!
THE ATLANTIC CROSSED IN THREE DAYS!!
Signal Triumph of Mr. Monck Mason's Flying Machine!!!

" Arrival at Sullivan's Island, near Charleston, S.C., of Mr. Mason, Mr. Robert Holland, Mr. Henson, Mr. Harrison Ainsworth, and four others, in the Steering Balloon ' Victoria,' after a passage of seventy-five hours from land to land! Full particulars of the voyage!"

Every one was on the *qui vive.* " The rush for ' the sole paper which had the news,' " says Poe, " was something beyond even the prodigious; and, in fact, if (as some assert) the Victoria *did* not absolutely accomplish the voyage recorded, it will be difficult to assign a reason why she *should* not have accomplished it." It is not a little curious that the New York *Sun* was the very paper in which, nine years before, in September, 1835, the celebrated " Moon Hoax" had appeared, overshadowing and interrupting forever the story of " Hans Pfaall's Journey to the Moon," which, by an extraordinary coincidence, Poe had begun three weeks previous in the *Southern Literary Messenger.*

Poe had originally intended his own story as a hoax, but his friends, who had less faith in the gullibility of the public than himself, persuaded him to give up the idea of deliberate deception. " I fell back upon a style half plausible, half bantering, and resolved to give what interest I could to an actual passage from the earth to the moon, describing the lunar scenery as if surveyed and personally examined by the narrator." The success of the " Moon Hoax" showed that Poe was right and his friends wrong. The former took up the very idea which Poe claims to have abandoned,—that of accounting for the narrator's acquaintance with the satellite by the supposition of an extraordinary telescope. The "Moon Hoax"—so called, of course, after its bogus nature had been discovered—opened with an account of how Sir John Herschel, with Sir David Brewster's assistance, had invented an apparatus (minutely described) by which the magnifying power of an immense telescope could be sufficiently increased to detect minute objects in the moon. Sir John was sent out to the Cape of Good Hope at the expense of the English, French, and Austrian governments. " Whether the British government were sceptical concerning the promised splendor of the discoveries, or wished them to be scrupulously veiled until they had accumulated a full-orbed glory for the nation and reign in which they originated, is a question which we can only conjecturally solve. But certain it is that the astronomer's royal patrons enjoined a masonic taciturnity upon him and his friends until he should have officially communicated the results of his great experiment." This was a clever explanation of the circumstance that nothing had before been heard regarding the gigantic instrument taken out by Herschel. That he was actually at that time at the Cape of Good Hope was generally known.

On the night of January 10, 1835, the telescope was ready to be employed upon the moon. The first things observed were basaltic rocks covered with poppies ; then fields, trees, and rivers ; then amethyst mountains and verdant valleys ; then animals like bisons, a unicorn-goat, pelicans, sheep, etc. All these things were described with a gorgeous wealth of detail. At last winged creatures were seen to light upon a plain, something between a human being and an orang-outang in appearance, with wings like those of a bat. These beings were at once christened the Vespertilio-homo, or Bat-man. They were doubtless innocent and happy creatures, but some of their ways were unpublishably singular and were reserved for a scientific book by Herschel. Meanwhile, several ministers, on a promise of temporary secrecy, were allowed a peep at these things which were unfit for the laity.

Such was the substance of a narrative which astounded all America. Many were deceived, many were only perplexed. Poe himself wrote an examination of its claims to credit, showing distinctly its fictitious character, but was astonished at finding that he could obtain few listeners, " so really eager were all to be deceived, so magical were the charms of a style that served as the vehicle of an exceedingly clumsy invention. . . . Not one person in ten discredited it, and (strangest point of all!) the doubters were chiefly those who doubted without being able to say why,—the ignorant, those uninformed in astronomy,—people who *would not* believe because the thing was so novel, so entirely 'out of the usual way.' A grave professor of mathematics in a Virginia college told me seriously that he had no doubt of the truth of the whole affair." Many prominent newspapers fell squarely into the trap. The *Mercantile Advertiser* thought the document bore "intrinsic evidence of being authentic." The New York *Times* thought it displayed "the most extensive and accurate knowledge of astronomy," was "probable and plausible," and "had an air of intense verisimilitude." The Albany *Daily Advertiser* had read the article with "unspeakable emotions of pleasure and astonishment;" while the *New Yorker* considered the discoveries "of astounding interest, creating a new era in astronomy and science generally." The hoax was reprinted in pamphlet-form, and, though by this time its bogus nature had been discovered, an edition of sixty thousand copies was readily disposed of. Lately a single copy of that edition sold for three dollars and seventy-five cents.

One effect of the hoax was to deprive us of the conclusion of "Hans Pfaall." "Having read the Moon Story to an end," says Poe, "and found it anticipative of all the main points of my 'Hans Pfaall,' I suffered the latter to remain unfinished. The chief design in carrying my hero to the moon was to afford him an opportunity of describing the lunar scenery ; but I found that he could add very little to the minute and authentic account of Sir John Herschel. I did not even think it advisable to bring my voyager back to his parent earth. He remains where I left him, and is still, I believe, the man in the moon." It is worth noting that Poe, who was ever morbidly keen on the subject of plagiarism, distinctly says, "I am bound to do Mr. Locke the justice to say that he denies having seen my article prior to the publication of his own : I am bound to add, also, that I believe him."

Mr. Richard Alton Locke, a clever New York journalist, was the author of the hoax. Not for many years, however, was the secret divulged. Some of the New York journals, indeed, published the "Moon Story" side by side with "Hans Pfaall," thinking that the author of one had been detected in the author of the other. Subsequently suspicion settled down upon Nicollet, a French astronomer who had come to America after the revolution of 1830, and whose object, it was said, was to raise money and to deceive his enemy Arago. It was added that he succeeded in doing both. But Mr. Proctor discredits the Arago story, and states that no astronomer could have either written or been deceived by the hoax. He adds that as gauges of general knowledge scientific hoaxes have their use, just as paradoxical works have. "No one, certainly no student of science, can thoroughly understand how little some people know about science, until he has observed how much will be believed if only published with the apparent authority of a few known names and announced with a sufficient parade of technical verbiage ; nor is it as easy as might be thought, even for those who are acquainted with the facts, to disprove either a hoax or a paradox." He therefore notes without any wonder that in January, 1874, he was gravely asked whether an account in the New York *World*, purporting to describe how the moon's frame was gradually cracking, threatening eventually to fall into several separate fragments, was in reality based on fact. "In the far West, at Lincoln, Nebraska, a lawyer asked me in February, 1876, why I had not described the great discoveries recently made by means of a powerful reflector erected near Paris. According to the Chicago *Times*, this powerful instrument had shown buildings in the moon, and bands of workmen could be seen with it who manifestly were undergoing some kind of penal servitude, for they were chained together." It is singular how often these pseudo-scientific hoaxes refer to the moon.

Of bibliographical hoaxes the most complete and artistic was the Fortsas Catalogue. In 1840, bibliographers were electrified by the appearance of a pamphlet purporting to be a catalogue of the library of the late Count J. N. A. de Fortsas, of Binche, Belgium. It contained only fourteen pages, to be sure, and described only fifty-two books; but each of these was unique: no book mentioned by any bibliographer was to be found in the collection. The count, it was represented, " pitilessly expelled from his shelves books for which he had paid their weight in gold—volumes which would have been the pride of the most fastidious amateurs—as soon as he learned that a work up to that time unknown had been noticed in any catalogue." The publication of the " Nouvelles Recherches" of Brunet had caused the destruction of one-third of the count's library and broken the collector's spirit. From that time he made no further acquisitions ; but the bulletin of Techener " from time to time still further thinned the already decimated ranks of his sacred battalion." Weary of books and of life, he had died, September 1, 1839, and his library was now offered for sale. The bibliographical world was fairly agog. The titles in the catalogue were of the most tantalizing description. Orders poured in from all parts of Europe. The most expert bibliographers were deceived. Charles Nodier, indeed, suspected a hoax, but Techener laughed at his doubts, and ordered No. 36,—" Evangile du citoyen Jésus, purgé des idées aristocrates et royalistes, et ramené aux vrais principes de la raison, par un bon sans-culotte." Van de Weyer and Crozat ordered the same book. The Princesse de Ligne, for the honor of her family, ordered No. 48 at any price,—" a catalogue more than curious of the bonnes fortunes of the Prince de Ligne," with a title that is hardly quotable. The director of the Royal Library of Brussels obtained an appropriation to purchase all the Fortsas treasures except seven, which were considered a little too *free* for a public library. A number of Parisian bibliophiles met in the stage for Brussels, and there discovered that they were all possessed with the same intention of stealing away unnoticed, each hoping by this means to have the game all to himself. In the course of the affair there were the usual illustrations of human mendacity and self-deception. Men remembered seeing books that had never existed. The foreman in Casteman's printing-office at Tournay had distinct recollection of a bogus volume credited to his press, and recalled its mythical author " perfectly."

On the 9th of August, 1810, the day before the sale, an announcement appeared in the Brussels papers that the library of the Count de Fortsas would not be sold,—that the people of Binche, in honor of its collector, had determined to buy it entire. Eventually it transpired that catalogue, library, and Count de Fortsas himself were all the invention of one René Chalons, a humorist living in Belgium. His ingenious catalogue begot quite a literature of its own, which was collected and published in a volume entitled " Documents et Particularités historiques sur le Catalogue du Comte de Fortsas," Mons, 1850.

Theodore Hook was a famous practical joker, and once, at least, he perpetrated a jest that disturbed all London and amused all England. This was the famous Berners Street hoax. Berners Street in 1810 was a quiet street, inhabited by well-to-do families living in a genteel way. One morning, soon after breakfast, a wagon-load of coals drew up before the door of a widow lady living in the street. A van-load of furniture followed, then a hearse with a coffin, and a train of mourning-coaches. Two fashionable physicians, a dentist, and an accoucheur drove up as near as they could to the door, wondering why so many lumbering vehicles blocked the way. Six men brought a great chamber-organ ; a brewer sent several barrels of ale ; a grocer sent a cart-load of potatoes. Coach-makers, clock-makers, carpet-manufacturers, confectioners, wig-makers, mantua-makers, opticians, and curiosity-dealers followed with samples of their wares. From all quarters trooped in coachmen, footmen, cooks, housemaids, and nursery-maids, in quest of situations. To crown all, dignitaries came in their carriages,—the Commander-in-Chief, the Archbishop of Canterbury, the Lord Chief Justice, a Cabinet minister, a governor of the Bank of England, and the Lord Mayor. The latter—one among many who speedily recognized that all had been the victims of some gigantic hoax—drove to Marlborough Street police-office, and stated that he had received a letter from a lady in Berners Street, to the effect that she had been summoned to attend at the Mansion House, that she was at death's door, that she wished to make a deposition upon oath, and that she would deem it a great favor if his lordship would call upon her. The other dignitaries had been appealed to in a similar way. Police-officers were despatched to maintain order in Berners Street. They found it choked up with vehicles, jammed and interlocked one with another. The drivers were infuriated. The disappointed tradesmen were clamoring for vengeance. Some of the vans and goods were overturned and broken ; a few barrels of ale had fallen a prey to the large crowd that was maliciously enjoying the fun. All day and far into the night this state of things continued. Meanwhile, the old lady and the inmates of adjoining houses were in abject terror. Every one soon saw that a hoax had been perpetrated, but Hook's connection with it was not discovered till long afterwards. He had noticed the quietness of the neighborhood, and had laid a wager with a brother-wag that he would make Berners Street the talk of all London. A door-plate had furnished him with Mrs. ——'s name, and he had spent three days in writing the letters which brought the crowd to her door. At the appointed time he had posted himself with two or three companions in a lodging just opposite, which he had rented for the purpose of enjoying the scene. He deemed it expedient, however, to go off quickly into the country and there remain *incog.* for a time. Had he been publicly known as the author of the hoax he might have fared badly.

William Shepard.

THE TEMPERANCE REFORM MOVEMENT.

INEBRIÉTY is a vice of civilization. Only a few native instances of it are known among savage and barbarous tribes. This, however, is due to savage ignorance, not to aboriginal virtue, for the untutored soul of uncivilized man has everywhere received the rum-bottle of the whites as a gift from the gods, and graduated into intoxication with an abnormal rapidity that has done much to clear the land for the "progress of civilization."

In the annals of civilized man intoxication fills a prominent space. We are told of its existence in the very ancient records of China, while the Vedas of India, the Avestas of Persia, and the Biblical narrative yield evidence of its general existence at a very early date in the era of civilization. As soon, indeed, as it was found that fruit-juices would ferment and yield a liquid capable of producing intoxication, the long revel of mankind began, and it has been continued to the present time with a steadily increasing vehemence.

We may trace through the ages the gradual development of inebriety. Beginning with the pure fermented juice of the grape, intoxicants of greater potency in time came into use,—the fiery " rice wine" of India and China, the drugged wines of Palestine, Greece, and Rome, —until effects emulating those of distilled spirits were produced. Yet the drunkenness of the ancient world was due to fermented liquors only. It is not known when the art of distillation was first discovered, but it has been practised in Europe for some six centuries only, and the general use of ardent spirits as an intoxicating beverage has existed for not more than half that period.

On the continent of Europe, indeed, wine and beer still continue the favorite intoxicants, except in the most northerly regions, though spirituous liquors are now gaining ground in Germany and France with an alarming rapidity. Spirit-drinking gained its first strong development in the British Islands, and intoxication reached its climax in England in the early part of the eighteenth century. This was the era of the "gin-drinking mania," that frantic outbreak of intoxication which for a time threatened to sweep half of England into the drunkard's grave, and was checked only by the adoption of stringent license-regulations.

Intoxication in America has had the same history of gradual development. In the early days of the colonies the religious fervor of many of them, and the police regulations of others, strongly opposed intemperance, and throughout the seventeenth century sobriety was the general rule. During the eighteenth century appetite gradually broke down the wholesome regulations of the early colonists, and the dominion of the bottle grew apace, aided greatly by the wars of that century. New England, the home of Puritanism, became the centre of the importation and manufacture of rum, and distributed this death-dealing beverage far and wide throughout the world, as if to negative the wholesome effects of its older example.

Within the first quarter of the nineteenth century the drinking-habit grew in a frightful ratio, and by the year 1825 the United States as a nation of drunkards had reached a climax equivalent to that attained by England a century before, but never surpassed, if equalled, elsewhere in the world. In the succeeding year, 1826, began that active effort at temperance reform which has produced such striking effects in this country and has made its influence felt so far through foreign lands.

We have here given in brief the story of the growth of the habit of inebriety, from a remote period until its culmination in the early years of the present century. The story of prohibitive efforts may be given with equal brevity. In the far past many such efforts were made by rulers and priests, but of popular measures of temperance reform we have few instances. Several emperors of China made strenuous attempts to do away with drunkenness, one going so far as to order that all vines should be uprooted in the kingdom, a radical measure which seems to have been effective for a considerable period.

In India and Persia the priesthood made similar efforts, but apparently with no great effect until the rise of the Buddhistic sect of India, in whose declaration of principles was a vigorous total-abstinence plank. The later extension of Buddhism throughout eastern and northern Asia proved very effective as a temperance reform movement in that ancient land, and placed a barrier against the growth of the drinking-habit which yet retains much strength. A work of similar efficacy was performed by Mohammed when he prohibited wine-drinking in the Koran. In most of the remainder of Asia and in a considerable part of Africa Mohammedanism now prevails, and wherever it is the ruling faith intemperance has never become prevalent.

Nowhere else have such effective efforts to repress intoxication been made, though spasmodic prohibitive measures were adopted from time to time in the regions of Greece and Rome and in Middle-Age Europe. For ancient total-abstinence societies we must seek the land of the Hebrews, where several such societies arose from time to time, comprising the Nazarites and the Rechabites of the older era, and the Essenes and the Therapeutæ of the time of Christ. Of the temperance sentiment of the Hebrew priesthood the Bible contains many striking evidences.

Coming down now to modern times, we find that the repressive movement is active only in those lands in which distilled spirits are the favorite intoxicants. It has gained no foothold in the wine- and beer-drinking countries. In Sweden, where ardent spirits had produced a frightful state of inebriety, prohibitive laws were passed on two different occasions during the eighteenth century. They remained in force, however, for a few years only, and effective for much less time. During the present century more efficient prohibitive measures have been adopted in Sweden, local option repression exists in many districts, and the spirit of temperance reform there is far in advance of its condition in any other region of continental Europe.

With this preliminary glance at the general history of intemperance we proceed to the consideration of the temperance reform movement in America, a movement which has produced extraordinary effects and is rapidly inoculating all foreign civilized lands with its fervor. It is essentially different in character from any preceding measures of temperance reform, and in this lie its strength and promise for the future. It is, in fact, distinctively a movement of the people,—not of rulers, legislators, or the priesthood, as in the past. It comes not from above, but from below, and among its most active advocates are those who have themselves been drunkards, and whose influence on their fellow-inebriates is of necessity a hundredfold greater than would be that of any authoritative mandate from the powers that be.

We do not propose to review the history of the American temperance movement. It is probably very well known to most of our readers, and it is our purpose simply to point out its results, to contrast the condition of the United States in this respect in 1825 with that now existing. The difference is far more striking than is generally supposed, and the gain for temperance much greater than would be imagined from the amount of inebriety which still exists.

It was in 1826 that the temperance reform movement in this country first actively began, in the organization and labors of the American Temperance Society. Societies had been formed previously, and a strong temperance sentiment existed among the clergy, but the first effective work was done by the society above named, whose efforts were of such remarkable efficacy that by 1835 there were more than eight thousand societies in the country, and hundreds of thousands of drinkers had signed the pledge. The people of America seem suddenly to have become convicted of sin and in haste to repent. In 1840 began the ardent labors of the Washingtonians, a band of reformed drinkers, whose lectures had an extraordinary influence upon the inebriate community. Since then the temperance work has been manifold, and consists in the development of the various orders of temperance, the work of reform clubs, of the Catholic Total Abstinence Union, and the Woman's Christian Temperance Union, the establishment of homes and reformatories, temperance teaching in public and Sunday schools, active efforts at legal prohibition, and various similar measures, the total of which have had a vigorous influence upon the general temperance sentiment of the land.

What has been the effect of this temperance reform crusade on public opinion and on the drinking-habits of the community? That is what we have next to consider,—to present a general contrast of the status of liquor-drinking in the United States in 1825 with that of 1888.

There are two reasons why we take the year 1825 as a starting-point of comparison. It was the year immediately preceding the era of active temperance propagandism; and it represents the climax of intoxication in America. Statistics show that in 1790 the annual consumption of spirituous liquors in this country was two and one-half gallons per capita of the population. This was a greater consumption than had previously prevailed, but it was destined to be soon far outdone. By 1810 the number of distilleries had increased from two thousand five hundred to more than fourteen thousand, and the consumption of spirits was four and one-half gallons *per capita*. In the succeeding years intemperance advanced at a frightful rate, and it is computed that in 1823 seven and one-half gallons of this fiery beverage were consumed for every man, woman, and child in the country. It is doubtful if this was ever surpassed, even in the days of the gin-drinking mania of England.

Such a condition of affairs could not have existed had it not been strongly sustained by public opinion. In fact, in 1825 few voices were raised against the drinking-habit, and intemperance occupied a position of the highest respectability in the land. Distilled spirits were classed among the "good creatures of God," and looked upon as necessary to the health, happiness, and endurance of the community, while few, from the clergy downwards, objected to the free imbibing of whiskey, or looked upon such indulgence as a vice or a weakness. Many, indeed, deprecated drunkenness, but it was widely viewed as an excusable fault, the misfortune of having too weak a head, and the drunkard did not lose caste in society from this cause alone. Only when intemperance brought in its train some of its attendant evils—immorality, crime, profanity, loss of self-respect, etc.—was there a decline of the drunkard in social position ; but intoxication alone, free from these consequences, was winked and laughed at, rather than abhorred.

This sentiment was a direct resultant of the habits of society. Where every one drank, no one could be contemned for drinking. Let us glance at the situation. The church, the censor of morals, set an example of indulgence which the world was not slow to imitate. Drinking was common not only with the members of the church, but with its highest officials. The deacon and his wife felt that their daily eleven- and four-o'clock drams were necessities of existence, lubricants to the wheels of life, which would creak frightfully without them. Many deacons, indeed, made the manufacture and sale of whiskey a principal item of their business. Similar indulgence in intoxicants was common among the clergy. `A pastoral ordination, according to the testimony of the Rev. Lyman Beecher and others, was often little short of a debauch, and though open drunkenness was not common with the clergy it was by no means unknown. Only the most radical and energetic reformers ventured to preach against the prevalent custom.

Outside the church affairs were ten times worse. The rulers of the nation, Congressmen and legislators, governors and officials of every class, drank with impunity, with no loss of station or public respect. Rum played an essential part in the law-making of that epoch. In the highest circles of society the same habits prevailed. Every social meeting became a revel, in which wine and brandy flowed freely, and in which the guests not only as a rule became drunk, but were usually expected and often forced to become drunk. To lock the door and refuse to permit any one to leave the room except through the gate-way of intoxication, was an ordinary trick, considered by many of our ancestors as a commendable display of hospitality.

While such were the habits and sentiments of the higher grades of society, those of the lower were almost unmentionable. Rum was an essential requisite of every public occasion,—the marriage, the funeral, the merrymaking, the election, the races. Every special occasion of industry, from the harvesting to the church-raising, was sanctified by the rum-bottle. Whiskey was necessary to overcome the heat of summer and the cold of winter. It was considered absolutely requisite to the endurance of hard labor. It was the solace of infancy and age, the medicine for almost every disease, the inspirer in every joy, the comforter in every grief. The tavern tap-room was the common meeting-place of the male members of the community, and to visit it daily entailed no loss of self- or public respect. Moderate drinking was universal, immoderate drinking exceedingly common, and the extreme of drunkenness so ordinary a spectacle in the streets as hardly to excite a comment. When men of high respectability could fall dead-drunk in the streets (and instances might readily be cited), what was likely to be the condition or the feeling of the laboring-classes?

This indulgence in intoxicating beverages was not confined to men. It was not uncommon among women and children. The young were taught to drink from early childhood, and often graduated as drunkards before reaching manhood. Drunkenness was not usual with the women of the higher ranks of society,—it never has been, except in some instances of utter national demoralization,—but drinking was an ordinary custom, and the present strong sense among women of the moral obliquity of drunkenness had hardly begun to exist. With the women of the lower classes the habit of drinking to intoxication was much more common, and though the inebriety of women never equalled that of men, it was often much more base and vile in its manifestations.

In regard to Congressional intemperance we may quote from a speech made by Senator Vest, of Missouri, in 1882. He prefaced his remarks by the following testimony as to former drinking-habits in the West: "I remember when, in my boyhood days in Kentucky, the first rite of hospitality was to extend alcoholic drink to guests, both coming and parting, and it was found upon my father's table as regularly as a bowl of milk, or bread and butter, for home consumption. The victims of intemperance in those days were numbered by the hundreds and thousands; public men in the country fell from it in the halls of Congress. . . .

"To-day, I say here as a fact, that out of seventy-six Senators in the Congress of the United States, more than half, and I believe more than fifty of them, do not touch, taste, or handle alcoholic drink in any shape whatever. And I say more than that. A member of the House of Representatives or of the Senate who would ever dare to show himself in a state of intoxication in the public councils would never disgrace his seat again in either house. One of the most brilliant, one of the most fascinating, of all the public men I have met in my career in Washington in those years was guilty of excess publicly, and at the renominating convention he received not one single, solitary vote. . . . I remember when free whiskey and free votes were the mottoes of both parties."

In corroboration of the above statement may be given the following trenchant remarks, attributed by the New York *Independent* to General D. E. Sickles, in which are clearly indicated the habits of Congress in the period preceding the war :

" The war of the rebellion was really a whiskey war. Yes, whiskey caused the rebellion. I was in the Congress preceding the war. It was whiskey in the morning,—the morning cocktail,—a Congress of whiskey-drinkers. Then whiskey all day ; whiskey and gambling all night. Drinks before Congress opened its morning session, drinks before it adjourned. Scarcely a committee-room without its demijohn of whiskey ; and the clink of the glasses could be heard in the Capitol corridors. The fights, the angry speeches, were whiskey. The atmosphere was redolent with whiskey,—nervous excitement seeking relief in whiskey, and whiskey adding to nervous excitement. Yes, the rebellion was launched in whiskey. If the French Assembly were to drink some morning one-half the whiskey consumed in any one day by that Congress, France would declare war against Germany in twenty minutes."

As a contrast to the picture we have drawn, let us now look upon the present condition and sentiment of society as regards intemperance, —the outcome of the temperance reform agitation. The merest glance at the two periods shows a remarkable difference,—so great, indeed, that it is difficult to conceive that a half-century of work could have produced so radical a change in public opinion.

To consider present conditions in detail, as we have those of the past, the state of the Church first forces itself on our attention. Here the reform has been almost absolute. The drinking of ministers and high officials has ceased entirely, and they could commit few sins more repugnant to the moral sense of the community. In church-membership also the use of intoxicants has almost ceased to exist. Most of the churches, indeed, have become great total-abstinence societies, and in an estimate of the strength of these societies that of the church-membership should in great part be included. These remarks, of course, do not closely apply to the foreign element in American religious societies. The temperance reform is in great measure an American movement, and the most difficult element it has to deal with is that of the adult immigrant.

As regards the habits of the higher officials of the nation, it may be said that the pictures above drawn of Congressional intemperance no longer apply. The wines which of old times profusely graced the Presidential table have, in some of the recent administrations, been banished therefrom, partly in response to the temperance sentiment of the ladies of the White House, partly in deference to the general sentiment of the community. Where, in public dinners, they are retained, it is significant to perceive that it is done out of respect to the tastes and opinions of the representatives of foreign nations ; or, at least, this is offered to the people of America as an excuse for their use. Here again we find the lower stage of temperance sentiment in Europe dragging us down to its level.

Abundant testimony might be brought, were it necessary, in evidence of the improvement in the habits of legislators and officials as regards drinking, while it has become as difficult to buy a vote with whiskey to-day as in former times it was to obtain one without. Closed saloons on election-day indicate the popular sentiment in this respect, and the disgraceful drunken election-riots of the past have ceased to exist.

In judicial circles no judge to-day would remain long on the bench who deemed it necessary to prime himself with brandy as an aid to the administration of justice, while to furnish a jury with liquor would in itself be deemed a crime worthy of legal punishment. Yet in the past liquor formed part of the ordinary supplies to judge and jury alike, and whiskey had often as much as wisdom to do with the verdict of the jury and the judgment of the court.

In professional circles a similar growth in habits of sobriety is visible. The medical profession, for instance, was notable in the past for the number of drunkards which it embraced. As an evidence of the truth of this statement may be quoted a remark made by Professor Gibbons, of Philadelphia, in an address delivered before the graduates of one of the medical colleges of that city. He asserted that of all the graduates from the medical schools of the United States during the present century, fully one-half had sunk into the grave of the drunkard. Habits of inebriety are not yet weeded out of the profession, but a statement of this stringency applied to the medical profession of the present day would be absurdly inexact. There has been a striking reform among our physicians in this respect.

If we now consider the drinking-habits of society at large, and the existing state of public opinion upon this subject, as marked an improvement will be manifest. It may be said that in all but the lowest grades of society drunkenness has ceased to be respectable. This remark may seem to some of no special importance, yet in reality it is full of significance. Public opinion is a strong lever, and to the average man and woman nothing is of more consequence than the maintenance of a position in society. Yet few things would now lower a person in the social scale more suddenly and decidedly than indulgence in open drunkenness, and this vice, where it exists, takes diligent care to hide itself from public view. There is yet a degree of indulgence for some of the gilded crimes; there is growing to be no indulgence for the beastliness of intoxication. The one lowers a man morally, the other degrades him physically; and at present, with society in general, physical repulsion weighs more heavily than moral abhorrence. We have reached that stage of social development in which we shrink with pain and disgust from physical deterioration; we are but slowly approaching that higher stage in which moral delinquency in its more *respectable* forms will be equally repulsive.

Moderate drinking is still very common among persons of high social standing, but the moderate drinkers of to-day are the lineal descendants of the immoderate drinkers of the past, while their former analogues are represented by our advocates of total abstinence. So much, at least, the temperance movement has done: it has replaced drunkenness by moderate drinking. And in wide ranks of society even this degree of indulgence is severely disapproved, while drunkenness is hidden from the public eye as sedulously as a robber might hide a stolen treasure.

The force of public opinion, in fact, has become a powerful agent in mitigating the drinking-habits of society, and we owe to this more largely than to anything else the marked difference between the social customs of 1825 and 1888. This, however, is saying nothing in derogation of the special efforts at temperance reform in the intermediate period, since principally to them is due the public opinion which is now so effective in restraining men from intemperance.

This influence bears more strongly upon women than upon men, and among the women of American birth drunkenness has almost ceased to exist, and the habit of drinking has in great measure vanished. The women of America have advanced further than the men in this respect. They are restrained to a greater degree by a sense of the moral obliquity of intemperance, and their social and moral influence is one of the strongest forces in the temperance propagandism of the present day.

Among the members of the laboring-classes of American birth the improvement is little less marked. The women of these classes are as earnest in their sobriety as those of higher social rank; and American mechanics are, as a rule, as ashamed to be seen in the streets drunk as are their so-called social superiors. It is as important to the most of them as to any members of the community to retain their standard of respectability and the respect of their associates.

That drunkenness is, therefore, a far less frequent spectacle in our streets, and a much less prevalent vice, than of old, scarcely need be said. And of what is still visible much the greater part is the drunkenness of foreigners. It is due to the activity of immigration, and to the fact that the lower classes of Europe are much below those of America in self-respect, and have grown up under the influence of a very different public opinion in regard to inebriety.

Intemperance has by no means ceased to exist among Americans. There is far too much of it at the present day. But it is driven to hide its head, to lurk in secret places, to cringe in shame from the eyes of that searching public opinion which has become a power of such mighty mould. The open, flaunting drunkenness which we now perceive is in great part that of persons of foreign birth or of recent foreign descent, and is largely a resultant of the sharp class-demarcation of European countries, and the consequent lack of any high standard of respectability in the laboring-classes. In America the mechanic is not prevented by his profession from mingling on terms of equality with the capitalist, and not only feels himself the equal of the latter, but endeavors to dress as well, to live as well, and to behave as well. With the first two of these efforts his limited means must interfere. The last is often more than realized. So far as regards drinking, indeed, many of the industries of the country require sobriety in their employees. This is particularly the case with the railroad service, in which intemperance is so dangerous a fault that many companies will not employ a man who tastes liquor. And the great workingmen's union of America, the Knights of Labor, has spoken in decided accents in favor of temperance, its leading spirit, General Master Workman Powderley, being a total abstainer of the most radical stamp.

It would appear, then, from the above considerations, that the habit of inebriety in the United States now finds its chief strength among the new citizens who are flocking here in such vast droves from Europe. It is in this class of our population that intemperance presents its most obnoxious features and the liquor interest finds its chief strength. But for this fact of incessant immigration the temperance cause would be far more advanced than we find it in the United States of to-day; and the fact that the liquor-sellers of our country are in great part men of foreign birth forms another strong evidence of the sentiment with which Americans in general regard this business. They look upon it as disreputable, and leave it, with its gains, to those who are below their level of moral elevation and self-respect.

The fact above cited, that our drinking population is largely of foreign birth, has brought about certain striking changes in the character of the intoxicating beverages used. The consumption of distilled spirits has declined till it is now but one and a quarter gallons annually *per capita* of population, or but one-sixth its rate in 1825. The consumption of wine has varied but slightly; but that of beer has increased enormously. In 1840 the people of the United States drank but 1.36 gallons of beer *per capita.* In 1886 they drank 11.18 gallons, or nearly nine times as much. This is still but one-third the rate of consumption in England; yet the rapid increase is not a satisfactory element of the problem, particularly in view of the fact that the drinking-area has been much reduced by the enactment of prohibitive laws in several States and many counties, so that it argues a considerably greater *per capita* consumption in the localities in which the saloon is still freely open. This increase in the quantity of malt liquors imbibed is undoubtedly due to the rapid augmentation of our population by persons of German birth.

Much certainly remains to be done by the advocates of temperance reform ere they can succeed in overcoming the vice of intemperance in America. If we could have a law to prohibit the importation of foreign drunkards, like that which applies to foreign paupers, the problem would be greatly simplified. But as matters now stand, the temperance cause must extend its proselyting labors to the class in Europe from which our population is annually recruited, ere it can hope to have full success upon American soil. The reform movement, to be successful, must become universal.

We have said nothing in regard to the present active prohibition movement. It was no part of our purpose to discuss liquor legislation. But it seems evident that, apart from this, the cause of temperance reform has made remarkable progress in America, while the existing moral suasion and educative methods can scarcely fail to yield equally good results in the future, even if all prohibitive and restrictive methods prove ineffective.

Charles Morris.

OUR ONE HUNDRED QUESTIONS.

6. *Cite some famous instances in literature where a lie is applauded.*

Out of the five hundred and more answers sent in to this question, for no one of them all failed to get a mark, we choose the following by " One of a Thousand" :

In Tacitus, Hist., iv. 50, we read that Piso incurred the wrath of Festus, who sent a band of assassins to kill him. When the murderers arrived at Piso's house the door was opened by a slave, who guessed their errand, and, when they asked for Piso, said, "I am Piso," and was immediately slain, while his master escaped. Tacitus comments, " Egregium mendacium."

> Horace, Carm., iii. 11:
> "Splendide mendax et in omne virgo
> Nobilis ævum."

This refers to Hypermnestra, daughter of Danaus. Her father had learned from an oracle that he would be slain by his son-in-law : so when his fifty daughters married the fifty sons of Ægyptos he made them all promise to kill their husbands. All obeyed save Hypermnestra, who permitted her husband Lynceus to escape. She was imprisoned for breaking her vow, but the people unanimously declared her innocent.

> Tasso, " Gerusalemme Liberata," ii. 22:
> " Magnanima menzogna, or quando è il vero
> Si bello che si possa a te preporre."
> (O noble lie! was ever truth so good?
> Blest be the lips that such a leasing told!)

The occasion of this apostrophe was the lie of Sophronia. The king, having had some reverses, was advised by a renegade Christian in his service to take a certain statue of the Virgin Mary from a church and place it in the mosque, where it would serve as a talisman of good luck. The king accordingly had the statue placed in the mosque; but the next day it had disappeared. Suspicion naturally fell upon the Christians, and the king decreed that the thief should lose his life. No traces of the culprit were found, and the king resolved to kill the whole Christian population, for then he would be sure that the thief would suffer. On hearing this, a virgin, Sophronia, falsely declared herself guilty of the theft, and, to save her people, gave herself up to execution.

Other less famous examples of ancient literature applauding deceit, etc., are—

Æschylus (Fragm. Incert., ii.), " God is not averse to deceit in a just cause."
Sophocles (Antigone, 74), " Doing a holy deed in an unholy way."
Euripides (Helen., 1633), " To commit a noble deed of *treachery* in a just cause." (Also Sophocles, Philoct., 108.)
Cicero (Pro Milone, 27), " Mentiri glorioso."
Seneca (Ep., 55), " Gloriosum scelus."

> Horace, Ars Poetica, 9 (Poetic license defended) :
> " Pictoribus atque poëtis
> Quidlibet audendi semper fuit æqua potestas."

Lucian has a similar remark : " 'Tis an old story that poets and painters are accountable to nobody."

The familiar phrase " Pia fraus" may be classed as an applauded lie or deceit.

In the Old Testament we have several instances of deception used in a good cause. Passing by Jacob's frauds, which, though crowned with success, are certainly not applauded, we have—

Joshua ii., Rahab's lie, denying that she had concealed the two spies of Israel in her house.

Judges iii., Ehud, "the deliverer raised up by the Lord," obtains access to Eglon, king of Moab, by a lie, and stabs him.

Judges iv., Jael invites Sisera into her tent, bidding him "fear not," and kills him. Deborah and Barak sing, " Blessed above women shall Jael be."

In the Apocrypha, Judith gains the confidence of Holofernes by a series of lies in order to kill him, for which act she is applauded by the governor, the high-priest, the ancients, and all the people of Israel.

In the Talmud is a curious story illustrating the importance of phylacteries, which I translate from Buxtorf's Latin version: "The Roman government once forbade the Jews to wear phylacteries, and decreed that any Jew found wearing one should lose his head. The Rabbi Elisæus continually wore one upon (or around) his head, but once when in danger of arrest by a lictor he took it off and concealed it in his hand. The lictor asked what he had in his hand. He replied, 'I have the wings of a dove.' The lictor having threatened him with death if he did not reveal what he held, Elisæus opened his hand, and the wings of a dove were actually found therein." I mention this because it bears such a strong resemblance to the lies of hagiology, which may be called "applauded," since the liars have been canonized.

St. Elizabeth, Landgravine of Hungary (1207–1231), was charitable against her husband's wish, and, meeting him when her apron was filled with bread for the poor, declared on inquiry that it contained roses. He insisted on examining it, and the crusts were miraculously changed to roses.

Almost precisely similar is the legend of St. Rosaline of Villeneuve (1263–1329) ; and like incidents are recorded of minor saints.

The most touching lie in English literature, though deceiving no one and not applauded in the text, is that of Desdemona (" Othello," Act V. Scene 2). Emilia cries, " Oh, who hath done this deed?" and Desdemona answers, "Nobody; I, myself. Commend me to my kind lord," and dies.

Perhaps the most famous lie in modern literature is in " Les Misérables." Sydney Carton's sacrifice of himself in place of his friend Darnay, in " A Tale of Two Cities," is a well-known instance of noble deception.

A like *motif* is found in "Mademoiselle Mathilde," by Henry Kingsley,—a story of the Commune. The sister of the heroine is denounced as an aristocrat; but Mathilde declares herself to be her sister, and is executed in her stead.

Both these novels, and perhaps others, recall the story of Piso. Several incidents are recorded in history where a servant or a friend, representing himself to be his master or friend, has suffered the death intended for another; but these have not all been fortunate enough to have their heroism celebrated by a Tasso or even a Tacitus.

Less known than Dickens's hero are " Evan Harrington" (by George Meredith), who upholds and confirms a lie told by his ambitious sister to advance her interests, and the heroine of " Mauprat," by George Sand, who lies at the trial of her lover to save his life, although she supposes him to have been intent on her murder.

A poem by Adelaide Anne Procter, " Milly's Expiation," is a little like this last instance. Milly's lover is accused of murder; though innocent, circumstances are against him, and Milly swears falsely to save him. But Miss Procter condemns the lie.

To close with an American instance, " Madame Delphine," by George W. Cable. She is a quadroon, consequently her daughter Olive cannot legally marry a white man, Lemaitre. Madame Delphine perjures herself, swearing that Olive is not her daughter. She dies at the confessional, acknowledging her lie, on the evening of Olive's wedding-day.

7. What is the origin of the word " mascot" ?

The word " *masqué*" in the French language means literally " masked," " covered," " concealed," but I find, upon looking at a French encyclopædia, that it is also applied (from the derivation) to " one born with a caul." The old superstition attributes good fortune to the caul, and very high prices have been paid for one, the possessor being regarded as certain of good luck when he owns a caul. Of course the child fortunate enough to have been born with this lucky appendage would be regarded as especially favored, a "masqué," who would be always fortunate and bring good fortune to others.

In Brand's "Popular Antiquities" I find that in Scotland a caul is called a "holy cap" and a "fortunate hood." In France the superstition is proverbial, the expression " être né coiffé" being used to denote that a person is extremely fortunate.

Another origin of the word "mascot" is as follows:

There seems to be a legend prevalent in many countries that the seventh son of a seventh son will bring good luck, have powers of healing, etc. In Scotland the "spae-wife" always announces herself as the seventh daughter of a seventh daughter to imply her mystic power.

In France the seventh son of a seventh son was called a "marcou," branded with the fleur-de-lis, and supposed to be endowed with healing power. There was a famous one in Orleans called "Le beau Marcou," his power being supposed to be particularly strong during Holy Week. On Good Friday hundreds are said to have visited him between midnight and sunrise. From "marcou" *might* come "mascot;" but this seems to me rather fanciful.

According to Dies, "mascot" means a "witch," or, in a good sense, a fairy who brings good luck.

Worcester gives "masca, a sorceress,—from the Goth." This might be the origin of mascot,—one who brought good fortune by magical powers. My own preference is for the first derivation,—from "masqué."—OLIVE OLDSCHOOL.

"Chif's" answer is also very good, and furnishes some additional items as to the superstition of the caul:

Mascot comes from the same root-word as our word *mask*, the French *masque*, the Spanish and Portuguese *mascara*, and the Arabic *maskharat*,—meaning a cover for the face.

The word *mascot* was applied originally in France to one born with a caul. This was thought to be an omen of good luck to the possessor.

The word has sprung into common use through Audran's popular opera, in which the heroine is a Mascot,—"a gift of God,—a child of great blessing, and one that will bring good luck to her family," etc.

Ruddiman, in his Glossary to Douglas's Virgil, says, "In Scotland the women call *a haly* or *sely how* (*i.e.*, holy or fortunate cap, or hood, or net) a film, or membrane, stretched over the heads of children new-born; . . . and they give out that children so born will be very fortunate." Speaking of these cauls, which are generally like veils, masks, or hoods, Riolan, Du Laurens, and other anatomists believe that infants which are born thus (*né coiffé*) are "lucky," and superstitiously attribute great virtues to them. All times and all countries acknowledge this superstition. Ælius Lampridius, in his History of Diadumenus, who came to be the emperor Antoninus, remarked that "this emperor, who was born with a band or thin skin on the brow, in form of a diadem, from which he took his surname Diadumène, enjoyed perpetual felicity during all the course of his reign and life."

The "wise women" (midwives) sell these cauls to lawyers, advocates, etc., who believe that they carry with them a persuasive force which neither judge nor jury can resist. The ancient custom which decreed that judges sitting in the King's Court should wear a white coif of silk may have taken its rise from the superstition of carrying cauls as a charm.

In France the expression " *être né coiffé*" is proverbial to signify that a person is extremely fortunate. "This caul is estimated as conferring some power of seeing into the future, for good." "It is sold for magical uses." "It is an infallible preservative against drowning."

Weston, in his "Moral Aphorisms from the Arabic," 8vo, London, 1801, p. xii., gives the following: "The caul that enfolds the birth is the powerful guardian, like the seal-ring of the monarch, for the attainment of the arch of heaven, where, in the ear of a bright luminary, it is crowned and revolved." In a note he says, "The superstition of the caul comes from the East; *there are several words in Arabic for it.* It is not out of date with us among the people, and we often see twenty-five and thirty guineas advertised for one."

8. *Whence arose the expression "breaking a butterfly"?*

This phrase comes from the three-hundred-and-seventh line of Pope's "Epistle to Dr. Arbuthnot" (being the Prologue to the Satires): "Who breaks a butterfly upon a wheel?" meaning, Who would take the trouble to destroy an insignificant, harmless insect on an instrument of torture, when it could be so easily crushed in some simpler manner? In China the expression is familiarized by the sayings, "He fells a tree to catch a blackbird," and "He shoots a sparrow with a cannon." The context all refers to Lord John Hervey, and the passage has been said to rank "among the deadliest pieces of satirical writing in the language." Lord Hervey, the victim whom Pope lashed so unmercifully as "Lord Fanny" and "Sporus," was the son of a distinguished peer, a writer of able political pamphlets, and the favorite of George II. and Queen Caroline; one who appeared to possess all that the world envies. But one bitter drop in his cup of life made every draught unpalatable. His health was feeble, he was subject to epileptic fits, his temper was nervous and uncertain, and he regarded all about him with suspicion. Pope's venomous caricature of him contained sufficient truth to wound and cling to him. To prevent the frequent attacks of his disease, he made his diet chiefly of asses' milk and flour biscuits; and to conceal the ghastly pallor of his complexion, he rouged with an unsparing hand. His literary style, though elegant, and at times even brilliant, was marred by a love of antithesis and exaggeration. Thus we see why Pope stigmatized him as "that mere white curd of asses' milk," "this painted child," "one vile antithesis," etc. The quarrel which gave rise to Pope's attack was occasioned, it is supposed, by Hervey's espousal of the cause of Lady Mary Wortley Montagu, upon whom Pope had turned after a friendship of long standing. Although Hervey's "Memoirs," published in 1848, have given him the title of "the Boswell of George II. and Queen Caroline," he has been handed down to posterity as the "Sporus" of Pope. This nickname is the more humiliating when we recall the character of the original Sporus. He was a Roman youth of mean origin, to whom Nero devoted himself. Dressed as a woman, and adopting the name of Sabina, he accompanied the emperor in all his journeys, and after the latter's death was handed over to his successor, and finally terminated a degrading existence by committing suicide.—DAVUS.

In searching for the answer to this question I have found the following curious story, entitled "Breaking a Butterfly on the Wheel."

"In the republic of Quito, and some other parts of South America, there is a small insect called the comejen, whose destructive qualities are so active that in the space of one night it will penetrate the hardest wood or any other similar substance. In that short period it has been known to penetrate through and through a bale of paper containing sixteen reams. . . .

"In the archives of Quito there is a curious royal decree of Carlos III. respecting this insect. A number of cases of gun-flints had been sent to Panama from Spain for the purpose of being forwarded to Lima, but their non-arrival at that place caused the viceroy to repeat his request to the court for the necessary supply. This gave rise to an investigation: the flints were traced to Panama, and the governor was ordered to account for them. In his answer to the minister he stated that the comejen had destroyed the cases in the royal magazine. The minister being ignorant of what the comejen was, an order was issued under the royal seal commanding the governor of Panama to apprehend the comejen, to form a summary process on the crimes he had committed, then to send the prisoner and documents to Spain, that he might be dealt with according to the extent of his criminality."

In Lincolnshire, England, the first butterfly seen in spring should be crushed with the foot, insuring the crushing of all enemies during the year.—GUNN'S HILL.

9. *What is the Saint Baddeley Cake?*

Robert Baddeley, a low-comedian, attached for many years to the Drury Lane Theatre, London, died November 20, 1794, and left a peculiar will. He bequeathed his cottage to a theatrical fund, in trust, that there might be chosen four of the fund pensioners who might not object to living sociably together at Hampton (his home). He also requested that a sum of three pounds should be annually expended upon a cake, to be divided on Twelfth Night, in the green-room of the Drury Lane Theatre, among the actors.

The first cake was cut on Twelfth Night, 1796, and on successive anniversaries there have gathered to celebrate its cutting many celebrated actors of the English stage, among them Mrs. Siddons, the Kembles, Mrs. Jordan, Braham, and many others. At the cutting there was also offered a strange toast: "To the skull of the founder,"—supposed to be a respectful allusion to the brains from whence issued this kind attention to the actors of Drury Lane.

Twelfth Night, or Epiphany, has been celebrated for many years, throughout England, by the cutting of a bean cake, a cake in which a bean is cooked, the finder of which is made King of the night and the following day. It was, of course, in commemoration of this custom that Baddeley left this otherwise strange bequest. At present the cake-cutting has grown into a protracted feast, ending in a supper after the play.—OLIVE OLDSCHOOL.

10. *What was the Fortsas Catalogue?*

William Shepard's article on "Famous Hoaxes," in the present number of *Lippincott's*, contains an account of this extraordinary sell. Some of the most intelligent and painstaking competitors failed to give a satisfactory answer to this question. The following by "Olive Old-school" contains all the essential particulars:

The publication in 1840 of a catalogue purporting to be that of the Count J. N. A. de Fortsas created immense excitement among bibliophiles. This was a volume of only fourteen pages, and the count's collection consisted of only fifty-two books, but these were unique; not one was mentioned by any previous bibliographer; and these rare treasures were to be sold at Binche, a village in Belgium. Each bibliophile was trying to steal a march upon the rest in order to be possessed of some rare book. One bookseller came from Amsterdam just to see No. 75,—"Corpus Juris Civilis," printed by the Elzevirs on vellum. The Princess de Ligne, for the honor of her family, wrote to purchase No. 48 at any price. The Roxburghe Club sent orders. M. Van de Weyer ordered Nos. 7, 8, 12, 36, 47, 64, 78, 142. Téchener, half suspecting the joke, still sent commissions. The catalogue was printed in an edition of one hundred and thirty-two copies. of which two were upon vellum, ten upon colored paper, and one hundred and twenty upon white paper.

The day before the sale the announcement was made that this wonderful library would not be sold,—that the people of Binche would buy it, and include it in the public library! Binche is an insignificant little village, and the idea of its purchasing this library of rare wonders was absurd enough.

The author of this most successful hoax was M. René Chalons, of Brussels; the publisher was "M. Emm. Hoyois, bibliophile, member of the Société des Bibliophiles Belges séant à Mons."

M. Chalons and M. Hoyois, who had been warm personal friends, quarrelled afterwards over the question of a reissue of the catalogue.

There is in the Congressional Library at Washington, D.C., a copy of the original "Fortsas Catalogue."

11. *Who was the probable original of Lancelot du Lac?*

There is every reason to believe that the historical Lancelot was King Mael, or Melruas, of Britain, who appears to have been elected by the native tribes, in A.D. 560, after the triumph of the Saxons in southern England. Mael in Welsh means a servant, and l'Ancelot (diminutive of *ancel*) would in the Romance tongue signify "the little servant." Moreover, early Cymric tradition makes Mael the nephew of King Arthur, whose wife Guenever he carried off. Arthur besieged him, was defeated, and concluded a disgraceful peace which restored him his wife. Like Lancelot, Mael closed his career in a convent. But the Mael of real life was a very different being from the courtly and polished Lancelot of romance and poetry. He was a coarse barbarian, redoubtable in arms, and notorious for his crimes of unchaste violence, who seized Guenever by lying naked under an ambush of leaves in the wood she was to pass through, then rushing out on her as a satyr, from whom her attendants fled in terror.

Few of our correspondents mention this theory, which is certainly plausible, and is supported by Villemarqué and Henry Morley (" English Writers before Chaucer"). M. A., who alludes to a possible identification between Lancelot and Mael, says that the latter's surname Paladr-ddellt "has the same meaning as Lancelot,—*i.e.*, splintered lance." But Villemarqué's etymology is far more likely. M. A. also suggests that as Sir Thomas Malory finished his history of King Arthur "in the ninth year of King Edward IV.," the date of the battle of Barnet and of Edward's celebrated landing at Blackheath with only seven followers, we can scarcely doubt that in Lancelot's return from France attended by the same number of kings, and in Sir Ector's eulogy of the hero, the courtly knight intended a veiled compliment to his sovereign.

The possibility of a classical prototype for Lancelot, suggested by comparative mythologists, has been treated by many competitors. Here is the answer by " One of a Thousand" :

Paris of Troy was the probable original of Lancelot du Lac, the story of his life having many points of resemblance to the mediæval hero, and Guinevere corresponds closely to Helen. Guinevere is called "a destroyer of many knights," and similar taunts were applied to Helen. Paris grows up in ignorance of his father, so does Lancelot; the ingratitude of Paris and his treachery in carrying off the wife of his host are rivalled by Lancelot's connection with the wife of his king and trusting chief.

Max Müller and George W. Cox both advance this theory, and say further that Paris is the Vedic Pani and Ravana.

Rama, the seventh incarnation of Vishnu, marries Sita. Ravana, king of Lanka, loves Sita, and carries her away to the island where he dwells. Rama pursues them, and rescues Sita.

Pani seduces Saramâ in like manner. The whole story is finally reduced to a sun-myth.

With regard to Paris, as compared with Lancelot, Cox says, in his "Popular Romances of the Middle Ages," "We have falsehood and treachery on one side, and faithlessness on the other ; in other words, we have in Lancelot and Guinevere the counterparts of Saramâ and the Panis, of Paris and Helen ; and the taking away of Guinevere from the court of Arthur, who had cherished him as his friend, answers to the taking away of Helen from Menelaos by the man in whom he had placed a perfect trust. The character of Lancelot precisely reflects that of Paris ; and the words of Menelaos before the walls of Ilion are echoed in those of Arthur in the supreme strife before the gates of Joyous Gard : ' Fie on thy fair speech ; I am now thy mortal foe, for thou hast slain my knights and dishonored my queen.' In short, Lancelot is throughout a man of fair words, who disclaims all thoughts of treason, even while he knows that he has shamefully deceived his friend. It is the picture of Paris as drawn in the Iliad ; and if it be said that in that poem, as we have it, Paris does not exhibit the unfaltering courage or invincible strength of Lancelot, we have only to remember that the portrait given to us in our Iliad is not the only mythical picture of the treacherous son of Priam. (*Note.*—The story of the birth and early years of Paris, his irresistible prowess at games, his redoubtable exploits against thieves and evil-doers, are not,less parts of the great myth of Paris, as it has come down to us, than those portions of it which are related in our Iliad.)"

In an article on the Arthurian romances in the "Encyclopædia Britannica," they are said to be in the main a recast of the legends of Charlemagne: "Lancelot, Tristan, Gaurin, personify languor fatality, pleasure." These attributes would seem more appropriate to Paris than to Lancelot. Cox considers the latter to be substantially the same as Tristan (I believe).

12. *Who was Old King Cole, and what is the probable date of the nursery rhyme which celebrates him and his fiddlers three?*

Nearly all our correspondents agree with Halliwell in identifying this monarch of the nursery rhyme with Cole, Coël, Coil, or in Latin Coilus, the semi-mythical king of Britain who, according to the doubtful testimony of Robert of Gloucester, Geoffrey of Monmouth, and other old chroniclers, succeeded Asclepiad on the throne of Britain about A.D. 255, was the reputed father of St. Helena, and built the walls round the city of Colchester,—so named in his honor. In addition, " Eidon" and others remind us that the Scotch have also an "Old King Coul" in their traditional history, who flourished in the fifth century and was the father of the great Finn MacCoul. The territory of Coila (Ayrshire) was under his rule, and the name of Coila is often poetically applied to the whole of Scotland. Green and Freeman both recognize as indubitable a British king called Cole or Coël, who ruled in the sixth century and was the founder of a short royal line.

"Ad Astra per Aspera" throws out a suggestion that the "merry old soul" may be identified with Edwy, the brother of the Saxon king Edmund, surnamed Ironsides. This Edwy, on account of his great popularity with the peasants, bore the title of *"King of the Churls,"* a designation implying no real dignity, but merely a nickname bestowed by a populace which loved him. The title might easily enough have been subsequently abbreviated to "King Cole" by the populace.

M. A. thinks

The character of King Cole was undoubtedly derived from King René of Anjou (1409–1480), who throughout a life of war and misfortunes found pleasure in the study of music and what we should call the drama. He composed music and poetry, and arranged splendid spectacles for his people. His description of these "tournois" is still extant, and has been printed from the original manuscript in the Royal Library at Paris. The rather caricatured portrait of him in Scott's "Anne of Geierstein" helps us to understand how he appeared to the English, who were unable to comprehend his Latin elasticity of temperament, and mocked at his poverty and empty titles; for he was

> King of Naples,
> Of both the Sicilies and Jerusalem,
> Yet not so wealthy as an English yeoman.

"Bibota" and others send as an alternative answer the suggestion that King Cole was identical with "Old Cole," a famous cloth-manufacturer of Reading, one of the "Six Worthie Yeomen of the West," whose name became proverbial through an extremely popular story of the sixteenth century, and appears in several plays, the first of which was published in 1602. Deloney, an old chronicler, describes the riding of Henry I. towards Wales, and his meeting ever so many wains of cloth, which he was told all belonged to Old Cole. In consequence of this, he sent for him and received him at court.

Bibota, McNox, and several others refer to an amusing skit by Richard Grant White in the *Galaxy*, showing from the internal evidence of the ballad that King Cole was probably no other than the " Merry Monarch" Charles II., and that the nursery rhyme dates from his reign, when most of these old rhymes, and many of the so-called ancient ballads, really appeared.

Mr. White's points [says " McNox"] were that King Cole's pipe fixed the date after Raleigh's introduction of tobacco,—*i.e.*, after Elizabeth's reign; that violin-players, or " fiddlers," were not held in sufficient esteem to be musicians to a king, and, indeed, were scarcely known, before the time of Charles I.; that Charles II. raised them to higher honor, and used to have a band of them play to him while at table; moreover, that Charles was especially the "merry" king, and that the epithet " old" need not be taken as literally descriptive of the king's age here, any more than in Charles's well-known nickname " Old Rowley."

But the pipe may mean a musical instrument; and in any event it does not appear in the earlier version which Halliwell refers to the seventeenth century :

> Good King Cole,
> He called for his bowl,
> And he called for his fiddlers three:
> And there was fiddle-fiddle,
> And twice fiddle-fiddle,
> For 'twas my lady's birthday ;
> Therefore we keep holiday
> And come to be merry.

" The exact date of the song," says Bibota, " is unknown, but part of the words are quoted by Dr. William King, who was born in 1633. The air, therefore, is certainly as old as the seventeenth century."

13. *With what saint may Mother Hubbard be identified, and why ?*

Several competitors have named St. Elizabeth, though acknowledging with " Curious" that it is almost an insult to the sweetest of all the saints of the Roman calendar to give her name as the answer to this question.

And yet [continues " Curious"] from the " Mater Pauperum"—" Die Mutter von Ungarn"—the transition to "Mother Hubbard" is simple enough. In the "cupboard was bare," of the nursery-tale, we find the "empty treasury" of Hungary, exhausted by Elizabeth to supply the wants of the poor. In her seeking clothing for "her poor dog," we see the fair saint giving away her own robes,—even tearing off her rich mantle to bestow upon a beggar. In the search "for white wine and red," we find Elizabeth's charity and visits to the hospitals which she had founded; in the sickness of her four-footed companion, the sick and suffering whom Elizabeth relieved with her own hands, and the leprous child for whom she cared, laying him in her own bed. Even in the nursery-tale Mother Hubbard thought of another, not of herself, so Elizabeth's unselfishness and self-denial shine forth like stars. The " bare cupboard" may also indicate the famine which afflicted Thuringia in 1226, which was followed by a plague, in which Elizabeth herself nursed the sufferers. She was born in 1207, and died November 19, 1231, being canonized four years after her death. The most celebrated picture of Elizabeth is that painted by Murillo for the church of La Caridad (Charity) at Seville.

Other theories are thus summed up by "Eidon," who is undoubtedly right in giving the preference to St. Hubert,—a theory first broached by Prof. John W. Hales in the *Athenæum*, February 24, 1883 :

The question of the identification of

The widowed dame of Hubbard's ancient line

with one of the saints of the calendar opens a wide field for conjecture. Do we find the prototype of our familiar "Mother Hubbard and her Dog" in St. Margaret and *her* dog, St. Collen and her cat, or—rash supposition!—in St. Agnes and her lamb? Probably in none of these, but rather in St. Hubert himself, the patron of dogs and the chase. The grounds of this conjecture are these: The representations of the saints in painting and sculpture were familiar to a class which knew nothing of the orthodox legends concerning them. Among this class originated a large number of pseudo-legends, sometimes couched in rhyme, which were evidently framed to meet the vulgar understanding of the representation. St. Hubert is depicted in a long robe,—a veritable Mother Hubbard gown, in fact,—with long hair, so that the uninitiated observer might easily be doubtful as to his sex and make an old woman of him at a venture. Further, he was the patron saint of dogs, and was often represented with a canine attendant, so that the "prick-eared companion of the solitude" of the ancient dame was naturally assumed. St. Hubert was appealed to also to cure the ailments of a favorite or valuable dog, and bread blessed at his shrine was believed to cure hydrophobia. Given the character popularly accepted as Mother (or Saint) Hubbard (or Hubert), and the attendant dog, may not the rest of the tale be left to the untutored but active imagination of some rhymester or story-teller of the village green or servants' hall, which has often produced even more startling results from much slighter material?

It may be remarked, in passing, that the legend of St. Dominick and his dog, who were starving and had their larder replenished by supernatural means, doubtless was insensibly woven into the foundation of the nursery-tale in question.

14. *What is the origin of the phrase " The Queen of Spain has no legs"?*

The following answer, by "One of a Thousand," is similar in substance with a hundred others, although the name of the monarch is variously given :

Philip III. of Spain, surnamed "The Pious" (1578–1621), married Margaret of Austria April 18, 1599. This queen on her first entry into Spain passed through a town famous for its manufacture of silk stockings; the authorities, wishing to compliment her, sent her a costly pair as a present, which was, however, indignantly refused by the queen's chamberlain, who informed the delegation that "the Queen of Spain had no legs." The Queen, on hearing of this remark, burst into tears, exclaiming, "I will go home again! I would never have come to Spain had I known that my legs were to be cut off!" When the story was repeated to her husband, he is said to have laughed for one of the only two times in his life. Since then there has been a popular saying that officially the Queen of Spain has no legs. Etiquette was so strict at this time that Philip's death is said to have been caused by his sitting too long by an excessively hot fire because the proper official to remedy the trouble was absent.

The story, like the story of Philip's death, is probably apocryphal, invented to burlesque the rigid etiquette of the Spanish court. "The custom," says "Incognita," "of concealing the feet of Spanish women, dates back to the Spanish Goths and Germans described by Tacitus. Mediæval artists were forbidden to paint the feet of the Virgin, and it was contrary to court etiquette to allude even to the possibility of the

Queen of Spain having legs." It is said that Mirabeau, when offered a petition to be laid at the feet of majesty, replied, "Majesty has no feet." "Mary Andrews" has another story to tell in explanation of the proverb:

> This saying probably arose from the strict court etiquette of Spain, which forbade any man whatsoever on pain of death to touch the queen of Spain, and especially her foot. The queen of Charles II. almost lost her life from this custom. She was fond of riding, and, having received several fine horses from Andalusia, she had a mind to try one; but had no sooner mounted than the horse pranced, and, throwing her, dragged her over the ground, her foot having caught in the stirrup. All the court were spectators, but dared not touch her on account of this court rule. Charles II. saw the accident and the danger his wife was in, and called out vehemently; but the inviolable custom and untouchable foot restrained the Spaniards from lending a helping hand. However, two gentlemen, Don Luis de las Torres and Don Jaime de Soto Mayor, resolved to run all hazards despite the law of the queen's foot, the law *del pié por la reina*. One caught hold of the horse's bridle and the other of the queen's foot, and in taking it out of the stirrup put one of his fingers out of joint. This done, the dons immediately went home. The queen, recovering from her fright, desired to see her deliverers. A young lord told her majesty they were obliged to flee from Madrid to escape the punishment they deserved. The queen, who was a Frenchwoman, knew nothing of the prerogative of her heel, and thought it a very impertinent custom that men must be punished for saving her life. She easily obtained their pardon from the king.

15. *Who was Rübezahl?*

A number of answers were selected as worthy of publication. "Davus," "Veritas," "Box 211," "Owego," "Mayflower," "Hohenfels," "Œdipus," "McNox," "Ulm," "Lillian Walsh," "Ray le Brun," "Queue," "Elsie Marley," "Quill,"—any one of these, or a score of others, would do to quote. Instead, we will make up a composite article from the contributions of "One of a Thousand" and "Olive Oldschool," leaving out what is mere reduplication, and inserting that part of each article which is complementary to the other.

Here is "One of a Thousand's" description of the gnome:

> A famous spirit of the Riesengebirge (Giant Mountains), which separate Prussian Silesia from Germany, corresponding to the English Puck. He is celebrated in countless tales and ballads, which represent him as fond of playing tricks, sometimes good-natured, sometimes malicious, leading travellers astray, laming horses, breaking wagon-wheels or axle-trees, blocking up the roads, raising tempests to bewilder his victims, etc. He punishes the wicked, hating pride, injustice, covetousness, and disobedience, but is always ready to help the poor and oppressed, guides lost wayfarers, and rewards the virtuous. His presence is invoked at peasant weddings, where a ribbon given by him is transformed into a costly gift. In one of the stories of his munificence, a black pudding which he gives a workman is found to be filled with gold pieces; and others relate how seemingly worthless presents from him, such as sloes, skittles, leaves, or curds in the milk-pan, turn into gold. Once he aided an innocent man, condemned to death, to escape, and, assuming his form, was hanged in his stead, which penalty, needless to say, did no injury to the goblin.
>
> He appears under various forms, as a miner, huntsman, monk, dwarf, giant, or most often as a sooty collier, with long red beard, fiery eyes, and a pole like a weaver's beam; sometimes as an animal, dragon, wolf, or bear, or the fabulous leopard-like hyson. It is dangerous to hunt on his mountains, for he punishes interference with his sport, and also to call him Rübezahl; instead the peasants allude to him cautiously as "The Lord of the Mountains," "The Warden of the March," or "Herr Johannes."
>
> The legends of this mountain-goblin are to be found in "Volksmärchen der

Deutschen," 5 vols., 1782, by Johann Karl August Musaeus (1735–1787), who collected them from the peasantry; the same whom Kotzebue called "the good Musaeus." Some of them have been translated by Mark Lemon under the title of "Legends of Number Nip" (1864), and translations of single tales have occasionally appeared in periodicals, etc.

The origin of his name, both "Davus" and "Olive Oldschool" tell us, is etymologically obscure; but the following is "Olive Oldschool's" synopsis of the legend which popularly explains it:

Once upon a time this "Lord of the Mountain," as he called himself, became enamoured of a lady of noble birth, and persuaded her to go with him to his mountain-home. In order to supply her with servants, he planted turnips, which when they had sprouted he changed into little people. After a while the lady began to sigh for companions: so the devoted lover, anxious to please her, planted more turnips, which he promised to change into people when they should have sprouted. The lady, becoming impatient while waiting for the turnips to grow, ran off one day while her lover was looking after and counting his turnips. From this he obtained the name of *Rübezahl* ("turnip-counter"), which name, however, always angers him, as it reminds him of how he was tricked.

Gehe has taken this legend for the plot of his opera "Der Berggeist" ("The Mountain-Sprite"), and Fouqué and Menzel have introduced it into their dramatic stories.

William J. Thoms, in his interesting book "Three Notelets on Shakespeare," says, "The readers of the beautiful German tales of Musaeus doubtless remember his story of Rübezahl, or, as the translator of the selection of them (said to be no less a person than Mr. Beckford) which appeared in 1791, under the title of 'Popular Tales of the Germans,' anglicized his name, 'Number Nip.' They cannot have been otherwise than struck with the resemblance between this tricksome spirit of the Giant Mountains and our own Puck, but may probably have ascribed no small portion of this resemblance to the manner in which Musaeus has told his story. The resemblance is, however, very great, and is perhaps still more so when read in the simple legends in which Rübezahl figures, than in Musaeus's witty and spirited tales. These traditions were first collected by Practorius, in the middle of the seventeenth century, in a work entitled 'Dæmonologia Rübinzalii Silesii,' the third edition of which was published at Leipsic in 1668."

An extract from this book, too long to insert here, "seems to establish the resemblance between Puck and Rübezahl, and to show that the transformation which poor Bottom underwent was a common incident in works of popular fiction."

SONG.

BE firm, my heart, nor let the world torment thee;
    Be true, my heart, nor do thyself torment;
Let not a windy fortune cry she rent thee,
    Nor be with wine or rebel passions spent.
·Bear thou against the wind, a banner flying
    Before our army with quick folds of fury;
Or a storm-breasting eagle, cloudy, crying,
    With wings of darkness and a head all hoary;
Or the storm's self, all mighty in its anger:
A Storm, a Banner, an Eagle, and a Clangor!

               Langdon Elwyn Mitchell.

OUR MONTHLY GOSSIP

WITH READERS AND CORRESPONDENTS.

THE Prize Questions, to which a fresh instalment of answers is presented in this number, seem at least to have given a great deal of amusement to a great many people, and possibly a good deal of instruction as well. A large number of the competitors, even those who, from the limitations of their library or of their available time, hardly dared hope for a prize, have thanked the Gossip for the many hours of real delight they have spent in hunting up answers. Here, on the other hand, is a good-natured account, by one of our most intelligent contributors, of the trials and difficulties in the way of the inquirer.

"Some of your readers may care to hear of the trials and tribulations which a country cousin has had in seeking for knowledge. How one short moment can change the tenor of one's life! A few months ago, I was accounted a moderately sensible middle-aged woman; *now* I am looked upon as a monomaniac, and it will require years of extreme sober-mindedness to regain my former reputation, if I *ever* wholly do. *Lippincott* must bear the whole blame, for publishing what a friend called 'a fiendish set of questions.' They enchanted me like a siren when I first overlooked them, because I knew none of them, and my curiosity was excited. I began to question every one. One person said, confidentially, 'My cousin Ann, in the States, can tell you all about Mother Hubbard, and I am sure my friend Lucy in St. John *must* know all about the peacock's feather, because she is afraid to have one in her house.' Letters went forthwith to the two parties. Weeks after came kind answers, regrets, but *no* information. One busy friend made fair promises, but, like a Waterbury watch, needed winding up every time I met him; but, bless his heart! his books have been invaluable to me. One sent me *wrong* answers, rather than confess his ignorance. One gentleman, who was considered a fount from whence all knowledge flowed, was consulted, but *these* subjects were the only ones of which he was in almost total ignorance. I heard of a gentleman in Halifax who was such a close student of Thackeray that he almost knew his secret thoughts; wrote to *him;* a polite answer came saying he was the wrong man, referring me to another, to whom I wrote; he was charmingly interested, longed for information on the subject as much as I did, consulted every literary person of his acquaintance in the city, and sailed for England, promising to consult others there; if he has any light upon the Thackeray questions it is still locked in his own bosom. I have not heard from him since.

"Then there stole over me sweet recollections of days spent with a friend of undoubted ability in Washington, of talks about books, of hours spent in libraries. Happy thought! I wrote to her of my difficulties, asked if she would join me in the quest; her answer came prompt and firm, 'I am with you for the fray;' and my mind became easier. I found as many as I could, as each set of questions came, and sent the rest to her. One gray-haired pomposity thought the questions 'very silly,' 'a waste of time;' another said, 'they seemed framed on purpose to puzzle. What odds about King Cole and Mother Hubbard?' forgetting that some of the profoundest minds of the day are making folk-lore a study. My children called me a 'note-gatherer,' refused flatly to carry a missive to any one, unless assured that a '*Lippincott* question' did not lurk within. My husband rolled on the floor, in agony, when one of them was mentioned, and threatened a divorce; my best friends turned street-corners when they caught a glimpse of me coming; my *known* correspondents trembled when they saw my handwriting, my *unknown* ones wondered who that crooked-writing crank could be. I found myself only valuing persons according to their ability to answer questions, regarding them simply as notes, myself as a query. The trial of verifying slip-shod quotations was no small one. When college professors failed, I turned to a friend in a small country village, who gave me much valuable information. I have been snubbed and frowned upon, helped and smiled upon, alternately, till the extremes of fears and hopes have fairly addled my brain. My assisting friend wrote, 'Sixty boys are nagging sixty fathers for the Barbara Frietchie answer,' and adds an account of *her* trials. Whenever I have wished to consult fathers, babes have either just been born or babes have died. Libraries which have remained *in statu quo* since the foundation of the government, became chaos and were to be moved, if I wished to get access to them; people who knew and could help me were enlisted for others; people who knew little and *pretended* to know a heap snubbed me and the whole business, denouncing the questions as rubbish, time wasted, time much better spent in acquiring a language. Then again friends did help me cheerfully, thinking, 'Poor old lady, it amuses her.'

"After I had safely consigned my answers to the post-office, wishing them 'bon voyage' across the rough old Bay of Fundy, I thought, 'Now for a good night's rest!' But vain hope! sleep did not flee, but in my dreams all the characters visited me. The Gabbon Saer flirted with the Lady of Kynast. The 'Frost' and 'Vintage' saints peered from corners upon the archangel Abdiel, and would not tell their names. The Brides of Enderby, in their weddinggowns, smiled upon the Mascot. All the 'broken butterflies' cried for their pretty wings. Warrington and Blanche Amory feasted off the Baddeley cake. Lancelot du Lac and King Cole carried old Mother Hubbard and her dog in an arm-chair. Soapy Sam and Sam Weller played chess. The rest of the characters heaved sighs as profound as ever the spirits in Limbo did for the blessings of Paradise; and, finally, all who were mentioned in the questions donned long black veils and danced in a circle on the Great Wall of China, and then were exiled to the islands of Jack-a-Dan and Kick-em-Jenny. I have been threatened with brain-fever, and ordered a trip to Europe,—my ambition for years: so, if I don't get a *Lippincott* prize, I still shall have proved that 'man may have his *will*, but woman has her *way*.' So three cheers for *Lippincott!*

Was Holger Danske, whose name gives the title to one of Andersen's "Tales," an historical character? J. W.

Ogier or Olger the Dane [*Fr.* Ogier le Danois; *Dan.* Holger Danske; *It.* Uggero or Oggero] was a famous hero of Carlovingian romance, and one of the Twelve Paladins. According to the most usual tradition, he received his surname from his Danish birth, though some authorities claim that it is a contraction of L'Ardennois, and that he was a native of the Ardennes, while others again represent him as originally a Saracen, who, being converted to Christianity, was informed by his quondam associates that he would be damned, whence he was facetiously styled Le Damné by his French comrades. A not very successful attempt has been made to identify him with the Helgi of the Edda. Under any aspect Ogier seems to be a purely mythical character. His deeds of prowess are celebrated in the cycle of romances relating to Charlemagne, in two poetical romances of the thirteenth century, "Les Enfances d'Ogier," by Adènes, which narrates the events of his youth, and "La Chevalerie d'Ogier de Danemarche," by Raimbert, which tells of his quarrel with his royal master Charlemagne, and, more fully, in the anonymous prose romance "Ogier le Danois."

In Denmark this hero has been accepted as a national patron, and, under the name of Holger Danske, has won for himself a distinct individuality which presents only faint traces of resemblance to the original French legends. According to mediæval Danish ballads and romances, Holger was indeed a Paladin of France, but his greatest fame was won under the Danish standard. He made a crusade into India, and fell in love with the heathen princess Gloriani, but she preferred Prince Carvel, and Holger vowed he would never love another. After filling Europe and Asia with the fame of his exploits, he disappeared, and is said to be still lying in a magic slumber in the vaults of the castle of Elsinore, there to remain till Denmark shall need his aid.

Once, a Danish peasant, wandering through the dungeons of the castle, came upon a huge oaken door, and drew out the bar that secured it. Instantly the door swung slowly inward, while from the gloom came forth a mighty voice, asking, "Is it time?" The faint light that entered through the door-way revealed a giant form reclining against the wall, arrayed in rusty armor, and with a long white beard overspreading his ample breast. Again the question was repeated, and the peasant, rallying his courage, answered, "No." "Give me thy hand, then," said the figure. The other, unwilling to trust his hand in that tremendous grasp, extended the iron bar. Holger (for it was he) gave it a grip which left the print of his fingers in the iron as if it had been clay, and exclaimed, with a grim smile, "Ha! I see there are still *men* in Denmark; I may rest yet awhile!"

Like other popular heroes, Holger has been magnified by the folk-lore of the peasantry into a giant of enormous size. Twelve tailors, says one legend, once came to take his measure for a new suit of clothes. As they were perched on various parts of his body, one of them slipped, and pricked the hero's ear with his scissors. Holger, thinking it was a fly, lifted his hand and crushed the luckless tailor to death between his thumb and forefinger.

In answer to "C. G.'s" question in your April number, "What is the difference between a member and an officer of the French Academy?" I would say that there is not such a thing as an "*officer*" of the French Academy. There is the title of "Officier d'Instruction publique," and the *Government* gives this title to any one upon whom it wishes to confer an honor and to whom it seems too great an honor to confer the decoration of the "Légion d'Honneur." It is usually given to professors or literary men, though occasionally to commercial men.

The title of "Officier d'Académie" is less than the above, and generally only given to professors who have taught for a long time; "Académie" here has not any connection with the "Académie Française," which consists only of the forty Immortals, but it may be compared with English universities, several colleges and faculties being united under one institution and called an "Académie." There is the "Académie de Paris," the "Académie de Lyon," etc., etc. The

Government chooses the "officiers d'Académie," and gives the title as a reward, but only to professors; there is not any examination for it.

One says, "*membre* de l'Académie Française," which is a little higher than any of the above; or, "membre" of one of the four sections of the "Institut de France,"—1, "Académie des Inscriptions et Belles-Lettres," 2, "Académie des Sciences morales et politiques," 3, "Académie des Sciences," and, 4, "Académie des Beaux-Arts."

To be a member of the "Académie Française," or of either of the other four, is either a literary or scientific or artistic honor; and a new member to either is elected only by its own members; the *Government* has nothing at all to do with these "Académies," or with electing their members.

"Luigi."

Who was Svend Faelling? W. R. T.

Svend Faelling is a hero of popular Scandinavian folk-lore. He was born in the village of Faelling, and, as the roads were at that time greatly infested with trolls and other supernatural beings, he undertook the office of letter-carrier. There are many stories of his encounters with these uncanny people, one of which is interesting for its similarity to Tam O'Shanter's famous adventure. Riding home one night, he came upon a number of Elle-maids, who danced round and round him. One damsel reached him a drinking-cup, which Svend took, but warily flung its contents over his shoulder, singeing the hair off his horse's back where it fell. Then, with the cup in his hand, he clapped spurs to the steed and rode off, with the Elle-maid in hot pursuit. He dashed across a stream of running water, and, as she could not follow him, she conjured him to give her back the horn, promising him twelve men's strength in exchange. On regaining the cup she kept her promise, and Svend was consequently able to perform many wonderful feats, which made his name great in the world. In Zealand Svend is represented as an enormous giant, and a hill is pointed out near Steenstrup on which he used to sit while washing his hands and feet in the sea, a quarter of a mile distant. Grimm identifies this hero with Sigurd.

The meaning of *Felibre* (p. 170 of your current volume) is very clear. *Felibre* is composed of "*fe*" (the Provençal expression for "*faire*" = make) and "*libre*" (the Provençal expression for "*livre*" = book). Felibre means, therefore, literally "*book-maker*,"—that is to say, in the sense of *writer and author*, not in the sporting sense. A. H.

Who was the original of Kingsley's Saunders Mackaye? W. O. T.

Saunders Mackaye, in Kingsley's "Alton Locke," the philosophic Scotch bookseller, who occupies himself in denouncing things and people with savage humor, is doubtless drawn from Carlyle. Froude tells us Carlyle so dominated Kingsley that after visiting him Kingsley would unconsciously talk Carlylese for hours; and it must have been under the influence of this mood that Mackaye was evolved. Carlyle's own criticism on the character is interesting. "Saunders Mackaye," he says, "my invaluable countryman in this book, is nearly perfect; indeed, I greatly wonder how you did contrive to manage him. His very dialect is as if a native had done it, and the whole existence of the rugged old hero is a wonderfully splendid and coherent piece of Scotch bravura."

BOOK-TALK.

A MONTH or two ago the Reviewer made a general Apologia for not criticising certain books, on the ground that it might pain their authors to be told what he conceived to be the truth. Yet, after all, isn't it rather a curious weakness in human beings to care for one another's opinions? Why should Jones mind what you or I think of him, or say of him, when you and I are almost certain to be wrong? Nay, why should he mind what the majority think of him, when the majority are usually wrong? what the cultured minority think of him, when the cultured minority are seldom right? what an entire generation think of him, when the next generation may reverse the verdict?

An accurate history of criticism, for example, would be a delightful burlesque upon the fallibility of human judgment: only the historian should owe no fealty to what is current, he should stand so far apart from present human thought that all its most cherished conclusions should appear to him only shifting waves in an ocean of folly,—should recognize that our moralities may be vices, our vices virtues, our orthodoxies follies, our rascals heroes, our masterpieces daubs, our Shakespeares and Goethes and Virgils and Dantes the puerile intelligences that their contemporaries mostly believed them to be.

Let us take the case of Amélie Rives's "The Quick or the Dead?" Here and there a voice has been raised in its favor, here and there a critic has proclaimed that it is a work of real power and genius, but the majority are against it: the burlesquer and the caricaturist and the chivalric penny-a-liner seem for the moment to have carried the day. The opinion of the majority has little value, but the opinion of an individual has even less. Therefore the Reviewer, instead of saying that he thinks "The Quick or the Dead?" is instinct with power, that it has the worldly-foolish sincerity of genius, that it throws a lurid yet none the less a searching light into the awful deeps of two souls (exceptional, perhaps, but not ignoble souls) weltering in the strongest of human passions, and that the very frankness of its revelations is better than the timid concessions of so-called realists to the contemporary Anglo-Saxon attitude towards social questions,—instead of saying all this, which would express only his individual opinion, the Reviewer will appeal to literary history, and show why, holding that opinion, the fact that the critics are generally against him only increases his calm and serene confidence in his own superior wisdom.

The critics have always been against any new force in life or literature. For the critical is essentially the conservative, the Tory element in human nature, —the respecter of orthodoxies and conventions. The critical mind must have some fixed standard, some inflexible rule, by which to judge. It must love the right. It must hate the wrong. But Nature has no fixed standard, no inflexible rule, no right, no wrong:

> Known yet ignored, nor divined, nor unguessed,
> Such is Man's law of life. Do we strive to declare
> What is ill, what is good in our spinning? Worst, best,
> Change hues of a sudden; now here and now there
> Flits the sign which decides; all about yet nowhere.

So sing Browning's Fates. And some humbler poet (whose name the Reviewer would be glad to learn) has put the same thought into these words:

In men whom men declare divine
I see so much of sin and blot,—
In men whom others class as ill
I see so much of goodness still,—
I hesitate to draw the line
Where God has not.

Now, if the critic were not wiser than God he would cease to exist. He *must* draw lines, he *must* apply to present performances the tests which represent the accumulated experiences of the past. He *must* praise, he *must* blame. And because he does these things he justifies his existence. The Whig welcomes Christ, the Tory retains him. Towards the Whigs of the past the Tory can do something like justice, for it is he who profits most by the lessons of the past. The Whig has his eye on the future, he is a little too impatient of the past; in last year's harvest he would sacrifice tares and wheat alike. , To contemporary orthodoxies, though they owe their inception to Whigs of former days, he is apt to be unjust, for he is busy with heterodoxies which shall become the orthodoxies of the future.

Grammar, rhetoric, logic, rhythm, dogma,—all these mirages of the Infinite are the proper elements for the Tory; the Whig is absorbed in the effort to grasp the Infinite itself. The Tory is Wagner, the Whig Faust. In the former the intellect predominates, in the latter the soul,—at once the highest and the lowest in man, the First and the Last. Instinct was born before Reason, and still outruns the later, and in one sense the higher, development. The intellect has built up all social systems, all conventions, proprieties, and orthodoxies, in the effort to realize the dreams of the soul, but the soul recognizes their futility, sees that they are shadow, not substance, mirage, not reality, and is constantly engaged in reaching out for a higher ideal.

In the presence of men of exquisite literary instincts, men like Howells and James and Daudet, in whom the intellect dominates the soul, whose genius runs in the old grooves sanctioned by canon and convention, the critic is rarely at a loss. He has a rule and measure by which he can test them and determine their value. He is always the first to welcome them: his judgment is ahead of the public judgment. But in the presence of the great original force that transcends rule and custom, that rejects the past and prophesies the future, the critic is for the time being utterly at a loss. Only two such forces have appeared in America, —Walt Whitman and Emerson. Both fared badly with the critic in their earlier days, both reached the unliterary or at least the uncritical public before they won over the lettered minority. The New York *Nation* is justly looked upon as one of our highest critical authorities. As clever an article as it ever printed was a slashing review of Whitman's "Leaves of Grass" some time after the appearance of that epoch-making volume. It said some things that were true, many that were witty. The true things and the witty things are alike forgotten. "Leaves of Grass" is recognized as a monumental addition to American literature. Emerson's "Brahma," the most significant short poem ever written in this country, was laughed at from the Atlantic to the Pacific; the funny men of the press found it an inexhaustible subject for satire, parody, burlesque; the critics joined in the laugh; by advice of his publishers Emerson omitted it from the first collection of his poems. Satires, parodies, burlesques, and criticisms have alike disappeared and left not a wrack behind,—and not only no collection of

Emerson's poems, but no general compendium of English poetry, is complete without " Brahma."

In England one might make a choice collection of similar mistaken criticisms. The *Athenæum* has always been an authority in literary matters, but the *Athenæum* thought Carlyle was a madman, discoursing nonsense, and the *Athenæum* voiced almost the unanimous critical opinion of the period. For many years the *Edinburgh Review* and the *Quarterly Review* were the acknowledged guides of public opinion in literary matters. The *Edinburgh Review* advised Byron to quit versifying, told Wordsworth he would never do, thought Goethe was a writer whom no gentleman could tolerate, and deemed Ruskin a fool. The *Quarterly Review* characterized Shelley's " Prometheus Unbound" as " drivelling prose run mad," and his " Revolt of Islam" as " insupportably dull ;" looked upon Keats's " Endymion" as " gratuitous nonsense ;" said of Dickens, " he has risen like a rocket, and he will come down like a stick ;" sneered with clumsy irony at " the peculiar brilliancy" of " the gems that irradiate the poetical crown" of that " singular genius" Mr. Alfred Tennyson ; and thought that if that wicked book " Jane Eyre" were written by a woman, it must be by " one who for some sufficient reason has forfeited the society of her sex."

A good friend of the Reviewer, who admires Amélie Rives but regrets " The Quick or the Dead ?" writes that " it is its utter absurdity which amuses people whom the mere shock of its immorality would have alienated." Well, it was the utter absurdity of Wordsworth, Goethe, Emerson, Ruskin, and Whitman, which amused their early critics. And as to immorality, have not " Wilhelm Meister," " Jane Eyre," " The Scarlet Letter," " Pendennis," " Elsie Venner," all been accused of immorality by conscientious exquisites in the past? Let us make the analogy more complete. Amélie Rives's English has been lavishly criticised. Now, if we turn to the *Quarterly's* essay on " Endymion" we find exactly the same sort of criticism. After asserting that Keats cannot write a sentence or spin a line, the *Quarterly* goes on to find fault with the new words with which, " in imitation of Mr. Leigh Hunt, he adorns our language. We are told that ' turtles *passion* their voices ;' that ' an arbor was *nested*,' and a lady's locks ' *gordian'd-up ;*' and to supply the place of the nouns thus verbalized, Mr. Keats, with great fecundity, spawns new ones ; such as ' men-slugs and human *serpentry ;*' the ' *honey-feel* of bliss ;' ' wives prepare *needments ;*' and so forth. Then he has formed new verbs by the process of cutting off their natural tails, the adverbs, and affixing them to their foreheads ; thus ' the wine out-sparkled,' ' the multitude up-followed.' But if he sinks some adverbs in the verbs, he compensates the language with adverbs and adjectives which he separates from the parent stock. Thus, a lady whispers ' *pantingly* and close,' makes ' *hushing* signs,' and steers her skiff into a ' *ripply* cove.' "

Now, of course all this does not prove that because Amélie Rives has been attacked and criticised she is *therefore* a great genius, otherwise the Sweet Singer of Michigan might readily put in a claim on similar grounds. But it does show the valuelessness of contemporary criticism. And if a man believes in Miss Rives, he need not be disturbed in any way by contemporary criticism. He need only bide his time, in full confidence that a dozen or fifteen years hereafter he will have the opportunity to evidence his magnanimity by refraining from the exasperating " Didn't I tell you so ?"

Edgar Saltus is often classed with Amélie Rives as an offender against public morals. But there is a well-marked distinction between them. Miss Rives has doubtless been surprised and shocked to find herself improper. Mr. Saltus is brilliant and audacious, the Anglo-Saxon prudery amuses, its hypocrisy offends him, and he takes a mischievous delight in making the Philistine world open its startled eyes. But in his last book, " Eden" (Belford, Clarke & Co.), he has written a story that can offend no one. It is a simple story, apparently, yet as full of surprises as an electrical jar, and is told in a style that is the despair of a Reviewer anxious to hurry through his work : not a line can he skip, for fear of missing some delicious epigram or well-turned phrase.

"Mr. Meeson's Will" (Harpers) is a good example of how a writer with the art of narration and few other literary gifts can hold a reader's attention. Mr. Rider Haggard has stolen his plot from a French source, and spoiled it in the stealing, his characters are well-worn types in fiction, his philosophy is of the weakest, and the main object of the book, which is to teach the wicked publisher how to conduct his business on a more generous basis, shows a *naïve* and preposterous ignorance that is too amusing to be ever offensive ; yet with all these faults you read the book through in a half-hour, and though you say to yourself that the time has been wasted you know in your heart that it has passed more rapidly (and perhaps more pleasantly) than if it had been devoted to some more improving study. "Maiwa's Revenge" (same publishers) is another new novel by Haggard, in which our old friend Alan Quatermain makes a reappearance. There are some vivid battle-scenes ; but, to tell the truth, Alan is getting to be a bore. Didn't he die in some former book? For Jesu's sake, Mr. Haggard, forbear to disturb his bones.

"A Winter Picnic," by J. and E. E. Dickinson and S. E. Dowd (Holt), is described by its sub-title as "The Story of a Four Months' Outing in Nassau, told in the Letters, Journals, and Talk of Four Picnicers." It is chatty and rather entertaining. The same publishers send us "In Hot Haste," by Mary E. Hullah, a good story of German life. Is it a translation?

All of us who take a pride in the national game of base-ball are glad to know that among the professional brotherhood so cultured a gentleman as Mr. John Montgomery Ward may be found. His book entitled "Base-Ball. How to become a Player. With the Origin, History, and Explanation of the Game" (Athletic Publishing Co.) is a brochure of unusual interest, written in plain, straightforward, yet excellent English, and containing a great deal of sensible advice and reflection,—the product of many years of training and experience on a mind that sees below the surface and co-ordinates facts into philosophy.

Mr. Andrew Lang is a perpetual marvel. Is there nothing he can't do, one whispers, nothing he doesn't know? He is poet, novelist, critic, wit, essayist, philosopher, and comparative mythologist, and he adorns everything he touches in any one of those capacities. His edition of "Perrault's Tales"—the famous "Contes de Ma Mère l'Oye," together with the "Peau d'Asne" and other tales in verse—is an excellent piece of book-making (Macmillan). The preliminary essay on Perrault is touched with a light and graceful pencil, and the essays on the various Contes are entertainingly written and present the latest results of scholarship. To every student of comparative folk-lore the book is indispensable.

EVERY DAY'S RECORD.

SEPTEMBER.

When the year began in March, as it did in old Roman days, the months from July to December were known by numbers only, September being the seventh month, from Latin *septimus*, "seventh." Subsequently July and August were renamed in honor of the emperors Julius and Augustus Cæsar, and several Roman emperors sought to give their names to September, but in this case the old name was retained. When Julius Cæsar revised the calendar, he made the months from March onward, with the exception of February, successively thirty-one and thirty days in length, September having thirty-one days; but it was subsequently reduced to thirty days by Augustus, who changed the lengths of all the months after August, in order to make the latter month, to which he had given his name, as long as that named after his predecessor. The Saxons called September *Gerst Monat*, or barley month, this crop, from which their favorite beverage was brewed, being then gathered. It is still called *Herbst Monat*, or harvest month, in Switzerland. The harvest moon comes in this month, being the full moon nearest the autumnal equinox. For several evenings the moon rises near sunset, thus enabling the harvesters to extend their day's work. This phenomenon is less marked in the United States than in England and Northern Europe, where it is aided by the higher latitudes.

Late in September the sun enters the constellation Libra, and passes the equator in its southward journey. This constitutes the autumnal equinox, which occurs about September 24. The period of the vernal equinox is about March 21, so that the winter season is somewhat shorter than the summer. Stormy weather often attends this period, but by no means always, for September is occasionally pleasant throughout, though the summer

temperature is apt to overflow into its first half and render it oppressively warm. In the closing period of the month morning and evening bring creeping chills, to remind us that the season of the flower and the leaf is passing away, while that of frost and snow is advancing. The month of September has much to render it enjoyable. The season of the blossoming has gone, but that of the fruitage and the harvest is at hand. The orchards groan with their weight of red-cheeked apples, and are heavy with the rounded perfection of luscious peaches and pears. The vines hold out their purple clusters to our hands, while the threatening spines of the chestnut, the browning globes of the walnut and hickory, and the opening clusters of the hazel-nut give invitation to the coming festival of the nutting-season,—a festival to which the nimble-footed squirrel must look forward with the same eager zest as his human competitors. In the fields the harvesters are busy gathering the golden-eared maize; in meadow and by brookside the flowers of autumn—the asters, the golden-rod, the blue gentian, and their modest companions — are in bloom; the trees are slowly putting on their autumnal robes of crimson and gold; and the birds are preparing for their southward flight to the lands of perpetual summer. In the depths of verdant groves, or by the flower-strewn sides of prattling streams, the lovers of nature still lie and dream, bidding farewell to the season of the flower that has brought them so many happy days. It is the month of the ripening, of the fulfilment of the promise of summer, of the breathing-pause of nature before it enters the winter's frosty realm, and that in which man throws off the lassitude of the dog-days, and prepares to vigorously begin again the battle of business life.

444

EVENTS.

September 1.

1715. Louis XIV., the "Grand Monarque" of France, died at the age of seventy-seven, after a reign of seventy-two years, he having come to the throne at five years of age. This monarch, through his ambition, his incessant wars, and the encouragement which he gave to commerce, art, literature, etc., played a great part in modern history. Yet the victories with which his reign began were followed by a series of defeats, while his wars and extravagances brought France into a condition of distress which was one of the causes of the Revolution. As a master of the art of kingcraft, however, he has had few superiors, while his patronage of literature made his age the most brilliant in an intellectual sense that France has known.

1827. The *Journal of Commerce* was issued at New York in the interest of abolition. It afterwards became a conservative organ, and vied with the *Morning Enquirer*, started in the same year, in seeking advertisements. They established swift schooners and pony expresses to get the commercial news, and were called "blanket sheets" from their efforts to surpass each other in size.

1830. Charles Kean, the celebrated actor, began his first engagement in this country, at the Park Theatre, New York.

1858. The laying of the first Atlantic cable was celebrated in New York by a public ovation to Cyrus W. Field and the officers of the expedition. The celebration surpassed anything of the kind that had ever been seen in that city, while in all parts of the country the event was celebrated by fireworks, illuminations, the ringing of bells and firing of cannon, and other demonstrations of joy. Yet the rejoicing was premature. After a few messages were sent, the cable ceased to work, and it was not until 1866 that a successful cable was laid.

1858. On the night of September 1, the quarantine buildings on Staten Island, which had been used for yellow-fever and smallpox patients against the protests of the people, were attacked by a mob, the sick carried out, the officers and physicians driven away, and the buildings burned. The woman's hospital was spared, but was burned the

next day, thirty-two buildings in all being destroyed. The island was declared in rebellion, and troops were sent there; but no further trouble occurred.

1858. The government of India, which had hitherto been held by the East India Company, was transferred to the Crown, which has since then governed India as a province of the British Empire.

1870. The final defeat of the French army in the Franco-Prussian war took place at Sedan. War had been declared on July 19, and a single month of fighting left France at the mercy of Germany, and brought the reign of Napoleon III. to an end. On September 2 he surrendered to the King of Prussia, and his army capitulated.

1880. A novel experiment with powerful electric lights took place at Nantasket Beach, near Boston. Three towers, one hundred feet high and five hundred feet apart, arranged in a triangle, were provided each with a circle of twelve electric lights of 2500 candle-power, thus concentrating a light of 90,000 candle-power on a limited space. The purpose was to discover the efficacy of this method of lighting cities. The light given was about equal to that of the full moon, and the experiment proved of no decisive value.

1881. A singular duel took place at Steinmühle. A young lawyer's clerk named Francis Waldeck fought a so-called "American" duel with Baron von R——, in which the contestants drew lots as to which should shoot himself. Waldeck drew the fatal blank. He twice asked a respite from his antagonist, who on the second occasion brutally replied, "Coward and rascal, I am waiting to attend your funeral." The young man thereupon killed himself with a pistol-shot.

1883. The "Black Flags," Chinese guerillas of Tonquin, were defeated by the French.

1884. During the preceding night a serious outbreak took place in the Snake Hollow mines, Hocking Valley, Ohio. The guards were attacked by a body of strikers and one shot dead. The strikers were finally driven off, more than one thousand shots being exchanged.

1886. The Severn tunnel was completed and opened for traffic. It had been thirteen years in building, in consequence of difficulties from springs.

September 2.

1666. The great fire of London, one of the most noted conflagrations in history, broke out, and raged with fury for several days, being fanned by a violent wind. Nearly the whole city was destroyed, thirteen thousand two hundred houses being burned and four hundred streets laid waste. Two hundred thousand people were left homeless. London had been for months desolated by the plague, and the distress was extreme. Yet the city was much improved in rebuilding, particularly by the use of brick and stone in place of timber as building-materials.

1792. The terrible "September massacres" of the French Revolution took place on the 2d and 3d, the prisons of Paris being emptied of their captives, who were slaughtered by the mob as they left the prison doors. There were in all 1085 prisoners massacred, among them the celebrated Princess de Lamballe.

1801. The French army evacuated Egypt, Napoleon's campaign in the East having proved a serious failure.

1807. The bombardment of Copenhagen by the English army began. Its university buildings and numerous other edifices were destroyed.

1864. The city of Atlanta was occupied by General Sherman. From this city began his famous "march to the sea."

1884. The Electrical Exhibition opened in Philadelphia, with a highly interesting and varied display of electrical apparatus.

1885. The Chinese coal-miners were driven out of Rock Springs, Wyoming Territory, by a mob of white miners, fifty houses being burned and fifty Chinamen killed. Five hundred Chinamen were dispossessed. Another attack on Chinamen took place on the 12th at Seattle, Washington Territory. They obtained no redress for the injury done them.

September 3.

1651. The battle of Worcester took place, in which Cromwell completely defeated the royal army under Charles II. and ended the contest for the throne. Just one year before, September 3, 1650, he had totally defeated the Scotch at Dunbar.

1658. Oliver Cromwell, the "Lord Protector" of England, died on the anniversary of his two greatest battles. His life had been one of extraordinary diversity, and he had risen on the wave of revolution from the lowest to the highest station. No greater military genius ever appeared in England, and in statecraft he has had no equal on the English throne.

1783. The treaty of peace between Great Britain and the United States was signed at Paris. At the same time a treaty of peace was concluded between Great Britain, France, and Spain, the war between which nations was an outcome of the American Revolution.

1855. Rachel, the eminent French actress, made her first appearance in this country at the Metropolitan Theatre, New York.

1877. Louis Adolphe Thiers, the eminent French statesman and historian, died, at the age of eighty. He bore a prominent part in recent French history, and was president of the republic from February, 1871, to May, 1873. Of his works, the most important are "History of the French Revolution" and "History of the Consulate and the Empire."

1878. The Princess Alice, a passenger-steamboat, was run into on the Thames by the steamer Bywell Castle, and immediately sank. Of nine hundred persons on board, only two hundred were saved.

1883. Ivan Turgenieff, the celebrated Russian novelist, died. He began his literary career with a poem, "Parascha," and wrote many novels of a high order of merit, besides short stories, poems, and dramatic sketches.

September 4.

1870. The deposition of Napoleon III. and the establishment of a republican government in France were proclaimed, as a consequence of the defeat at Sedan. The United States recognized the new republic on September 8, Spain on the same day, and Switzerland on the 9th. This constitutes the third establishment of republican government in France.

1878. The "Joseph II. mining adit," at Schemnitz, Hungary, was finished. This tunnel, begun in 1872, is 16,538 metres, or over ten miles, long, twelve feet high, and ten wide. The mines, which yield gold, silver, lead, copper, iron, sulphur, and arsenic, extend under the ground, and are connected by nearly three and a half miles of passages. The tunnel runs below the mines, and may be used either as a canal or as a railroad.

1881. Great forest fires raged in Eastern Michigan, spreading over one thousand square miles of territory. A large amount of property was destroyed, and more than two hundred lives were lost.

1884. The cashier of the National Bank of New Jersey, at New Brunswick, committed suicide. An examination of the books showed a deficit of about $300,-000. A few days afterwards the president of the bank killed himself.

1885. The seizure of the Caroline Islands by Germany created intense excitement at Madrid, Spain. A serious riot was threatened, and the mob had to be dispersed by troops. Spain had an old claim on the islands, and sent an expedition to take possession, when a German gunboat slipped in ahead, and hoisted the German flag, thus gaining prior possession.

1886. Fresh shocks of earthquake took place at Charleston, and along the coast. No damage done. The great shock occurred on August 31, and laid Charleston in ruins, 96 persons being killed, and $8,000,000 in value lost. This earthquake extended from the Atlantic coast to Omaha, and from Detroit to Mobile, Charleston being its centre.

1886. Prince Alexander of Bulgaria was forced to abdicate. He had been driven from the throne by a conspiracy on August 21, and on his return was enthusiastically received by the people, but the hostile attitude of the Czar of Russia obliged him again to give up the throne.

September 5.

1752. The first theatre in Virginia was opened at Williamsburg, with " The Merchant of Venice."

1774. The First Continental Congress met at Philadelphia, delegates from eleven colonies appearing. It agreed on a declaration of rights, adopted a resolution against commercial relations with the mother-country while the oppression continued, and prepared an address to the King and the people of Great Britain.

1795. The first exclusively commercial newspaper in the United States was issued at Boston. It was named *The Boston Prices Current and Marine Intelligencer, Commercial and Mercantile.*

1800. The island of Malta was surrendered to the British by the French garrison, Napoleon having taken it in 1798. At the peace of Amiens it was stipulated that it should be returned to the Knights Hospitallers, its old owners, but the British retained possession, and it was guaranteed to them by the treaty of Paris, 1814.

1808. John Home, the author of the tragedy of " Douglas," died. The play was first brought out in 1756.

1863. James Glaisher, an English scientist, made a balloon-ascent at Wolverhampton, in which he reached the extraordinary height of seven miles. At five and three-quarter miles he became insensible, and Mr. Coxwell, who accom-

panied him, lost the use of his hands, but was able to open the valve with his teeth. They descended safely. He made many other ascents, reaching the height of five miles in his first ascent, July 17, 1862.

1887. The Theatre Royal, of Exeter, England, was burned, with a loss of about one hundred and forty lives, mostly of those in the gallery. The fleeing audience became choked in an angle of the stairway, and were unable to escape from the rapidly-spreading flames.

1887. The Ninth International Medical Congress met in Washington, more than four thousand physicians being present, many of them of the highest standing in the profession. It adjourned on the 10th, the next congress being fixed for Berlin, in 1890.

1887. Labor Day was observed as a general holiday by the working-people of New York, in which State it had been made a legal holiday. Little attention was paid to it elsewhere. A great parade is arranged for this day in 1888.

September 6.

1620. The Mayflower sailed from Plymouth, England, for America, having on board one hundred and one emigrants, afterwards known as the Pilgrims. It cast anchor in the harbor of Cape Cod on November 9, a landing soon after being made at Plymouth, Massachusetts. This place had been named by Captain John Smith, on a previous voyage of exploration.

1769. A grand Shakespearian festival, devised by David Garrick, the celebrated actor, was held at Stratford-on-Avon on the 6th, 7th, and 8th of the month, with feasts, processions, illuminations, fireworks, masquerades, etc. This was the first of the authors' commemoration festivals.

1838. Grace Darling, daughter of an English light-house-keeper, with her father, rescued fifteen passengers from the wrecked steamer Forfarshire, venturing out in a tremendous sea. Her name has become famous through this noble action.

1839. A destructive fire took place in New York, forty-six buildings being burned, with a loss of $10,000,000.

1865. A great fire occurred in Constantinople, about twenty-five hundred buildings being burned. At the same time, a severe epidemic of cholera raged in that city, which carried off fifty thousand people in August. It ended during the month of September, probably in consequence of the conflagration.

1869. A serious disaster took place in the Avondale coal-mine, Luzerne County, Pa., one hundred and eight miners losing their lives. The shaft, which was built mainly of timber, took fire. All within the mine perished, no assistance or escape being possible, as the only avenue of entrance to the mine was filled with smoke and flame.

1881. A day of extraordinary darkness in New England, like the "dark day" of 1780. The weather was extremely hot, the air full of vapor, and the darkness such that vision was limited to short distances. Colors changed. The sun looked like the full moon, when visible at all. Schools were dismissed, factories closed, and gas and lamps everywhere lighted.

1883. A statue to the Marquis de Lafayette was unveiled at Le Puy, France, in the presence of an immense throng. The statue was decorated with American and French flags.

1887. The Apache chief Geronimo and his band surrendered to General Miles. This was an important event, as this band had been long pursued, and their capture seemed hopeless. It put an end to all danger of serious outbreaks of the savage tribe that had committed so many outrages on defenceless citizens and travellers.

September 7.

1792. The mint at Philadelphia was ready for operation. It had been built in accordance with an act of Congress, which provided that bullion should be assayed and coined free, or exchanged for coin at a discount of one-half per cent. Coining was done by horse-power until 1815, when steam-power was introduced.

1822. Brazil declared its independence of Portugal. Pedro I. was crowned emperor on December 1, a new constitution was adopted in 1824, and in 1825 Portugal recognized the independence of its former colony.

1860. The steamer Lady Elgin, engaged in passenger-traffic on Lakes Superior and Michigan, was run into at night by a schooner, and quickly sank. There were nearly four hundred persons on board, of whom about three hundred were lost.

1867. Amnesty to the Southern officials, with some few exceptions, was proclaimed by the President. Jefferson Davis, who had been imprisoned in Fortress Monroe, was soon after arraigned for high treason, and released on bail. His trial, fixed for November, but postponed, never came off.

1881. Sidney Lanier, a distinguished poet of the Southern United States, died.

1884. A great fire broke out in the lumber district of Cleveland, Ohio. Fifty acres of lumber-yards were burned over, and more than forty million feet of lumber destroyed. Twenty-seven cars loaded with merchandise were burned. The loss was estimated at $1,500,000.

1885. The first international yacht-race for the America's cup took place between the American sloop Puritan and the English cutter Genesta. The vessels fouled, and the race was put off to the 14th, when the Puritan won. The Puritan won in a second race on the 16th, thus settling the best-two-out-of-three contest in favor of the American yacht.

1886. The second international yacht-race came off between the American yacht Mayflower and the British yacht Galatea. The Mayflower won in this, and also in a second race on the 11th, thus deciding the contest in her favor.

September 8.

1397. Thomas of Woodstock, Duke of Gloucester, and uncle of Richard II., was treacherously seized and murdered by order of that king, on suspicion of taking part in conspiracies.

1565. The city of St. Augustine, in Florida, was founded by Don Pedro Menendez, who had been sent by the King of Spain to drive the French from Florida. It is the oldest town in the United States, and was the scene of the massacre of the French Huguenot settlers, which soon after took place.

1760. Montreal was surrendered to the English. This completed the conquest of Canada from the French, who, by treaty, gave up all their possessions on the North American continent.

1819. The Vauxhall Garden, at the northeast corner of Broad and Walnut Streets, Philadelphia, was destroyed by a mob. A balloon-ascension had been advertised, but there was such great delay that the mob in the street outside became impatient and riotous, and set fire to the buildings, which were completely destroyed.

1825. Lafayette set sail for France, after his visit to, and tour through, the United States, in which he was everywhere received with the greatest honor and rejoicing. Congress granted him $200,000 and 24,000 acres of land in Florida, as recompense for his services in the Revolution.

1842. The queen of Otaheite, or Tahiti, was forced to put herself under the protection of France. She retracted, and France assumed the protectorate of the island in November, 1843. The island was formally annexed to France June 29, 1880.

1850. Lieut. Gale, an Englishman,

made a balloon-ascent with a horse from the Hippodrome of Vincennes. On descending, and releasing the horse, the people who held the ropes let go too soon, and the unfortunate aeronaut was borne into the air before he was ready, and dashed to the ground a mile distant.

1855. The Malakhoff at Sebastopol was stormed and captured by the French. The British, at the same time, stormed the Redan fort, but were unable to hold it. During the night the Russians withdrew from that part of the town. No further defence was made, and the siege, which had lasted for a year, came to an end.

1883. The Northern Pacific Railroad was opened to traffic. The last spike, a golden one, had been driven on August 22, in the presence of a large assemblage. The road is 1674 miles long, from its eastern terminus, Superior City, near Duluth, Wis., to Walhalla Junction, on the Columbia River. From this point, extensions have been built in several directions.

September 9.

1513. The celebrated battle of Flodden Field was fought by the English and Scotch armies. It was caused by James IV. of Scotland taking part with Louis XII. of France against Henry VIII. of England. James was killed, with thirty of his nobles and more than ten thousand of his army. The English loss was small.

1846. Telegraphic communication was opened between New York and Albany. During the same month a telegraph line was completed between Philadelphia and Harrisburg, which was extended to Pittsburg by the end of the year. Telegraphic communication between New York and Boston had been completed on June 27, and between Boston and Buffalo on July 3. In January of this year Philadelphia and New York were connected by telegraph, with the exception of the Hudson River, over which the messages were taken by boatmen. A copper wire covered with cotton saturated with pitch, and enclosed in a lead pipe, had been tried as a conductor of the current under the river, but proved a failure.

1848. A severe fire broke out in Brooklyn, N.Y., which consumed about three hundred buildings and destroyed property to the value of $1,500,000.

1850. California was admitted into the Union as a State. It had been ceded by Mexico to the United States in 1848, but its progress in population was phenomenally great, owing to the discovery of gold, and it was ready for admission in two years.

1860. The allied English and French armies began their advance on Pekin, which city was surrendered to them on October 12 and evacuated on November 5. The celebrated summer palace of the Emperor of China was pillaged and burned, an act of wanton destruction which has called forth severe reprobation. Its professed purpose was to revenge on the government its cruel treatment of the commissioners sent to treat for peace, thirteen of the twenty-six having been murdered and the others treated with great indignity.

1873. The Alabama award was paid by England to the United States. This grew out of the depredations of the Confederate steamer Alabama, which had sailed from an English port to prey on American commerce. The claim of the United States for redress was settled by a court of arbitration, England being adjudged guilty of remissness, and damages awarded to the amount of about $16,000,000.

1882. Arabi Pasha attacked the British army in camp at Kassassin, Egypt, but was repulsed with loss. On the 13th General Wolseley's army advanced and made an early morning attack on Tel-el-Kebir, the camp of the Egyptian army. The surprise was complete, and the works were carried in twenty minutes, the Egyptians flying in all directions. Fifteen hundred were killed and wounded and several thousand taken prisoners. On the 14th the British entered Cairo, and Arabi surrendered unconditionally. This brought the war to an end.

September 10.

1087. William the Conqueror died. Great as were the power and fame of the Norman conqueror of England, all respect for him vanished with his death. His corpse was deserted by his servants and court officials, and left almost naked on the floor while they looked after their interests with his successor. No coffin was provided, and as the masonry grave prepared proved too small, the body was forced into it with such rough vigor that it burst asunder.

1609. Hudson River was discovered by Henry Hudson, an English captain in command of a Dutch vessel. He sailed up the river as far as the site of Albany. This discovery gave Holland a claim to the adjacent territory, of which she was forcibly deprived by England in 1664.

1797. Mary Wollstonecraft (Mrs. Godwin), author of the "Rights of Woman," died. She also wrote "Vindication of the Rights of Man," in answer to Burke's "Reflections on the

Revolution in France," and a "Historical and Moral View of the French Revolution." But she is best known for her advocacy of the theory that marriage should cease with the cessation of sympathy between the parties, and that no ceremony is necessary. She left one daughter, who became the wife of the poet Shelley.

1813. The battle of Lake Erie took place, in which Commodore Perry attacked the British squadron on the lake and captured the entire fleet. In this engagement he performed the daring feat of leaving his sinking flag-ship and crossing under the British fire in a small boat to another vessel of his fleet.

1846. The Howe sewing-machine patent was granted. Elias Howe, the inventor, found great difficulty in the introduction of this useful invention, and went to England, where he was met with the same spirit of scepticism. On his return to the United States he found that imitations of his patent were in use, and entered into law-suits which were not settled until 1854. The decision was in his favor, royalties were paid to him by the several patentees, and he became in the end very rich, after having passed through periods of great depression of fortune.

1849. Edwin Booth, since so celebrated as a tragedian, made his first appearance on the stage at the Boston Museum. He was not quite sixteen years of age.

1881. A suspension-bridge near Pittsburg was nearly destroyed by fire through a singular cause. On examination it was found that thousands of sparrows had been in the habit of building their nests in the wood-work of the bridge. The dry and inflammable material of the nests was kindled by a spark from a passing steamer.

1884. The cholera alarmingly increased at Naples. Three hundred and sixty-five deaths took place, and four hundred and thirty on the 12th. Heavy rains on the 13th and 14th were followed by a notable decrease of the epidemic. In all Italy, during this outbreak, the deaths were 7974. In September, 1886, there was a severe cholera epidemic in Japan, there being 37,000 deaths out of 50,000 cases. It was still more destructive in Corea.

1885. Severe floods took place in the province of Bengal, India. Many lives were lost.

September 11.

1777. The battle of Brandywine was fought, between the American army under Washington and the British under

Howe. The defeat of the Americans in this engagement opened Philadelphia to the British, who soon after occupied it.

1814. A naval battle took place on Lake Champlain, in which Captain McDonough with an American fleet encountered a superior British squadron and sunk or captured the entire fleet.

1823. David Ricardo, a celebrated writer on political economy, died.

1882. The "Star Route" trial ended in a disagreement of the jury. This was one of the most noted trials in the history of the country. Extensive frauds had been discovered in what were known as star routes in the postal service, and several of the contractors were arrested for perjury, it being shown that the bonds they had given for the faithful performance of their contracts were fraudulent and worthless. The jury brought in some of the accomplices guilty, but disagreed concerning the principal offenders. A new trial began in December, and lasted six months. It ended in the acquittal of the principals.

1883. Hendrik Conscience, the most notable of Belgian novelists, died. Of his many stories, the best-known is "The Lion of Flanders," an historical romance.

September 12.

1642. Cinq-Mars, the favorite of Louis XIII., was executed at Lyons by order of Cardinal Richelieu. He had been introduced at court by the cardinal as a spy on the king, whose favorite he soon became. Enmity grew up between him and Richelieu, against whom he entered into a conspiracy. He was arrested and executed at the age of twenty-two. His history has formed the basis of plots for romance-writers and dramatists.

1649. Drogheda, Ireland, was taken by storm by Cromwell, and nearly all the garrison massacred. This Cromwell described as a " righteous judgment" and a "great mercy."

1683. The siege of Vienna was raised. It had been besieged by a Turkish army two hundred thousand strong, and was weakly garrisoned. But the King of Poland and the Duke of Lorraine hastened with armies to its relief, and the Turks withdrew without fighting. This event is of importance, as it relieved Europe from the danger of being overrun by the Turks.

1814. Baltimore was attacked by the British fleet, an expedition from which had just before captured Washington and burned its principal buildings. The American land-forces were defeated near Baltimore, but Fort McHenry repulsed the British attack, and the fleet withdrew in discomfiture.

1847. The heights of Chapultepec, near the city of Mexico, were stormed and captured by the American army under General Scott. The next day the city was taken and the war brought to an end. The storming of Chapultepec is looked upon as an exploit of remarkable boldness and daring, the hill being very steep and high, while it was crowned with a fortress of great strength.

1857. The California passenger-steamer Central America was lost at sea, with great loss of life. It had left Havana on the 8th for New York, but encountered a severe storm and sprung a serious leak. The pumps were set to work, but the water gained rapidly. A vessel which drew near on the 12th took off more than a hundred of the passengers, including all the women and children; but about eight o'clock in the evening the water swept over the deck, and the vessel went down with a plunge, carrying with it all on board. A few more were saved, but over four hundred were lost, together with a treasure in gold of more than two million dollars.

1874. Francis Guizot, the celebrated French historian, died. Of his numerous historical works the best-known and most valuable is "History of Civilization in Europe."

1881. Professor S. A. King started on a balloon-voyage from Minneapolis to the East. There accompanied him Mr. Upton, of the Signal Service, and five reporters. The enterprise failed from lack of wind, and the aeronauts were obliged to come down near the Mississippi.

1884. The cholera epidemic raged severely in Spain. From September 1 to 12 the cases numbered 23,644; deaths, 6379.

September 13.

1592. Michael de Montaigne, the celebrated French essayist, died. As he himself tells us, he began to write for lack of something to do, and jotted down whatever came into his head. As a writer he is frank, easy, and rambling in method, full of practical wisdom and sagacity, and ranks as the first and one of the best of essayists.

1598. Philip II. of Spain died. He is noted for the vast amount of human suffering to which his merciless bigotry gave rise. During his reign the Inquisition flourished in Spain, while terrible misery and great destruction of property arose from his vain efforts to reduce the Netherlands. The most celebrated event of his reign was the attempt to invade England with the "Invincible Armada,"

which proved a total failure. After his death Spain sank to the position of a second-class European power.

1759. The capture of Quebec by the army under General Wolfe took place. This city, from its position on a lofty hill, was deemed impregnable; but Wolfe led his army by night along a narrow path up the steep bluff, and defeated the French army the next morning. Wolfe was killed on the field, while Montcalm, the French commander, was severely wounded, and died the next day. This victory put an end to the power of France in America.

1806. Charles James Fox, one of the most celebrated of English orators and statesmen, died.

1858. The steamer Austria, of the New York and Hamburg line, was burned at sea. The boatswain had been ordered to fumigate the steerage by thrusting a hot iron into a bucket of tar. The tar caught fire and set fire to the vessel, the flames spreading with great rapidity, rushing through the gangways and hatchways, and cutting off the retreat of all those on the forward part of the vessel. All the boats but one were swamped in launching, and when the engines stopped working the vessel's head swung round, so that the flames were driven forward by the wind, forcing most of the passengers to leap overboard. Of more than five hundred persons on board, only ninety-nine were saved, being picked up by two vessels which hove in sight during the fire.

1880. A severe earthquake took place at Valparaiso. At Illapel, Chili, about two hundred perished. Other disastrous September earthquakes were the following. In 1186 a city of Calabria with all its inhabitants was overwhelmed in the Adriatic Sea. Thousands perished in an earthquake at Constantinople, September 14, 1509. In September, 1693, a terrible earthquake took place in Sicily, which destroyed fifty-four cities and towns and three hundred villages. More than one hundred thousand lives were lost. Not a trace remained of Catania and its eighteen thousand inhabitants. September 1, 1726, Palermo was nearly destroyed and nearly six thousand lives were lost. In 1754 half the houses and forty thousand of the inhabitants of Cairo were swallowed up. In 1789, at Borgo di San Sepolcro, more than one thousand lives were lost. September 26, 1800, the royal palace and many buildings were destroyed at Constantinople. September 8, 1874, Antigua and other places in Guatemala were destroyed, with great loss of life.

1881. Sergeant John Mason fired at

Charles J. Guiteau, the assassin of President Garfield, in prison. His shot missed its aim. Mason was condemned to one year's imprisonment for breach of discipline, but was pardoned before his sentence expired.

September 14.

1321. Dante Alighieri, the most celebrated of Italian poets, author of the "Divina Commedia," died. Dante ranks with the few great epic poets of the world, while his history has a melancholy interest which has added to the celebrity of his great poem.

1741. Charles Rollin, the French historian, died. He is notable in literature for his "Ancient History," which remained a standard work until antiquated by the recent great discoveries in the history of the past.

1851. James Fenimore Cooper, the noted American novelist, died. He is celebrated for his romances of Indian life and his sea-stories, the latter of which are very true to nature, though his Indian characters have been severely criticised. He was familiar with ocean life, while his Indians were creatures of the imagination.

1852. The Duke of Wellington died. This celebrated general first distinguished himself in India, where he gained important victories, and afterwards in Spain and Portugal, which countries he skilfully defended against Napoleon's armies. But his greatest celebrity was gained at Waterloo, at which place he defeated Napoleon's last army and put an end to the career of the greatest military genius of modern times.

1882. The steamer Asia foundered on Lake Huron, nearly one hundred lives being lost.

1882. A four-oared race on the Thames, between the Hillsdale club of Michigan and an English rowing club, ended in the defeat of the Americans. They kept in advance till near the goal, when an accident caused them to stop rowing, and the English boat shot ahead.

September 15.

1615. Lady Arabella Stuart died. Her story was a very interesting one. She was next in succession to James VI. of Scotland, who became James I. of England, and a conspiracy, which proved abortive, was devised to raise her to the throne. She was then forbidden to marry, but did so in defiance of the prohibition. She and her husband were arrested, but both escaped. Seymour, her husband, succeeded in making his way to Flanders, but his wife had made her flight in a different vessel, which was taken, and

she confined in the Tower. Here she was held prisoner from 1609 till her death.

1784. The first balloon-ascent in England was made by a man named Lunardi. An ascent had been made in Edinburgh before, and several in France. Most of these were in what are known as fire-balloons; Lunardi's balloon was inflated with hydrogen gas.

1804. A balloon-ascent, for scientific observation, was made by Gay-Lussac at Paris. He reached the height of 22,977 feet, or over four miles, the highest point reached to that date.

1812. The city of Moscow was burned. It had been entered by Napoleon's army on the previous day, and this conflagration is supposed to have been started to prevent the French from finding winter-quarters. Eleven thousand eight hundred and forty dwellings, besides palaces and churches, were burned. This was the turning-point in Napoleon's career. His power from that time steadily declined.

1830. The Liverpool and Manchester Railway, the first on which steam locomotion for traction-purposes was fully established, was formally opened. Locomotives had been tried before. The first locomotive constructed by George Stephenson, in 1814, travelled six miles per hour. The Rocket, built by him in 1829, made from twenty-five to thirty-five miles per hour. It took part in the opening of the L. & M. road, and won the prize of five hundred pounds offered for the best locomotive. William Huskisson, a distinguished political economist, was killed by the Rocket on this occasion.

1882. Harper's Ferry surrendered, with its garrison of eleven thousand men and a great quantity of military stores, to Stonewall Jackson.

1885. The elephant Jumbo was killed near St. Thomas, Ontario. It was being loaded on a train, when a freight-train backed on it and injured it so severely that it died in half an hour. This elephant was of the African species and one of the largest known in captivity. It was about twenty-five years old, having been taken to the London Zoölogical Garden when quite young, whence it was purchased by Barnum, in opposition to the vigorous protests of the English press.

1887. The three days' centennial celebration of the adoption of the Constitution of the United States began in Philadelphia. On the first day there was an industrial parade of remarkable extent and brilliancy. On the second day a grand military procession took place.

The third day was given to orations and other ceremonies, Hon. Samuel F. Miller, of the United States Supreme Court, delivering the principal address, while a new national hymn by Francis M. Crawford was recited.

September 10.

1701. James II., the deposed king of England, died. In a reign of three years this monarch succeeded in so thoroughly disaffecting his subjects that William of Orange was called in and the tyrannous ruler driven from his throne. The remainder of his life was spent in France.

1736. Gabriel Daniel Fahrenheit, the deviser of the thermometer, died. The year of his death is not certain, and may have been 1740, but is usually given at the above date. His thermometer was completed about 1720. For reasons which he gives at length, he fixed the number of degrees between the freezing- and boiling-points of water at one hundred and eighty. The greatest cold he was able to produce by a mixture of ice, water, and sal-ammoniac was thirty-two degrees below the freezing-point, and this he chose as the zero-point of his thermometer. The Centigrade thermometer, of later date, is much more simple in these particulars.

1795. The Cape of Good Hope, where a Dutch colony had existed since 1650, was taken possession of by the English. It was restored at the peace of Amiens, in 1802, but taken again in 1806, and finally ceded to England in 1814.

1873. The final evacuation of France by the German army took place. The country had been held, after the close of the war, until the arrangements for the payment of the indemnity could be completed.

1875. A severe cyclone visited the Gulf of Mexico, and continued for three days. Much damage was done in Galveston, and in Indianola over one hundred lives were lost and nine-tenths of the houses were swept away. The town was flooded eight feet deep by the waters of the gulf.

1875. The system of fast trains for the delivery of the mails came into operation.

1887. A collision took place on the Midland Railway, in England, twenty-three persons being killed and sixty injured.

September 17.

1787. The Constitution of the United States was adopted by the convention at Philadelphia. The articles, which had been agreed upon after four months' deliberation, were afterwards ratified by conventions in the several States. Pre-

vious to this the States had been bound by a weak compact which could be dissolved at will, and Congress was almost destitute of authority. The Constitution first put into the hands of the government the power to enforce its laws.

1862. The battle of Antietam, or Sharpsburg, was fought between the armies of General Lee and General McClellan. This battle had been brought on by Lee's invasion of Maryland, and was desperately contested, the losses being about ten thousand on each side. It ended in a repulse of the Confederates, who retreated to Virginia on the 19th.

1871. The Mount Cenis tunnel was formally opened by the passage of a train of twenty-two carriages in twenty minutes. This great work had occupied fourteen years. The tunnel is seven and one-half miles long, and cost about $13,000,000. Compressed air was the principal power used in the boring.

September 18.

96. Domitian, one of the cruellest emperors of Rome, was assassinated by conspirators, after having been for fifteen years the terror and detestation of his subjects. He was stabbed by a man who was reading to him the particulars of a pretended plot, and quickly despatched by the other conspirators.

1772. The first dismemberment of Poland, by Russia, Prussia, and Austria, was arranged, about one-third of the whole kingdom being seized. This was done by a compact between Frederick the Great and Catherine of Russia, in which Austria was invited to take part. Two other partitions were made, one in 1793 and one in 1795, which last completed the work and took the whole of the kingdom. Poland had been long distracted by bad government, and became an easy prey to these imperial robbers.

1793. The corner-stone of the capitol at Washington was laid by President Washington. This city became the seat of government in 1800. The capitol thus inaugurated was burned by the British during their raid in 1814. The present one was built afterwards.

1830. William Hazlitt, a very distinguished writer on miscellaneous subjects, died. His works were voluminous and brilliant in style, and he was one of the ablest of critics on art and the drama. His largest work was a "Life of Napoleon," in four volumes. It is highly commendatory of Napoleon.

1868. The insurrection in Spain against Queen Isabella began. It ended in her flight and the adoption of a republican form of government. In the succeeding May the Cortes voted for a monarchy. Republican risings followed, but were suppressed, and the Spanish republic came to an end, after a very short term of existence.

1879. Daniel Drew, a noted New York stock-speculator, died.

1884. Jerry McAuley, a well-known missionary and reformed convict of New York, died. His efforts at reform were attended with great success, and many drunkards and criminals were redeemed.

September 10.

1356. The battle of Poictiers, between Edward the Black Prince, son of Edward III. of England, and King John of France, was won by the English over a great superiority of numbers. The French had sixty thousand horse, in addition to foot-soldiers. The English force was not over ten thousand in all, its retreat was cut off, and escape seemed impossible. Yet by a bold attack the French were dispersed, thousands of their knights and nobles slain, and their king taken prisoner and brought to London.

1648. The pressure of the atmosphere (discovered by Galileo in 1564) was found by Pascal to vary with the height above sea-level. This opened the way for the measurement of the heights of mountains by means of the barometer.

1665. During the week ending September 19 the great plague of London reached its height, more than ten thousand persons dying. Considerably more than one hundred thousand died during the whole period of the plague. The city was in a dreadful state, the dead being so numerous in comparison with the whole population that it was hardly possible to bury them.

1777. The battle of Stillwater, in which General Burgoyne was defeated, occurred. A second battle took place October 7, and Burgoyne with his whole army surrendered at Saratoga on the 17th, every chance of escape from the trap into which he had fallen being cut off.

1783. Joseph Montgolfier, the pioneer aeronaut, ascended in a balloon inflated with smoke from burned straw and wool. The first ascent was made June 5, 1783, in a fire-balloon. The first ascent in a balloon inflated with hydrogen gas was made by MM. Robert and Charles, at Paris, August 27, 1783.

1852. Severe inundations took place in the valleys of the Rhine and Rhone Rivers, overflowing the country to a great extent.

1863. The battle of Chickamauga took place on the 19th and 20th. The Confederates under Bragg attacked Rose-

crans and drove him back in disorder, but Thomas held his ground firmly against them and saved the Union army from a serious disaster.

1864. The battle of Winchester, between Sheridan and Early, was fought. Early was attacked, and, after an obstinate contest, driven out of the town and up the valley in utter rout. Sheridan followed, and destroyed the crops in the valley, with the purpose of rendering it incapable of sustaining an army.

1873. The great financial panic of this year reached its height during the ten days after the 19th. The New York Clearing-House suspended payment, and many great banking-houses failed. A very severe financial and industrial depression followed, whose effects lasted for several years.

1874. A great fire took place in the cotton-mills at Fall River, Massachusetts. About sixty lives were lost.

1881. President Garfield died. He had been shot at Washington on July 2 by Charles J. Guiteau, a disappointed office-seeker, and lay in a gradually sinking state, the sympathies of the whole country being deeply aroused by his suffering, patience, and courage. On September 6 he was removed from Washington to Elberon, New Jersey, in the hope that the pure sea-air would help him. Here he died on the 19th. No American was ever more widely and sincerely mourned.

September 20.

1415. Owen Glendower, the celebrated Welsh patriot, died. He had raised the standard of insurrection against England about 1400, claiming to be the lineal representative of the old Welsh kings. His power waned after the battle of Shrewsbury, in which his allies the Percies were overthrown, but he continued to annoy the English from mountain-fastnesses until his death.

1777. The surprise and defeat of General Wayne, known at that time in the army as the "Massacre of Paoli," took place. Wayne had concealed his force in the woods to harass the rear of the British army, but was surprised, and three hundred of his men were killed while making no resistance.

1858. Piccolomini, the favorite opera-singer, made her first appearance in America at the New York Academy of Music.

1863. Jacob Grimm died. His researches, in association with his brother, into the folk-lore of Germany, were of the utmost importance, and brought the study of popular legend and tradition into a prominence which it still maintains.

1870. The Italian troops occupied Rome. This brought to an end the long contest over the temporal power of the Pope, and Italy became once more a single kingdom, after having been broken into a number of minor states during the long period since the fall of the old Roman empire.

1875. William Perkins, at Lillie Bridge, London, walked eight miles in less than one hour.

1879. General Grant was received at San Francisco, after his two years' tour round the world, with a grand procession and public ceremonies.

1887. The Iron-clad Trafalgar, the largest ship in the British navy, was launched at Portsmouth. The register of this vessel is 11,940 tons, and its engines are of 12,000 horse-power. Its armament consists of twelve heavy guns.

1887. A test of automatic air-brakes took place. A train of twenty cars, running forty miles an hour, was stopped in a distance of four hundred and eighty-four feet, without shock, by the application of these brakes. One of fifty cars, running twenty miles an hour, was stopped in one hundred and fifty-five feet.

September 21.

1327. Edward II. of England was murdered in Berkeley Castle. The reign of this king is notable for the celebrated battle of Bannockburn, in which the English were defeated by the Scotch under Robert Bruce. Edward, whose course had given general dissatisfaction, was dethroned January 20, and assassinated the following September.

1558. Charles V., Emperor of Germany and King of Spain, died. This celebrated monarch, after a life of great warlike activity, abdicated his throne in 1556, and retired to a monastery, where he died two years afterwards.

1776. A severe conflagration took place in New York, shortly after it had been occupied by the British under General Howe. Four hundred and ninety-three buildings, including Trinity Church, were burned. This event interfered greatly with the British expectations of pleasant winter quarters.

1792. Royalty was abolished in France by a decree of the National Convention. It was replaced by a republican government, which was proclaimed on the 22d, and which continued in existence until overthrown by Napoleon in 1804.

1832. Sir Walter Scott, the great novelist, died. As a writer of historical novels this distinguished author has never

had an equal, and his works promise to become classics in the literature of fiction.

1860. The Prince of Wales entered the United States at Detroit, after his tour in the British provinces. He made a long journey through the United States, and was received with a grand military and civic display in New York on October 11. A grand ball was given in his honor on the 12th, and a torchlight procession of firemen on the 13th.

1886. A strike of ninety thousand cotton-spinners took place in England. Parnell's Irish land bill was defeated in the House of Commons.

1887. A severe hurricane at Brownsville, Texas. More than ten inches of rain fell, and great damage was done.

September 22.

479 B.C. The battle of Platæa was fought. This great contest went far to decide whether Persia or Greece should have the empire of the civilized world. It put an end to the Persian invasions of Europe, which were destined to be followed, in the next century, by a Greek invasion and conquest of Asia under Alexander the Great.

19 B.C. Virgil, the greatest of the Roman poets, author of the celebrated epic poem "The Æneid," and of charming poems of country life, died.

1736. Major John Bernardi died. The career of this man was a remarkable evidence of legal injustice. Arrested in 1696 as a conspirator in a plot to assassinate William III., he was kept in prison for forty years, in spite of the fact that there was not evidence enough to convict him, and of many efforts for his release. Long before he died his alleged crime had been forgotten.

1836. The Bowery Theatre, at New York, was burned. This theatre had the misfortune of being burned four times, the first time on March 26, 1828, the third on February 18, 1838, and the fourth on April 25, 1845.

1853. The first telegraph line in California was completed. It extended eight miles from San Francisco towards the ocean, and was intended to give early information of shipping-arrivals.

1882. A terrible explosion took place on the Russian war-ship Popoffka Novgorod, at Sebastopol. A torpedo exploded in the torpedo-magazine, shattering all the upper works of the vessel and rendering her unseaworthy. Two officers and twenty-two seamen were killed.

1882. A railroad-accident took place just outside the tunnel near the Grand Central Depot, New York. The axle of an engine broke and blocked the track, while an express entered the tunnel unsignalled and ran into the wreck. Four persons were killed, and fifteen severely injured.

1887. James A. Stewart, of Wichita, Kansas, was sentenced to seventeen years and four months' imprisonment and $20,-800 fine for violation of the prohibition law. This remarkable sentence was imposed on a clerk in a drug-store, who pleaded guilty to an indictment of 2080 counts.

September 23.

1779. Paul Jones, with the American frigate Bon Homme Richard, captured the British frigate Serapis. The engagement was one of the most memorable naval battles in history. Captain Jones fought his antagonist until his own vessel was ready to sink under his feet, and compelled victory where almost any other man would have acknowledged defeat.

1780. Major André was captured by American scouts. He was on his return from West Point, where he had been arranging with Benedict Arnold, the traitor, for the surrender of that post to the British. André was hanged (October 2) as a spy, though earnest efforts were made to save his life.

1886. Henry George, the advocate of free land, was nominated by the Central Labor Union for Mayor of New York. This event is notable as the first decided political movement made by the labor element of our population.

September 24.

1664. The Dutch province of New Netherlands was surrendered to a British fleet sent over by the Duke of York, in honor of whom the province was renamed New York. The seizure was a high-handed one, as the two nations were at peace; but the British took good care not to give up their acquisition.

1680. Samuel Butler, a noted English satirical poet, died. His political satire of "Hudibras" gave him at the time a great reputation, which its wit deserved. It is little read now, however, its local allusions having lost much of their point.

1846. The city of Monterey, Mexico, surrendered to General Taylor after a three days' siege, in which the soldiers mined their way through the walls of the houses.

1856. The steamer Niagara was burned on Lake Erie, more than fifty lives being lost.

1869. This day is memorable in the financial history of New York as "Black Friday." Gold, which was approaching

par value, was made the basis of a daring speculation by a clique of bold operators, who got under their control about $120,000,000 in gold and ran up the price from 131 to 150. On the 24th it made a further advance to 164. The value of all stocks was now seriously disturbed, fortunes were being rapidly lost and won, and the wildest excitement prevailed. At this perilous point the government announced that it would sell gold, and the price at once fell to 135. This broke the power of the conspirators and defeated the most daring plot ever known to Wall Street.

1875. Great storms took place in India from 22d to 24th of September. Ahmedabad was inundated and about twenty thousand persons left homeless.

1876. Hallett's Reef, one of the principal obstructions to navigation at Hell Gate, Long Island Sound, was blown up with dynamite. General Newton had spent seven years in excavating it, having mined ten tunnels into the rock, thirty-three feet under low-water mark. Numerous holes were bored along these passages and charged with twenty-eight thousand pounds of dynamite and twenty-four thousand pounds of other explosives. The explosion that followed rent the ledge to pieces, the fragments being afterwards removed by dredging. Another obstruction, known as Flood Rock, was removed in the same way, the explosion taking place October 10, 1885.

1883. A singular accident occurred in one of the buildings of the Royal Arsenal, Woolwich, England. This building, containing seven hundred and seventy fully-charged war-rockets, took fire, and more than five hundred and fifty of these rockets exploded, flying in all directions over the country to a distance of nearly five miles. There were many hairbreadth escapes and much damage to buildings, but only two lives were lost.

1887. William O'Brien, the Irish agitator, was found guilty of seditious language and sentenced to three months' imprisonment. Several other prominent Irishmen, some of them members of Parliament, have since then been punished in the same manner.

September 25.

1513. Vasco de Balboa discovered the Pacific Ocean. He was a Spanish adventurer, who had smuggled himself in a cask on board a vessel bound for the Isthmus of Darien, but became leader of an expedition across the isthmus, which, after encountering many hardships, reached an elevation from which the waters of the great Pacific could be seen. He claimed possession of this broad reach of unknown waters for the King of Spain. In the words of Keats,—

With eagle eyes
He stared at the Pacific,—and all his men
Looked at each other with a wild surmise,—
Silent, upon a peak in Darien.

1690. *Public Occurrences*, the first newspaper published in America, was issued at Boston. Its career was a very brief one, as it was suppressed by the legislature before the appearance of the second number.

1775. Montreal was captured by General Montgomery. In this enterprise Ethan Allen, the daring leader of the Green Mountain Boys, was taken prisoner and sent in chains to England.

1857. The siege of Lucknow, in India, was raised by a force under General Havelock. This siege is memorable for the persistent defence, under great distress, of the besieged, and the story of Jessie Brown, the Scotch girl, who heard the sound of the Highland pipes of the relieving column long before it came into sight. This story, however, is not credited by historians.

1886. A novel accident took place near Glasgow, Scotland. A great blast of seven tons of powder was made in the Crarae granite-quarries on Loch Fyne, which dislodged over sixty thousand tons of rock. About three hundred spectators hurried in to see the effect of the blast, many of whom fell prostrate and insensible, while others went into convulsions. More than one hundred were thus affected by the choke-damp, or gas produced by the explosion, of whom six died.

September 26.

1768. A garrison of British soldiers, under General Gage, entered Boston, with the avowed purpose of enforcing the payment of duties and keeping the people in order. This occupation was bitterly opposed by the Americans, and led to acts which were the immediately instigating causes of the Revolutionary War.

1866. Great inundations took place in France on this and several succeeding days, much property being destroyed by the overflowing rivers.

1879. Deadwood, in the Black Hills, Dakota, was almost destroyed by fire, the loss being $2,500,000, and two thousand persons being left homeless.

September 27.

1777. Philadelphia was occupied by the British army under Sir William Howe.

1825. The Stockton and Darlington Railway, constructed by Edward Pease

and George Stephenson, was first opened for passenger traffic. On this, the pioneer passenger railway, the cars were drawn by horses.

1854. The steamer Arctic was lost. This steamer, on her voyage from Liverpool to New York, with more than four hundred persons on board, was struck, when about sixty-five miles from Cape Race, by the Vesta, an iron propeller, and injured so seriously that she quickly filled with water, and went down in about three hours, carrying with her most of the persons on board. Less than fifty were saved. She was running through a dense fog at the time of the collision.

1871. The slave-emancipation bill was passed in Brazil. This was a measure for gradual emancipation. It has been supplemented (1888) by a bill for complete and immediate emancipation.

1876. The prizes to exhibitors at the Philadelphia Centennial Exhibition were awarded. There were about eleven thousand in all.

1879. The Astley belt in the New York walking-match was won by Rowell, an Englishman, who walked five hundred and thirty miles in five days, twenty hours, and twenty-five minutes.

1881. An autopsy on the body of President Garfield showed that the doctors were mistaken and that the bullet had taken an entirely unexpected direction. Its locality was such that it could not possibly have been extracted.

1886. John Esten Cooke, a favorite novelist and biographer of Virginia, died. Among his best-known works are the novels "The Virginia Comedians" and "Leather Stocking and Silk," and biographies of General Lee and Stonewall Jackson.

1887. The third international yacht-race, between the British cutter Thistle and the American sloop Volunteer, took place at New York. The Volunteer won. This race aroused much attention, being looked upon as a test of the British and American methods of building. The easy victory of the Volunteer excited much surprise.

September 28.

490 B.C. The great battle of Marathon took place on this day, or the 29th, between the Greeks and the Persians. The Greek army of 11,000 men, commanded by Miltiades, Aristides, and Themistocles, defeated the Persian army of 110,000, and forced it to retreat to Asia.

1789. Thomas Day, author of "Sandford and Merton," a child's book of long-continued popularity, died.

1849. The Turkish government refused to give up the Hungarian refugees Kossuth, Andrassy, and others, to the Austrians. They had escaped over the frontier after the close of the war for independence.

1885. A riot took place in Montreal, Canada, in consequence of the smallpox regulations, particularly that of compulsory vaccination. The ignorant French had been stirred up by mischievous persons, and a mob of them attacked the city hall. They threatened to burn the English newspaper offices, but were dispersed by the police and many of them hurt.

1887. The Yellow River of China overflowed its banks in the province of Honan, submerging an area of seven thousand square miles. This district contained numerous populous towns, which were overflowed, with a loss of many thousands of lives. A vast amount of property was destroyed, and several millions of people were left homeless, by this severe disaster, which was one of the most terrible known to history.

September 29.

Michaelmas Day, or, properly, the Day of St. Michael and All Angels. This has long been a great feast-day of the Church of Rome, and is also a feast-day of the Church of England. Michael, in the Christian world, is the chief of the angelic host. His history is obscure, but is a militant one. He is mentioned five times in Scripture, and always as fighting.

48 B.C. Pompey the Great was killed. This celebrated personage, after attaining great reputation in Rome as a military leader, joined Cæsar and Crassus in forming the first triumvirate. Afterwards a war arose between him and Cæsar, and he was defeated at the battle of Pharsalia (August 9, 48 B.C.) He fled to Egypt, where he was treacherously slain and his head cut off and taken to the conqueror.

1540. Gustavus Vasa, a celebrated king of Sweden, died. By his valor he freed Sweden from the Danish rule, and was raised to the throne of the new kingdom in 1523.

1613. The first general water-supply was introduced into the city of London. This supply was brought from New River, the work, which was begun in 1609, being performed against great difficulties and opposition by Hugh Myddleton, a celebrated engineer of that period. The water was distributed through the streets in pipes made from the stems of small elm-trees, cut in six-feet lengths, drilled, and one end tapered so as to fit into the bore of the other. Four hundred miles of such pipes were laid.

1813. The Americans took possession of Detroit, which had been abandoned by the British on the approach of the army under General Harrison. This city had been taken by the British at the beginning of the war (August 16, 1812).

1887. The prohibition constitutional amendment election took place in Tennessee. Prohibition was defeated by a majority of 27,693.

September 30.

1770. The Rev. George Whitefield, a celebrated itinerant preacher of the Methodist denomination, died. He was in the habit of making yearly rounds in the British islands, and repeatedly visited America, where he preached to great congregations. He died in America, near Boston.

1787. The ship Columbia started from Boston on a voyage round the world, the first performed by an American vessel. It sailed first by way of Cape Horn to the northwest coast of America, where it took on a cargo of furs and sailed for China. From the latter country it returned by way of the Cape of Good Hope, reaching Boston in 1790.

1811. Thomas Percy, a noted English scholar, died. He is best known for his "Reliques of Ancient English Poetry," a work which has been often republished, and which is the best collection extant of the old ballad poetry of England.

1851. The remains of Stephen Girard were removed to Girard College by the Free Masons.

1874. England took possession of the Feejee Islands. This group contains over two hundred islands, eighty of which are inhabited. The largest is about three hundred and sixty miles in circumference, with about sixty thousand inhabitants, twelve hundred of whom are Europeans. The islands had been offered by the king and chiefs to England in 1859, but not accepted.

CURRENT NOTES.

THERE has recently been published by the daily press of this city a list of the alum baking powders more prominently sold. This exposure is in the line of public policy heretofore commended in these pages. The most effective way to break up the manufacture and sale of adulterated articles of food is to publish their names.

It is stated that these alum baking powders are sold under the guarantee that they are pure and wholesome cream of tartar articles. This is criminal. Sold for what they are, the consumer has an opportunity to avoid them. But if poison is given when pure food is asked for, the danger to the public is appalling.

Alum, on account of its cheapness, is employed in the compounding of almost all the new brands of baking powder. Unscrupulous manufacturers who desire to reap all the profit possible from these powders for the short period during which only they know they can be foisted upon the public, naturally use the cheapest materials they can procure. Alum costs but three cents a pound, while cream of tartar costs from thirty to forty. The inducement to the business adventurer, who has no reputation to maintain, and is looking only for the present profit, when he finds that he can with this stuff make a powder at one-eighth the cost of a reputable article, is too great to be resisted.

It is hardly necessary to recapitulate the evil effects of alum upon the human system. It is well understood to be injurious in a high degree. Dr. Waller, of the New York Board of Health, in a warning to the public against the use of these alum baking powders, stated that the action of the alum in the stomach was precisely the same as in the mouth; it draws and puckers it up, producing unpleasant and dangerous disorders, dyspepsia, constipation, heart-burn, etc. Through the exposure made by the Royal Baking Powder Company of New York, which originally brought to light this practice of substituting alum for cream of tartar, the business was for a time largely checked, particularly in the East, where the highest medical and sanitary authorities condemned it in the strongest possible language, and earnestly seconded the efforts of the Royal Baking Powder Company to suppress it.

There now seems to be an effort to revive the business, and wealthy corporations, the owners of alum-mines, are engaged in the reprehensible business of trying to make a market for the alum baking powders, notwithstanding their well-known detrimental character.

At the time of the original exposure, Dr. Mott, Government Chemist, analyzed forty-two different samples of baking powder for the Government. He found more than one-half of these to contain alum or other injurious ingredients; and it is only fair to say, in passing, he found also that the Royal Baking Powder stood the test, and in his report to the Government placed it at the head of the list for purity and strength. The safety of the public lies in the use only of those baking powders of highest character and old established reputation.

THE criticism of Tennyson referred to in Book-Talk appeared in the *Quarterly Review* in 1833, and is a choice curiosity of literature.

The Reviewer in an ironic strain talks about introducing " to the admiration of our more sequestered readers a new prodigy of genius,—another and a brighter star of that galaxy or *milky way* of poetry of which the lamented Keats was the harbinger." Then he proceeds through fifteen pages to ridicule every idea and every expression which by ingenuity and malice prepense can be tortured into material for his banter. Thus, quoting this verse,—

> Sweet as the noise, in parchèd plains,
> Of bubbling wells that fret the stones
> (If any sense in me remains),
> Thy words will be, thy cheerful tones
> As welcome to my crumbling bones,—

he sees a very obvious possibility for jest in the words "If any sense in me remains." "This doubt," he says, "is inconsistent with the opening stanza of the piece, and, in fact, too modest: we take upon ourselves to reassure Mr. Tennyson that, even after he shall be dead and buried, as much *sense* will still remain as he has now the good fortune to possess." "The accumulation of tender images in the following lines appears not less wonderful:

> "Remember you that pleasant day
> When, after roving in the woods
> ('Twas April then), I came and lay
> Beneath those gummy chestnut-buds?

> "A water-rat from off the bank
> Plunged in the stream. With idle care,
> Down looking through the sedges rank,
> I saw your troubled image there.

> "If you remember, you had set
> Upon the narrow casement-edge
> A long green box of mignonette,
> And you were leaning on the ledge.

The poet's truth to nature in his gummy chestnut-buds, and to Art in the 'long green box' of mignonette,—and that masterly touch of likening the first intrusion of love into the virgin bosom of the miller's daughter to the plunging of the water-rat into the mill-dam,—these are beauties which, we do not fear to say, equal anything even in Keats." The strain of mockery is kept up throughout the remarks on the "Hesperides," "The Palace of Art," and "A Dream of Fair Women."

"Ducks and Drakes" is, in the words of an old author quoted by Brand, "a kind of sport or play with an oister-shell or stone thrown into the water, and making circles yer it sinke." If the stone emerges once, it is a duck, and increases in the following order:

> 1, 2, A duck and a drake,
> 3 And a half-penny cake,
> 4 And a penny to pay the old baker;
> 5 A hop and a scotch
>   Is another notch,
> 6 Slitherum, slatherum, take her.

From this game probably originated the phrase "making ducks and drakes with one's money,"—*i.e.*, throwing it away heedlessly. An early instance of the use of the phrase may be found in Strode's "Floating Island," Sig. O. iv. Butler in

"Hudibras" (Canto III. line 30) makes it one of the important qualifications of his conjurer to tell

> What figured slates are best to make
> On wat'ry surface duck or drake.

A somewhat similar game was known among the Romans, and is alluded to by Minucius Felix and other ancient writers.

"Conspicuous by its absence" is a phrase made popular in England by Lord John Russell. In his "Address to the Electors of the City of London," published April 6, 1859, he said of Lord Derby's Reform Bill, which had just been defeated, "Among the defects of the bill, which are numerous, one provision is conspicuous by its presence, and another by its absence." The expression was sharply criticised, and nine days later, in a speech at London Tavern, he justified it thus: "It has been thought that by a misnomer, or a 'bull,' on my part, I alluded to a provision as conspicuous by its absence,—a turn of phraseology which is not an original expression of mine, but is taken from one of the greatest historians of antiquity." This great historian is Tacitus. In his *Annales*, lib. iii. cap. 76, describing the funeral of Junia, he thus alludes to the absence of the images of her famous kinsmen Brutus and Cassius: "*Sed præfulgebant Cassius atque Brutus eo ipso, quod effigies eorum non videbantur.*"

J. Chénier, in his tragedy of "Tiberius" (Act I., Scene I.), translating the expression into French, gave it the form which is familiar in English,

> Brutus et Cassius brillaient par leur absence,

but which had already become familiar in France through its use by the Jansenists when their enemies had succeeded in securing the omission of the names of Pascal and Arnauld from Perrault's History of Illustrious Men. It was revived, too, in Talleyrand's observation when some one called his attention to the fact that Lord Castlereagh at the Congress of Vienna wore no decorations: "*Ma foi, c'est bien distingué.*" The latter story, however, is doubted by historians, and the late Prince Paul Galitzin received from his uncle, a member of the Congress, quite another version,—namely, that Galitzin and Castlereagh entered the council-chamber together, and the latter, noticing a gentleman in plain dress, inquired who he was, and, on being told, "An attaché of the Russian Embassy, just arrived from St. Petersburg," exclaimed, "*Comment! un Russe sans décorations! Il doit être un homme bien distingué!*"

"Beauty is only skin-deep," is a common saying that in one form or another may be found in the proverbial lore of all countries. In literature the following are early examples of its use. In "The Nosegay," by Thomas Becon (Edition Parker Society, p. 203), occurs the passage, "And to say the truth, is beauty any other thing than, as Ludovicus Vives saith, 'as [*sic*] little skin well colored? If the inward parts,' saith he, 'could be seen, how great filthiness would there appear, even in the most beautiful person!'" There is a similar quotation in "The Jewel of Joy," page 437. The passage from Ludovicus Vives is, "In corpore ipso quid forma est? nempe *cuticula bene colorata,*" etc. (Lod. Vivis. Valent. Op., "Introd. ad Sap.," 61, tom. ii. cols. 72-3, Basil., 1555.) Sir Thomas Overbury, in his poem "A Wife," says,—

And all the carnall beauty of my wife
Is but skin-deep.

Similarly Molière says,—

La beauté du visage est un frêle ornement,
Une fleur passagère, un éclat d'un moment,
Et qui n'est attaché qu'à la simple épiderme.
Les Femmes Savantes, III. vi.

THE last manuscript that came from the busy pen of the Rev. E. P. Roe (completed, indeed, only a day before his death) was an autobiographical sketch, in which he gives many interesting anecdotes of his literary career. Taking as his title a phrase from one of Matthew Arnold's attacks on America, "A Native Author called Roe," he improves the occasion to answer all unfriendly critics in a kindly and friendly way. The article gives a valuable insight into an exceptionally charming and generous character, and will warm many hearts towards the dead novelist. It will appear in the October number of *Lippincott's Magazine*, which will be a special "E. P. Roe number," containing this autobiography, his last story, "Queen of Spades," and personal reminiscences by a friend and acquaintance.

IT is now announced that the author of "From 18 to 20," the new society novel whose authorship has puzzled all Philadelphia, is Miss Elizabeth Jandon Sellers, the young daughter of David W. Sellers, Esq., one of the leaders of the Philadelphia bar, and law-partner of Judge Mitchell. The first edition of this book was exhausted within two days after publication, and the second was all sold in advance of delivery.

"The Quick or the Dead?" is still the most popular book of the season. For a time the presses found it hard work to keep up with the demand, but the number in every new edition has been materially increased, and though the presses are never idle, they are keeping just ahead of the demand (larger now than ever), and the book has rarely run out of print.

The *American Notes and Queries* (William S. Walsh, Publisher, 619 Walnut Street, Philadelphia) is invaluable to all keepers of scrap-books, from the mass of curious information which it contains that is unattainable in any other form. An interesting feature is the Prize Questions, for the best answers to which One Thousand Dollars are offered. Weekly. $3 per year; 10 cents per single number.

A NEW department, "Every Day's Record," is started in this number of *Lippincott's*, and will continue to be a monthly feature. It will be found full of information, told in an interesting manner, and invaluable for purposes of reference.

MR. JAMES HUNTER, well known as the editor of Ogilvie's Imperial Dictionary and of the Supplement to Worcester's Dictionary, has accepted an editorial position on the *American Notes and Queries*, of Philadelphia.